First published in 2025.

ISBN (ebook): 978-1-7644573-0-9
ISBN (paperback): 978-1-7644573-1-6
ISBN (hardcover): 978-1-7644573-2-3

A Life of Depravity

Sterile Hands. Dirty Mind

J. X. MIller

Table of Contents

The First Cut 1

Echoes of Discipline 13

A Summer You Don't Remember 23

Sterile Hands. Dirty Mind 35

The Club.. 53

The Body Keeps the Score... 63

When She Watched Me 80

The Dock.. 93

The Woman on the Shore 106

Reconstructed Desire 119

Not Clara 130

The Lake's Lesson.. 143

Unlearning Seduction 155

When Memory Fights Back 168

Reclaiming Agency.. 180

Refusal 198

Legacy Circle 214

Repetition.. 230

A Cut That Heals Wrong.. 249

Who Remembers Whom 263

Chapter One

———————∞———————

The First Cut

I always forget how fragile life looks when a skull is open, because on the MRI life appears tidy, reduced to clean slices and grids, color maps where a program pretends meaning lives. On the table, under retractors and hard white lights, it is far simpler, a pale animal breathing on command with its softest part turned toward me. Malik stands at the head of the bed and notes that the train is on time and the passenger is stable, meaning the woman whose name is taped to the bed in block letters like luggage. She is early thirties with drug-resistant temporal lobe epilepsy. Seizures bound to memories her brain cannot file without igniting.

I met her twice in clinic and remember her hands more than her face, ragged cuticles and raw knuckles, skin scrubbed too hard as if fear could be bleached away. She apologized three times for taking my time, and I told her it was my job. What I did not say was that I am good at cutting bad stories out of good brains. What makes a story bad is not its content but its velocity, the way it keeps returning at the wrong moments and hijacking a heartbeat or a hand. It can turn a quiet shower into a flood and a traffic light into a flare.

Good stories stay where they are put, while bad ones leak. They ignore the cabinets you build for them and show up anyway, bleeding into the present until you cannot tell what you are reacting to. In my line of work we call that a seizure. In private I know it is something closer to possession, a loop that will not let go. The brain is only a machine in theory, and in practice it is a hoarder that keeps every broken thing it ever loved.

Now she lies open in front of me with her skull hinged back and dura split, her cortex shining under the light. It is wet and wrong, like something meant to stay underwater rather than beneath plastic drapes and billing codes. When I ask about blood pressure Malik tells me she is rock solid and that she loves me, joking but only barely. Bodies treat me better than boards do, because patients I scarcely remember send cards and biscuits while boards send careful emails about my tone on television. I tell him to keep it that way as my hands hover gloved and steady above the field.

Cold OR air hits my wrists while warmth from her body fogs my loupes for a beat with the breath of something that does not know my name. The brain rises and falls with each pulse in a slow, damp tide that almost feels reciprocal if I stare too long. Lila asks whether I am good and I tell her I am just looking. I hear her smile behind the mask when she says it makes her nervous when I admire the view. I answer that the view is part of the job as she places the fine bipolar forceps in my hand before I ask.

We have done this often enough to move in a shared rhythm, like a nerve we both know by feel. To my left the fMRI glows with language, vision, and emotion. The focus in the left temporal lobe is lit like a warning, where circuits fire when certain images intrude. I tell Nguyen that this is where her past hijacks her. If we take it the seizures drop. If we leave too much, she keeps drowning in it. He nods, eyes jumping between scan and exposed brain, still hungry enough to show it, still new enough to believe the picture will line up with the flesh.

I lean in as the cortex shimmers slick under the beam. Suction keeps a tiny pool from forming while warm saline circulates. Not lake water, I tell myself. The word lake is a placeholder because it sounds harmless, a flat sheet of blue on a map where family's picnic and children wade. What I mean is depth and weight, the thick dark resistance that pulls at your ankles and asks whether you are sure you know how to swim. Water is the most efficient liar in the world, because it looks calm even when it is killing you.

I learned that long before medical school and long before EEGs and resection margins. No credential can overwrite it. The thought repeats more than it should as I say let us begin. The first touch is gentle by private rule, respect first, letting the brain return it. I set the tips of the bipolar above the focus and feel faint resistance through glove and steel, pressure not puncture and contact not attack. Brains rarely bleed if you do not treat them like enemies.

Lila announces coag on and my foot finds the pedal. It is a small switch that can change a life. When I press there is a hiss followed by a soft sizzle as current moves into tissue. A faint sweet smell of burnt protein rises. I register it not as disgust but as confirmation of depth and place. Malik murmurs approval while the EEG stays flat and well behaved. I remind him stepwise, that we remodel rather than erase.

Millimetres at a time I work, coag, suction, lift, each movement cutting another strand in the net of her seizures. The red cartoon on the fMRI is replaced by what happens here under my hands where no screen can see it. Malik asks what she is trying to forget, always choosing the edge for small talk. I reply that content is not the goal and circuits are, even though forgetting is never deletion but a kind of compression, the way the mind folds something too large into something portable so it can keep moving. Trauma does not disappear.

It only changes format into a smell, a color, a sound, a pressure behind the eyes.

Patients think they want erasure, when what they want is relief from constant unpacking, the suitcase to stay closed. When Malik pushes, I tell him I do not guess, half true because I keep theories where they belong inside my skull. Nguyen mentions nightmares, water, and a dock in the intake notes. My grip tightens by a hair as I remind him that notes are messy and that we use structured forms now. I cut him off when he tries to elaborate. We are not here to prove her story, only to stop misfires. The word story hangs in the air like smoke.

The OR settles into its usual rhythm with beeps, ventilator sighs, and soft clicks of passing instruments. The arterial line taps out its indifferent beat. For a heartbeat, the sound shifts into something else, not pulse but waves, soft and patient. I blink as the field tilts in that thin gap where the brain chooses which frame to show. Temporal lobe becomes plank and wet tissue turns into dark water with sky laid across it. A girl's laugh comes close enough that I could catch her wrist.

Lila's voice snaps me back, asking about suction tips. The dock drops away. The brain becomes the brain again as antiseptic replaces algae and copper stands in for mud. I draw a slow breath through my nose and say I am fine, just thinking. Malik asks what about, because he loves that game. I tell him I hate the word nightmares because it makes things sound pretty. Lila's shoulders loosen just enough for me to return to the field.

Cut, coag, suction, shape. It is an intimate job, editing a stranger's chance to relive her own life. Her pre-op form was reduced to one word, peace. She is tired of waking on shower tiles with her head ringing and knees bruised, unsure if she fainted or seized. What she did not write, but wore in her mouth and throat, was that she wanted amnesty too. A pass from the dock or whatever her brain has built from it.

When I ask for a clip Lila places the titanium jaws into my palm. Angle matters as I set it on a feeder vessel near the focus. I squeeze until flow stops and tissue pales by half a shade as blood finds a new route. The field clears. Malik praises the beauty of it. I tell him beauty is a function of whether it works. Reliability is what people buy from me, not charm and not genius.

I do what I say I will do. I take the part that is harming you and leave enough of you to live with what remains. It is a neat story that hospitals love, because neat stories fund programs. I smooth the resection edges and step back half a pace to look. The EEG stays calm at the margin of what I spared. I call phase one complete and tell them to let her coast before mapping. Nguyen exhales like someone loosened a fist around his throat.

Malik corrects him about names and Lila snorts, turning it into a cough. I let the outline of a smile show. They mean it as a joke, even when it is still worship beneath it. You have to dress worship in jokes, or someone calls HR. I peel off my gloves and call for a timer, ten minutes then stim. Malik adjusts the anesthetic mix as I cross to the sink. I do not need to scrub between phases, because need has nothing to do with it.

Water and soap and friction are the closest thing I have to confession. The tap squeaks as cool water sheets over my fingers and spills into the basin. Almost at once a ghost of a smell rises. It is not city water or sterile saline but something cold, green, and deep. Something tightens under my sternum as my hand stills beneath the stream. For a second the basin is gone and the sink edge is dock wood. The tile under my shoes becomes damp boards dark from years of soaking.

A young voice at my ear sounds bright and impatient, telling me to come on and not be boring. Malik calls my name and the room snaps back. Water is water and steel is steel. My reflection is a woman in a gown and cap rather than a dripping girl with goosebumps. I say I am good as I shut off the tap and dry each hand, each finger, each web space with motions cut into muscle by years. Inside my head something keeps moving. It is not a seizure but a ripple in the part of the brain that chooses what to keep and what to burn. The lake again. Always the lake.

I drop the towel and return to the table. When I say let us wake her, mapping means she needs to be halfway here and halfway wherever her memory drags her. We have that in common, even if only one of us pretends it is neat. Malik brings her up while the OR remains what it is, lights humming and machines blinking. Air moves through the vents with the cold indifference of weather. I ask Lila for the language cards and Nguyen for naming and repeat. I tell him if she gets lost to assume it is him first.

Her lashes tremble as the ventilator slows and her own breath takes over. A muffled sound slips under the tape at her mouth. Malik speaks warm and practiced, telling her she is doing great and that surgery is going well. He explains we will ask her to do a few simple tasks while I stimulate a bit. Her eyes open glassy and uncertain, trying to move toward the ceiling before they remember the frame has her pinned. Nguyen asks her name and where she is. She answers clearly enough. I tell her she is doing well and that I am Dr. Nile.

Her face tightens when she whispers that I said I would fix it. I tell her we are working on it and that I need her help. I warn her she might see or hear things that are not here. I tell her to say what happens even if it feels wrong. Nguyen holds the cards where she can see them. Malik watches the EEG like scripture. Lila's hands hover ready at the edge of the field. I call out stimulation at one milliamp left temporal for the record. The wand is thin and almost delicate as I lower it near intact cortex at the lip of the cavity.

I do not tap. I touch. I murmur for her to stay with us. We count and lift. Nguyen asks what she notices. She reports only being tired. We run the grid. Touch, count, lift. Prompt, answer, mark. We get the usual party tricks, buzzing lips and flashes of white and a metal taste that is not there. Then I shift a few millimetres back toward the hot zone. I call stimulation again. Her sharp breath answers contact. Nguyen asks what she notices.

She says water, lapping against wood. My mouth goes dry. I ask her to describe it. She says dark, blue black, a dock she is standing on. The edges of my mask itch as I keep my tone flat. I ask how she feels, scared or calm. A tear leaks as she says she should not be there but cannot move. I lift the wand and stop stimulation. The EEG calms. Her shoulders loosen. Nguyen asks where she is now. She says in the hospital, with us. He says perfect, too relieved. I move to a safer spot and continue. My hand is steady. My heart is not.

When I say I am going to repeat the one with the water she hesitates and then nods. Her fingers twitch under contact. Nguyen asks what now. She whispers that there is someone else. My heartbeat gets loud in my ears. That only happens when I sprint or lie. I ask who. She says a girl on the edge. Nguyen asks how old. She says fourteen or fifteen, laughing and not scared. Fourteen to fifteen lands like a weight. I ask if she knows her. She says no but that the girl looks like someone. Nguyen asks who. She whispers that the girl looks like me.

The room holds its breath. For a beat I am twelve and then fifteen and then nowhere at all. Wet boards are under bare feet. Dark water moves like muscle. A voice behind me sounds delighted and sharp. It tells me how beautiful I will be when I stop pretending I am good. I tell them to stop stimulation too fast. The wand lifts and the EEG settles. My pulse does not. Malik clears his throat and asks if I am okay. I say we have confirmed overlap at the focus and that it is enough. We will complete resection. Nguyen starts to object. I cut him off. He shuts his mouth. I cannot tell if that helps.

We finish the rest of mapping on habit. Motor is safe. Language is intact. Vision shows no loss. Under the clinical talk one-line loops in my head, that she looks like you. Patients project and pin masks on surgeons with steady hands, textbook behavior. But my nose does not smell chlorhexidine now. It smells like algae and old rain. It smells like the quiet before a storm decides what it is.

By closure she is back under full anesthesia. Bleeders are found. The bone flap is replaced. Plates are set. The scalp is closed in layers until only a curved red line remains under her hair. Nguyen remarks on the coverage. I tell him if she seizes again it is on me, not her brain. He gives a small unsure smile and asks if we ever wonder what they see when we push those memories. He asks if we make it worse before better. His face flushes because he hates that he asked. I tell him outcomes are tidy and people are not. He waits. I add that yes, I think about it.

I toss my mask in the bin. Cool air hits my face. I feel too exposed without it. I tell him the brain is not a cabinet. It tells stories. We do not delete scenes, we change how often they play. He asks what if the scene is defining. I tell him then it stays, even if the brain lies about details to keep it. He nods and turns to help Lila count instruments. I watch him a moment longer because residents are mirrors you can still adjust if you catch them early.

On a side monitor the intra-op scan is up. The focus is gone. In its place is a clean absence, like a sentence with one dangerous word removed. I stare at it. A piece of someone's story has been neatly cut out. I tell myself the first cut is correction, not harm. I am good at corrections. The hospital likes that about me. Administrators do not want visionaries, they want surgeons who bring problems back into alignment. My complication rates are low. My outcomes are tidy. My cases make for good conference slides. No one asks what it costs to maintain that level of order inside a skull.

In the locker room I step into the shower. Hot water stings. It is the one place in the hospital where my posture can drop. One hand rests on tile for balance while water runs over shoulders and spine. My mind replays the case. Position, exposure, resection, mapping. Her voice says there is a girl who looks like you. I tip my head back until the stream blurs the room. It would be easy to lean a few degrees and pretend the light is lower and the air wetter and the floor wood instead of tile. I do not. People call what I do courage, but it is not. Courage is walking to the edge of the memory and looking down. What I have is discipline. Discipline is building a life tall and busy enough that you do not have to look at the water unless you choose to.

The shower shuts off at ten minutes, ruthless and efficient. I dry off and dress. I rebuild Dr. Jacqueline Nile. Hair pinned. Clothes clean. Face composed. Three alerts glow on my phone. One from the hospital system praises an excellent outcome. One from my mother says God is using my mind for His glory. One from an unsaved number tells me to be in the VIP room at ten because I owe a story.

I read that one the longest. It is early afternoon. I still have post-op rounds and a new consult and a meeting where they will ask me to grow the memory program without saying out loud what it does to people. I could delete the text and pretend I never saw it. I could go home and eat something clean and joyless and sleep eight hours. Instead, I type that I will be there. Three dots appear almost at once. It answers good girl. Heat climbs the back of my neck. It is not shame. It is want.

I lock the screen. In the mirror above the sink my reflection looks back with no lag and no stutter. When I lift my hand she lifts hers in sync. I tell her there is no problem. She does not look convinced. Recovery is quiet. The patient is groggy but stable. Her partner sits folded into a plastic chair with fingers woven through hers and knuckles white. I tell him she did well and that we removed the focus. I say the next two days matter most but that I am hopeful. He exhales like he has been holding his breath for months. He thanks me with wet eyes. He says she was so scared of losing herself.

I tell him memories are stubborn. Even when we change the path around them they do not vanish. They soften and lose their teeth. He nods like that is enough. I do not tell him some memories never lose their teeth. They only learn new angles. He asks whether she will stop dreaming about the water. He has no idea I have stood in a version of that dream. I tell him her brain will have more room to build newer stories that will matter more over time. It is not a lie. He squeezes her hand. Her eyelids flutter. For a second her gaze catches on me like she knows me. She murmurs that I was on the dock. The floor tilts by a degree. I tell her gently that I was in the operating room. She blinks and drifts back under.

If her partner heard he files it somewhere he can live with. Or he pretends he did not. Either way he edits. We all do. By the time I escape the meeting about revenue and brand the sky has turned to that muted blue that makes windows into bad mirrors. I stand in the glass entryway and watch the doors breathe people in and out. Visitors and staff and patients with bandages like commas on their heads pass by. Beyond the lot the city flickers with pharmacy signs and headlights and a billboard selling a life that looks easy to hold. My phone buzzes again with a reminder not to be late because some of us do not have lives to save. There is no name attached. It does not need one.

The club is fifteen minutes by car and thirty by cab. It is fifty if I walk and pretend it is exercise rather than control. I run a quick list of what I am wearing and what is in my closet. I change the shirt and keep the slacks. I swap shoes and add lipstick. It is just enough to move from surgeon to the other version without a full shed. A nurse passes and nods good night. I nod back. She holds a whole story of me, driven and brilliant, a bit cold but kind to patients, married to the job and too busy for messy things. Lonely maybe, but fulfilled. It is not her fault. It is the version I give her.

Outside the air bites through my coat. Sirens and engines and footsteps and a crate scraping pavement layer the night. One hollow wood sound stands out for a beat. I look up. In the hospital glass I see myself twice. One stands where I stand. The other lags half a step behind. When I move the second hesitates and then catches up. I wait until they line up cleanly. I whisper stress and overwork. The lake does not answer. It never needs to. It has time.

There are cameras in the hospital lobby and in the parking garage and in the elevators. They record everything except intention. They would show me leaving in my coat and raising my hand for a cab. They would show another competent physician heading home after a long day. They would not show the calculation running under that image. They would not show the quiet decision to walk toward the other version of myself that waits when the scrubs come off.

I turn away from the building. There is a line I cross every time I leave here and head into the city. It is not on any map. There is no sign. It is just a point under my feet where one story stops covering the other. At ten someone in a dark room will call me by my name or my title or some other name I allow. I will step out of the day and into something tight and black and wrong for a hospital corridor. Hands will be on me instead of mine on someone else.

At some point after a drink and after a grip hard enough that I feel it in my teeth my brain will offer the same frame. A dock. A girl. Water black as deep space. Every time I choose not to follow it. Every time it follows anyway. The first cut I ever made was not with a blade. It was the moment I decided whatever happened at that lake belonged sealed behind a door marked do not enter. I have been operating around it ever since.

Tonight, will not be different. Probably. I step off the curb and raise my hand for a cab. The city moves brisk and blind around me. In the rearview the hospital shrinks, its blue logo glowing on the hill like a god that sells itself. Somewhere ahead the other life waits. It is not an accident. It is not a fall. It is a choice. And like any cut, once it's made, the tissue never goes back to what it thought it was before.

$$\sim\!\!\infty\!\!\sim$$

Echoes of Discipline

I woke with my neck set just right, and the rest of me wrecked, the pillow the kind the hospital pushes on surgeons because it held my head in line and kept my spine in its neutral curve with shoulders open and chin level. Everything else felt off, the dream staying in my body and not my mind as a weight at the base of my skull, a pull in the traps, tight ribs like I had spent hours braced against impact. I could not name the images. I only had the aftertaste. I lay still and watched light leak through the blinds in a pale grid.

Count breaths, in, out, again, because this was not comfort but a check, heart rate before thought could mess with it, normal and a bit high with no panic and no sprint. Just ready. Then I noticed my hands, left palm flat on the mattress and right hand on my sternum with fingers spread to feel each rise and fall. My mother used to do that when I had fevers, palm on my chest to count the breaths with silent prayer after and never during, numbers first and faith second. I let my hand drop and swung my legs out of bed.

The hardwood was cold, and I sat on the edge of the mattress with my spine tall and shoulders set, the posture coming without asking like a default. It is strange what the body keeps when the mind claims it cannot remember, because I can still see a pew with my feet not touching the floor and my father's hand at my lower back with pressure so light it was almost kind. Jackie, he would whisper, up, not harsh and not loud, just a fix and a shape. I stood and crossed to the window.

I rolled my shoulders until the left one clicked and the ache eased, and outside the city looked rinsed and thin, softened by distance, while my reflection floated in the glass. Straight spine, neutral stance, a body ready to be filled by the day, and we did not talk about bodies in my house, we talked about posture. That gap mattered, because bodies were private and a little shameful, they sweated and itched and needed things and interrupted church with coughs and bathroom breaks. Posture was moral. Posture showed who you were when you thought no one was watching.

At church my mother sat with ankles crossed and hands folded, her back one clean line that was not stiff but just composed, and my father matched her without effort so that it looked like nature. It was understood I would do the same, shoulders my mother would say in the car if I slumped and I would correct at once with vertebrae stacking and shoulder blades settling. Neck my father would say if my chin drifted toward my book at dinner, with no yelling and no hits and no sermons about my body belonging to God because we were not that kind of church. We were the quiet kind, the neat kind, where devotion meant taking up as little disruptive space as possible.

On Sundays the sanctuary smelled like wood and floral cleaner, light cutting through the high windows in pale bars so dust turned visible in it while the pews pressed hard through thin fabric. The sermons blur now into parables and letters and soft rules in a steady stream, a man insisting he held no power and only borrowed it, but what I remember is the weight along my spine. When the room rose to sing we did not just stand, we lined up with feet under hips and knees soft, chest open enough to carry sound and head level so the voice had a clean path out. I learned breath control there long before med school, not from a coach but from hymns everyone knew.

Inhale on the lift and exhale in long, measured lines, because the first time I felt my body as separate from the script I was nine, mid hymn when a small muscle between my shoulder blades seized just left of the spine as one tight thread. Clinically it was nothing and no scan would show it and no chart would note it, but the more I tried not to feel it the more it stained the whole moment. A note went flat and my breath snagged while my shoulders wanted to shift, so I held them still. My mother's fingers brushed mine on the pew as not a correction but a tether, and we stayed upright together.

The knot did not fade and joined the list of things I carried, so later I lay on the living room carpet with a library copy of Gray's open in front of me and tried to find that exact muscle. The diagrams were too broad and fibers implied but not named, yet the search mattered as spine, erectors, the structures that keep you from folding when gravity asks you to. I pressed my fingers into my own back, tracing lines from the page onto my body and cataloging tension without judgment. It never crossed my mind that other kids might be doing anything else that afternoon.

There is a quiet you only get in a church on a weeknight, because Sundays were full and timed and Wednesdays were youth group noise, but some evenings my parents stayed late with pews and budgets and meetings and plans while I sat in a side pew with homework. Stay where we can see you my mother would say, meaning stay inside and stay in range of your name said once at a normal volume. I would spread my books out like tools, with math coming easy and grammar too, rules and exceptions and clear parts that felt close to anatomy. The building smelled different at night with less people and more wood and cloth and cleaner, fluorescents humming so if I listened I could hear the place breathe as ducts shifted and pipes ticked and metal cooled.

When adults talked behind office doors I would slip into the center aisle just to stand, feet on worn carpet with knees soft and spine tall and shoulders back enough to open the chest. Without bodies beside me and without my parents bracketing me the posture changed, not imposed but chosen and held on purpose. My reflection flickered in the dark glass of the doors, a slim girl in a plain dress alone in a room built for together. If I leaned forward a fraction onto the balls of my feet I could feel movement coil in my calves and thighs and back.

Once I pushed further, not a jump but just enough that my heels lifted and my balance hovered, and in that narrow zone held and not falling I was not upright for them. I was upright because I chose it. It should not have felt as good as it did. Nothing dramatic and no fireworks, just a small clean thrill in the parts of the body that handle balance. Under that something was loosening and expanding, and I did not have a name for it then. Later I called it desire.

Most people remember adolescence as bad choices and betrayal by skin, but mine was posture checks and index cards, because puberty arrived on schedule and my parents treated it like biology and duty. Your body is a gift my mother said, handing me a box of pads and a list of steps, and you are responsible for how you carry it, not fear and not shame but a rule delivered like homework that you have been given something so do not waste it. Clothing rules came in small steps with hemlines fine at ten becoming not now at thirteen while necklines rose and sleeves got longer. Not because my parents hated my body, but because they did not trust the world.

It is hard enough out there my father said once, tying his tie before church, and we do not need to make it harder for anyone, so we contained it. Posture took on new work as a straight spine flattened curves and kept the chest from leading while slouching could look like attitude. In choir on risers between girls in drugstore perfume and hairspray, the director paced and told us to lift sternums and relax jaws and stop collapsing. Imagine a string she said from the crown of your head to the ceiling, and I did, feeling that string more than the music as it ran down through vertebrae into ribs and made me taller than gravity.

One rehearsal mid hymn I became aware of my own vertical line, how little space I took side to side and how much space I took upward, with notes buzzing in my chest while other voices blurred into harmony and mine felt sharp and close. I was not looking at anyone, but I felt eyes, the director's or a boy's or no one's at all and it was just hormones and nerves, with all three able to be true. What mattered was how my awareness narrowed along my spine with each vertebra distinct and stacked and charged. I sang, held posture, and did not move.

It was not romance and not even sex, but it was closer to the rightness I would later feel in surgery as a hard task done cleanly while a quiet part of me watched and approved. That was the first time I knew I liked being looked at if I set the terms. My parents never saw the split and they saw obedience and skill and felt proud. You have such presence an older woman said after a youth service, patting my hand, so composed for your age, and my mother said she always has been, never fidgety and always focused. I stood there like a specimen.

Presence, composed, focused, all true and not the whole truth, because at home I worked at a desk my father measured so my elbows made right angles. If I leaned my head into my hand my mother would pass and lift my wrist away, telling me I would strain my neck and that it ruins focus. Everything was function and not vanity, and we did not slump in front of the TV because we barely watched it while we did not sprawl on the couch because the couch was for sitting and talking. Slouching invited sleep, and sleep had its slot too.

I listened to muscles the way other girls listened to gossip, always checking and always taking notes, and in gym class while others hated drills I tracked the burn in my diaphragm and the pull in hip flexors and the difference between heel strike and rolling through the foot. In the locker room girls compared bodies as too this and too that, while I watched without staring and was less interested in shape than in how each girl lived in her skeleton. Some curled inward apologizing for space while others sprawled with limbs thrown wide and claimed room as if it was owed. A counselor once told me to try modeling and I laughed and said I did not like cameras.

Not true, because I just did not want to be made still and the whole point was movement, so looking back surgery was always coming even if at the time it felt like clean steps. I liked science and exactness and anatomy more than the soft fog of theory, because in biology rules had names and exceptions did too. In high school I shadowed a surgeon for a week with hours standing at the back of ORs, posture tall and watching. Surgeons were the extreme form of what I had been trained to be.

They stood for hours with hands where they needed to be and nowhere else, attention locked and bodies serving the work, so the first time I saw a craniotomy I did not fixate on blood. I watched the attending's stance, and he was not big and not dramatic, but when he leaned over the table with spine straight and head tipped into the scope the room shifted around him. Presence, the room orbiting him like a congregation around a pulpit, while nurses moved when he moved and residents matched his pace. Anesthesia tuned its calm to his.

When he spoke it was low and exact, retractor, suction, not there, here, hold, with no wasted gestures and no show. At the back of the room I mirrored him without meaning to, shoulders squared and neck set with focus angled down, because it was not gore that hooked me. It was the line from spine to wrists and the way his whole body became intention. That night I lay on my bedroom floor and stared at the ceiling, not faint and not high but feeling something quieter and worse as inevitability. A life shape I could wear without rubbing raw.

A straight spine, steady hands, and a soft voice with weight, a vessel for other people's fear, because church taught me how to be small in front of something larger while surgery offered the flip where you become the larger thing and serve it. I did not say any of that when I told my parents I wanted medicine, because they heard calling and helping and they smiled. We knew the Lord had plans for you my mother said, and you have got the discipline my father said, squeezing my shoulder. Discipline, yes, that part was plain.

What none of us saw was what grew beside it, because desire did not arrive late and my willingness to name it did. In college people tried things loudly with drugs and clothes and partners while I stayed near the edge and watched, not disgusted and interested. I watched posture shift when someone wanted to be seen, with backs arching a degree when the right person walked in and shoulders squaring, then either softening or locking. The first person I slept with barely mattered.

We had studied together for weeks with caffeine and stress and mutual obsession mistaken for closeness, and he was fine with a nice face and an easy body, while I did not picture him much. I wanted to see what would happen to my own structure if I let go, and when his hand slid under my shirt I did not feel heat first. I felt my spine change as a small curve forward and muscles that held me tall letting go in steps. I noticed it as breath changed and tempo shifted. Being less upright one notch at a time, after he slept I lay on my back and rebuilt my alignment vertebra by vertebra until I felt like myself again, with no guilt and no swept away glow because I felt informed.

I liked the knowledge more than the act, and it kept repeating as partners changed with some mattering and some not. The constant was not their voices but how my body reacted when I let it slip out of discipline. Pleasure peaked in the tiny moment my spine stopped obeying rules it never agreed to. Bent for my reasons and not theirs, the first time I noticed I could engineer it by tilting a hip and softening a knee and dropping shoulders to watch someone's pupils widen I felt the same quiet satisfaction as a clean closure. Input, output, confirmed. Desire was not a flood but a system and my body was willing.

Medicine hardened what church had started, so by residency posture was not just habit but survival. Hours in the OR demanded alignment because slump meant pain and pain meant drift and drift meant risk. I listened to fatigue the way I listened to that knot at nine, notice it, adjust, do not let it run the case, while an attending would mutter stretch your neck and think long game. I did, because I wanted to stand and to operate and to live in that narrow corridor where hands decide who wakes up whole. The OR became a new sanctuary with no hymns and no glass, just machines and blue gowns and the scrub ritual in place of prayer. I held myself tall over patients whose spines lay flat and exposed beneath drapes.

Sometimes late in a case I felt that old imaginary string again from the crown of my head to some point above the ceiling, and if I followed it down through skull and spine and pelvis and feet I could feel my weight settle. Stable, clear, and there was pleasure in that too, not sex but close enough to it to matter. Outside the hospital that same line became a dial, because in bars and in dim rooms where people hid their names and wore something else I learned how to shift it. Straight spine meant doctor and untouchable. A slight soften meant something else.

It did not take much, just a few degrees of hip angle or a head tilt that exposed the neck or a shoulder drop that read as open, and people noticed because they always do. Most seduction is posture plus timing, and I did not need low necklines or loud laughs because I could stand in a corner and shift my alignment by a fraction to feel attention swivel. Sometimes I let it land and sometimes I drew back into neutral and watched it fade. I thought that meant I was in control.

In some ways I was, but control only counts if you know what you are refusing, so the morning after the lecture after the dock slid across the room in my head I showered and dressed and moved through my apartment with surgeon speed. Coffee and toast I would forget and phone unlocked with emails sorted in my mind before I saw them, while the cut on my thumb from broken glass had healed clean as a thin pink line already flattening. Skin remodels well and memory does too, sometimes it does it wrong. I stood at the sink and tried to pull up the dock.

Not the ambush version and on my terms, I closed my eyes and scanned inward the way I read imaging, looking for what did not belong, and at first there was nothing. Just normal noise with cases and meetings and an avoided text and mild anger at comms posting me again, and then under it the echo. Not an image but a posture, a younger me outdoors with weight tipped forward and shoulders held in a tense balance, neither defiant nor collapsed, waiting. The floor under bare feet felt wrong for an apartment.

Not tile. Boards my brain offered, old wood warped by damp, and the moment it clicked my calves tightened as if they remembered balancing on narrow planks. In the present my fingers locked around the mug, and I could have stopped and logged it and labeled it and moved on. Instead I leaned toward it, toward the sense of being watched from behind the frame, while my adult system misread it the way it has learned to as attention and as risk and as a kind of oxygen. Heat crawled up the back of my neck.

Desire turning up late to a scene it did not earn, I opened my eyes and the apartment snapped back with coffee lukewarm and knuckles pale on ceramic and spine tall as always. Outside the city kept moving, and inside under bone and muscle and years of trained stillness a younger me stood on a dock and waited. Not saint and not victim but something harder to manage, the first self who learned you can choose how to stand even in a room built for kneeling. I rinsed the mug and tied my hair back.

I checked my reflection once more to make sure my body said what it needed to say, competent and composed and controlled. The other story stayed where it always has. Below the surface with the dock and with the lake and with whatever was watching.

Chapter Three

---◦◦◦---

A Summer You Don't Remember

T
here are nights my brain won't shut off unless I feed it something it can't label, and tonight is one of them. By the time I leave the hospital, Manhattan is wet-cold and wired, the air slipping through wool like it's thin paper as headlights smear on the street and neon stains puddles. The city looks flayed, glass and concrete humming like exposed cortex, and I could go home, microwave something with protein and no joy, skim an article, answer emails I shouldn't answer, and fall asleep on the couch while an algorithm drips comfort into my skull. Instead, when my building passes the window, I stay in the back seat.

"Keep going," I tell the driver, and he checks the mirror and asks where to, doc. "Lower East Side," I say, "Rivington and Orchard," and a small lift of his brows answers back with copy. I don't remember when that corner became shorthand, because it isn't an address and there is no address, just a black door under a blank awning and a camera you learn to look at a certain way. We head south as lights slide and break on the glass, and somewhere around Houston my shoulders drop an inch, like my body knows the route before I'll admit it.

I shouldn't do this tonight, because tomorrow is stacked with two resections and a consult that ends with "quality of life" spoken like a verdict. The responsible version of me would be home, screens off, in bed by eleven, and another part of me says I'll still be brilliant on three hours' sleep because I always am. The car stops and the driver twists a little and says we're here, and I tell him to give me ten minutes while he taps his phone and reminds me the meter's running.

I step out as wind comes down the cross street like a freezer door opening, music leaking from a bar window, thin pop that isn't loud, just present. A group of twenty-somethings crosses in a loose pack, laughing too hard with phones out and bare legs against the cold, and I turn away and walk east. The entrance is recessed between a shuttered florist and a stairwell to whatever "wellness" is being sold this month, and if you didn't know what to look for you'd miss it.

The awning is unlit, matte black canvas over a black door with no line and no sound, a small camera bubble above the frame and a faint rectangle where a bell used to be. I press my thumb to the seam where wood meets metal and a tiny click answers, then a soft buzz. "Good evening," a filtered voice says, asking for membership ID, and I reply Jax Nile, ending in thirty-two, as static crackles like someone is doing three things at once before welcoming me back.

The lock releases and the door opens just enough for me to slip through before closing behind me with a padded thud. The first corridor is narrow and dark, LED strips running low along the baseboards, guiding without showing much as my heels make dull sounds on concrete. The air is cooler than outside and smells faintly of steel, skin, and expensive alcohol, and at the end another door sits half-open with bass pushing through the gap.

My chest answers before my ears do as I push in. The club is underground in every way that matters, with a low ceiling, matte black walls, pipes and cables left exposed like a choice, and blue-violet light cutting the dark into angles. There is no marked dance floor, just a density of bodies that thickens and thins with the track, and the bass isn't loud enough to hurt as it settles into bone, a steady pulse somewhere between heartbeat and machine.

No one screams and no one stumbles drunk, because that isn't the point and this is where people go when daytime language runs out. I shrug off my coat and hand it to the attendant who tags it, gives me a token, and doesn't ask my name, because there are no phones, no cameras, and no questions. The rules are unwritten and absolute as I move in and shadows become faces, glances sharpening into offers that fade when I don't take them.

The bar glows from beneath with bottles lit like organs in glass, and I don't drink much here because alcohol blurs reaction time and I've trained my hands too long to risk that. "Sparkling water," I tell the bartender, and he nods once and slides a glass toward me with a lime wedge as condensation forms at once and runs down in neat tracks. I take it and turn my back to the bar so I can see most of the room.

Two men stand near the left wall, almost chest-to-chest without touching, close enough that the air between them has weight, and a woman in a silver slip dress leans against a pillar like she owns the building while scanning the crowd with patient hunger she hasn't spent yet. Couples, trios, and not-quite anything brush and align, staying an inch apart while everything between them hums. Control is the drug, knowing you could, and choosing not to yet.

I sip as bubbles gather at the back of my throat and pop bright, no taste, just sensation, and for half a second my brain tries to rename it, whispering lake. I swallow hard as the carbonation burns the word away before it can grow teeth, and the bass keeps going, steady and indifferent. I move off the bar line, not coming every week because I'm reckless, not stupid, but often enough that my feet know the map.

There is the slight rise where concrete gives way to rubber and the narrow ledge along the far wall where you can watch without being pulled in, and tonight my body chooses it before I finish pretending this is a choice made in the moment. From the ledge, the crowd looks like time-lapse cells bumping, splitting, and clustering, and the lights strobe now and then but never fast enough to scramble anyone. This place doesn't want chaos, it wants control with sharp edges.

That's when I feel it, being watched, not the general scan that follows anyone decent-looking through a room and not the lazy appraisal I've learned to ignore. This is narrow and focused, a beam, and I don't turn right away as I take another sip and let bubbles sting my tongue while keeping my eyes on the room and letting some older part of me map the angle. Left, I turn.

She's sitting just outside the main current on a low bench designed to discourage staying, one leg crossed with her foot pointed and heel hovering a breath off the edge. She wears a black sleeveless dress cut close without begging for it, no glitter and no shine, nothing that asks for the light, and her dark hair is gathered at the nape in a loose knot done without a mirror. A few strands escape and curl against her throat, her hands resting lightly on her knee with fingers loose.

She isn't watching the room, she's watching me, with no theater in it and no slow sweep up and down, just something that feels like an exam, calm, exact, and unhurried. A thin flare of irritation rises first because I spend my days under fluorescent light getting stared at by residents, families, nurses, and boards, all wanting my face to tell them how things end, and I didn't come here to be another case. That irritation is a top layer, and under it is something sharper, too close to relief.

Recognition hits hard enough to steal a breath, and I know that face, though not in any clean way that I can name. If she'd been a colleague, a patient, or a board member, if I'd cut into her life, I'd remember, because I remember most things I touch, and yet the angle of her jaw, the shape of her mouth, and the way she holds still inside a moving room make her feel like a fixed mark on a spinning image. My fingers tighten on the glass.

She tilts her head a fraction like she's clocked that I've seen her, a hint of a smile touching her mouth that is neither inviting nor mocking, just yes. My heart lands once, too hard, and I tell myself this is nothing, a pattern error as the brain overlays old faces onto new ones when it wants the room to make sense, running through med school, conference, and childhood without finding a match. Instead, vertigo unspools in my chest, like the floor has rotated a few degrees and my inner ear is waiting for the memo.

I realize I'm still staring, and she ends it for both of us as her gaze slides away, not a power move and not a flounce, just returning to the room like I've been scanned, filed, and shelved. The loss of her attention stings more than it should, because this was meant to be the place where I go anonymous. Instead, want sparks, small, unwelcome, and alive.

My feet move before the rest of me votes as I step down from the ledge and thread through bodies, aiming for her on a diagonal so it doesn't look like I'm hunting. My glass is half full and I leave it on a cocktail table as I pass because I want my hands free, and there's space beside her that is too tight to sit without acknowledging her and too wide to pretend it's chance. I stop just inside polite distance.

Up close, she looks the same, her eyes dark hazel, almost black in this light, with minimal makeup and lines that are deliberate rather than careless, a trace of gloss making her mouth look like a mouth and not a product. "Is this seat taken?" I ask, my voice coming out clipped and professional with the ghost of my consult tone that I hate. She looks up with nothing in her face reading surprise as she says no and that it's mine.

I sit, and we don't touch, my thigh inches from hers, close enough to feel heat and far enough that no contact can be an accident. She smells like clean skin and soap with nothing heavy, and my brain trained to sort scent into sterile, septic, anesthetic, and burnt can't place her. We sit for a few seconds facing the room.

"You don't come here often," she says, not a question, and I counter by asking if she does. She takes a beat and says often enough to see patterns, and the easy move is a joke about my schedule or trauma-bond small talk about surgeons' hours, but I don't take it. She doesn't feel like someone you impress with suffering.

"What pattern am I?" I ask, not knowing why I'm feeding this when I could stand and vanish, but I stay. She turns more fully and lets her attention move over me without flinching, and I catch a lighter ring around her pupils, a thin halo of amber. "The type who comes here to remember she has a body," she says, "not to forget."

A shiver runs under my skin as I tell her that's an assumption and she replies that it's an observation, her tone flat as if she's talking about posture. Most people here want to disappear into something, she continues, and then she lets the sentence hang as her gaze dips to skim my throat and the neckline of my black dress that could pass as dinner or conference depending on where you stand. My hair is still twisted like it was under a cap an hour ago. "You want to see yourself," she finishes.

It's unnerving to be read this cleanly by a stranger in a room built for masks, so I say maybe I like the music, light, and she lets out a small breath that could be a laugh. She tells me I didn't move, not once, hips, shoulders, spine, only my eyes, and she's right because when I let myself get pulled in I start near the center where contact can be denied, and tonight I stayed at the edges. I say she was watching me, and she replies that she was watching everything, that I was the only one standing still.

The bass rolls through the bench and through my sternum as someone near the center throws their head back like they're casting out a ghost. She asks if I always approach people who stare at me, and I shoot back asking if she always stares until they approach. This time she smiles properly, not wide, but it changes her face and tugs at something under my ribs. She says only when she's sure, and when I ask sure of what she tells me that they won't admit why they're here, but they know.

I feel irritation rise again, mostly as armor, and I ask why she thinks I'm here. Her gaze drops to my hands resting on my knees, nails short and faint glove marks still etched in the skin, and she says quietly that I spend all day trying not to shake, that I walk like I'm holding other people upright, and that this is the only place I let myself feel anything where no one dies for it. Something in me goes very still.

She shouldn't know I'm a surgeon, because there's no badge, no title, and no Doctor over the music, and then I remember the corridor, the camera, and the voice greeting me by name. I say membership ID, and she answers at once that she doesn't work here and they didn't tell me, her eyes staying on mine as she says she just watches. The way she says it makes watch sound like a role.

I ask her name, and she asks whether I want the one that's real or the one that hurts less, which should sound dramatic but doesn't, landing like a consent form. I tell her to start with the one that hurts less, and she thinks for a moment before saying Clara. The name hits like a cold hand at the base of my skull.

I've heard it before, somewhere just outside recall, and it rings through me like a chord my fingers used to know, dock, boards, water, a girl in a blue jacket laughing as light fades, Clara. The flash is so fast it outruns logic, and my body reacts before my mind can argue as my chest tightens, my fingers curl, and the room tips in that familiar half-degree slide. I force my breathing even and tell myself it's a common name, chance not fate.

"Jax," I say, short for Jacqueline, and she answers that she knows, as the bass drops out for a bar and slams back in. There is no good reason for her to know that, because down here I'm just Jax, no last names and no printed badges, the system using digits not syllables, and the people I've let press me into walls never asking for anything that could be written down. I ask how.

The track shifts, same tempo and different mood, like a heart finding a new rhythm after a shock, and Clara lifts her hand. For a second I think she's going to tuck hair back, but instead her fingers drift into the air between us, hovering a breath from my wrist. I feel heat before touch.

"If I touch you," she says, her voice barely cutting through the music, "you're going to decide I'm the problem," and the sentence is odd enough to pierce my defenses. I ask the problem with what, and she answers you, my pulse jumping. She asks if I want her to, small and direct, and it should not spike my adrenaline.

I should say no, because I have surgery tomorrow, my career runs on steady hands, and my public life does not include underground clubs and strangers named after half-remembered ghosts. Still, yes comes out, landing like relief and confession in one breath. Her fingers close the distance.

The touch is minimal, barely pressure, pads against the inside of my wrist where skin is thin and vessels run close, and it might as well be a wire. The room doesn't vanish, lights don't flicker, and music doesn't stop, but my nervous system decides this is a signal, and the rest is noise. Her skin is warm and smooth with no callus, and the contact isn't a grip, too light for that and too chosen to dismiss.

My pulse hits the back of her fingers like it's trying to push her away, and a smell rises that doesn't belong, cold, green, and deep, water. For a blink, the condensation on a mirrored column looks like it's running the wrong way, and somewhere in the wrong decade a gull cries. I blink again.

The present snaps back, slightly off, and Clara takes her hand away with no smug look and no win. She looks faintly sad, the way I look when a scan confirms what everyone feared but no one wants said out loud. She tells me I feel it, not a question.

I could lie, joke, or walk away and starve this moment by refusing it a story, but my own research sits in my head like a note in the margin that the brain doesn't store the past, it stores instructions for rebuilding a version you can live inside. In my version, there is no Clara, no lake, and no dock, yet my body seems to be working from a different draft. I say I don't know what she means, a compromise between denial and truth with a rough edge my voice almost hides.

"Yes," she says, "you do," and then softer, you always did. Always drops through me with no friction like a stone into deep water, and I say I don't know you. She accepts that as both fact and lie, telling me that's the part that isn't my fault.

The sentence lodges under my ribs, which implies some parts are, and I stand. I tell her I don't do whatever this is, and she asks remembering, one word with a clean impact. I grab my glass without recalling where I set it, the water gone flat and tiny bubbles clinging to the side, refusing the surface.

I say I came here to relax, not to be read, and she tells me I picked the wrong room. I should leave, walk the corridor, hit the cold, get in the car, go home, sleep, and label this stress plus hunger and be done. Instead, I hesitate.

If she knows me, I say, then she knows what I do, and her gaze drops to my hands again as she says yes, you cut. The word lands with a weight my bones recognize, and she adds that I cut other people's brains so they can live with themselves, asking if I've thought I might have done that to my own without a knife. Anger comes, clean and brief.

I tell her she doesn't know my past, and Clara looks straight up at me and says she knows I stood on a dock once with boards wet and bare feet, that I hated the water. The room goes quiet in my head even though the music keeps pounding. She shouldn't know that.

Those aren't even full memories, just flashes my brain has been using lately like it's borrowing images for metaphor, and a memory is a committee with one voice suggesting and another editing, tonight someone voting louder. I tell her she's drunk, thin, and her pupils are steady and her words are sharp as she tells me I'm scared. That hits with cruel accuracy.

I say I'm done, and she answers of course you are, with no grab, no chase, and no drama, just the sound of someone who has watched me quit the same fight before I've even named it. I turn away, the floor not tilting and everything feeling too level like someone overcorrected. I walk to the bar, set the glass down, and don't order anything else as my wrist hums with nerves rewiring around the ghost of her touch.

I collect my coat and the attendant hands it over without looking twice. The corridor out is colder than I remember, the LED strips making it feel like a scan, a narrow slice with clean edges that tells you to lie still while the machine reads you. Outside, the cold slaps my face and my breath ghosts white.

The car is still there, and the driver looks up from his phone and asks if I'm headed home, doc. I say yes, and as we pull away I look back at the blank awning with nothing to see, black canvas over a door that could lead to storage. The city slides past in streaks as streetlights stretch gold and a billboard paints someone else's drama across the glass and across my face.

I close my eyes, and inside my lids the club rebuilds with light, bodies, bench, and Clara. In the replay her touch is even lighter, a pinprick of warmth like a cautery point on a vessel, seal it before it can bleed. The driver asks if it was a rough night, and I say long.

He chuckles and asks if I saved any lives today, and I could say yes or no because both would be true depending on how you score it. I say I tried, and he answers that's more than most. We turn onto my street, and in the dark shop glass something flickers at the edge of my sight.

For half a second in the reflection I see myself, not in the back seat but on a dock with bare feet on wet boards and air cold enough to bite the lungs. Beside me at the margin of the frame is another figure with dark hair, bare legs, and a hand reaching out, not pushing or pulling, just hovering. The car moves and the reflection breaks into mannequins and sale signs.

We stop out front and the driver taps the meter off, telling me to sleep well, doc, the words hanging like an optimistic prognosis. Upstairs in the bathroom I brace my hands on the sink as the light turns harsh and flat, making my face all angles. I look at myself.

I am not drunk, with pupils constricting, breath steady, and cheeks only flushed from cold, and without thinking I turn my wrist palm-up. The skin where she touched looks normal, but when I press my thumb there the ghost returns, warmth and recognition, that liminal half-second when a patient starts to surface with a body awake and words not yet online. I tell the empty room I don't know you, and the mirror gives me my own face back without arguing.

Somewhere below the city the lake my mind calls a metaphor waits at whatever depth I left it, and somewhere under a blank awning a woman named Clara sits on a bench and watches people lie to themselves. We remember what we can live with, and tonight my body remembered something my mind hasn't agreed to survive. I switch off the light.

In the dark, for a fraction of a second, I could swear I hear water moving against wood, and then there's only the building hum and the small ordinary noises of strangers living lives I will never be able to cut my way into or out of. Sleep doesn't come fast, and when it comes at all it arrives in pieces, lake, dock, laughter, and always a hand on my wrist.

Chapter Four

---∞---

Sterile Hands. Dirty Mind

T he morning after the club, I follow a protocol. Not hospital protocol, mine. Step one is deny everything, and step two is move before thought can catch up. I wake before the alarm, heart already moving at a steady clip, and for seven, maybe eight seconds, I am no one. Just a body in a dark room pulling air in and out with no name, no degrees, no past, just blood moving.

Then the layers return, one by one, like PPE. Jacqueline comes first, then Doctor, then Surgeon, then Today's list, and I reach for my phone because phones are where consequences show up. The screen lights my face in a washed-out blue and my eyes skim while my brain does not read so much as sort. Fix later, present later, perform later, because those are the only categories that keep me upright.

No missed calls and no strange numbers, two urgent emails, one from a resident about a possible hematoma on a post op scan and one from the Chief's assistant, bright and chipper, reminding me the board talk is in a week and that everyone is very excited to hear about the memory program. Everyone is excited, which means donors are excited, which means administration is excited, which means I will be asked to make pain sound like progress. I flag both messages without answering, because answering is a commitment, and commitments are how you end up cornered. Only then does last night surface, like the brain saving its real content for the moment you have no defenses left.

The club, the black corridor, Clara on the bench, her fingers on my wrist like she was checking something under my skin that no atlas shows. My body reacts before thought, heat then cold, a spike of adrenaline with nothing to cut and nowhere to put it. The sensation is clean and wrong, and it brings my pulse up without bringing clarity with it. I do not like reactions I cannot assign to a cause.

For half a second, I picture texting someone, not knowing who, because there is no safe person in my life for I met a stranger in a sex club and she knows the smell of a lake I have never admitted exists. That sentence has no recipient, and even if it did, it would stain them with it. So I do not text anyone, and the decision feels like control even when it is only avoidance. I swing my legs out of bed as the floor is cold and the air is colder, gray light leaking around the blinds and flattening the room into a blank space like a hotel that forgets you the second you leave.

I shower longer than I need to, dial turned just shy of too hot, scrubbing until my skin goes pink and my muscles remember their job. Forward, not backward, not down, not into water, and my hands keep working as if diligence can cauterize memory. The spray takes sweat, smoke, and a faint trace of someone else's scent, and I let it because that part is honest. It does not touch Clara, because the thing she left was not on my skin.

Under the water, I turn my wrist palm up, the skin looking normal, veins pale blue under the surface with no bruise, no mark, no proof at all. There is only the memory of sensation replaying like it lives in the nerves and not the skin, as if she touched a switch rather than tissue. I tell the tile it is nothing, stress, pattern matching, you are tired, and the tile does not argue. The tile never argues, which is why bathrooms are where people confess.

By the time I am dressed, I look like the person the hospital thinks it hired. Dark pants, pale shirt, white coat folded over my arm like a shield, hair pinned up neat and tight to stay out of the field, and a trace of makeup to hide the broken sleep. I check myself once in the mirror and see competence arranged into a face. Then I turn away before the mirror can turn into a question.

In the elevator, I tear open a protein bar and chew like it is a task, chalk, sugar, and duty. I swallow without tasting because tasting means paying attention, and attention is the doorway. On the ride down, my shoulders settle into the posture that tells the world I am fine. The doors open and the day has already started without asking whether I am ready.

The ride to Meridian is short and the driver stays quiet, his talk in safe lanes about traffic, rain, and temperature, never feelings. When he says I am in early today, catching my eyes in the mirror like it is a compliment, I tell him big case. It is always a big case, because anything smaller gives the mind room to wander. He nods, satisfied, because people like simple narratives and I am paid to deliver them.

Meridian rises out of the street like every expensive promise, glass, steel, calm lines meant to reassure. The logo above the doors gleams with donor money and controlled miracles, and I feel the familiar irritation that the building is better branded than the people inside it are protected. Inside, cold air hits antiseptic and fluorescent light snaps across my eyes with the same harsh mercy it always has. The guard says morning, Dr Nile, and I answer morning, tapping my badge as the lock beeps and the building lets me in.

On the neurosurgery floor, my day clicks onto rails, scrub, review scans, brief the team, see the patient, repeat. The rhythm is a drug with no crash, and I let it take over because that is what it is for. The board can talk about wellness and balance, but the truth is this place runs on surgeons who do not stop. Stopping is where the old images get traction.

First case is a left temporal lobe tumor, operable but close enough to language cortex that a lazy millimeter could take his words from him. Mr Alvarez in his fifties watches me with a narrow, testing look like he is still weighing whether this is medicine or a billing trick. He has hands like he has spent decades fixing things, engines, wiring, other people's broken appliances, and the hands matter because hands tell you what someone believes about control. I like patients with hands that worked, because they understand what precision costs.

I ask how he is holding up and he rasps that he has been better, rough voice and clear eyes, then asks if I am the brain lady. I tell him I prefer neurosurgeon because brain lady makes me sound like I do birthday parties, and a short laugh slips out of him. Good, because patients who can laugh before we wheel them into machines and strangers tend to come back cleaner. Humor is a small sign the brain is still choosing, even with fear pressing on it.

He asks if I am going to take out the bad bits, and I say that is the plan, tapping the MRI where the lesion sits pale and wrong. I explain the tricky spot, how we mapped it, how he will sleep for most of it, then we will wake him for a few minutes to test language, then he will drift again while we finish. He says waking up with his head open sounds like a horror movie, and I tell him it is less dramatic than it sounds because he will not see anything, that is our job. I do not tell him that the horror movie is not the awake part, it is the part where a word disappears and never comes back.

He asks if I have done this before, the version of the question that really asks whether I am his worst day or his best shot. I say yes, many times, then watch him look for the lie under the yes. He studies my face for cracks, doubt, fear, ego, and I give him something else. I tell him I would not do this if I thought it would hurt him more than help, and his shoulders drop a fraction like his body wants permission to stop bracing.

He snorts and asks if that is my fancy way of saying he will be fine, and I tell him it is my way of saying I am very good at my job and he is not doing this alone. It is not kindness and it is not a performance, it is calibration, because people need a steady reference point. He nods, and the nod is not trust, it is consent, which matters more. All right then, brain lady, he says, do your thing, and I let it land because naming me makes him feel less powerless.

Later in OR 2, my world shrinks to the circle of light over his shaved scalp. Everything outside the field becomes useful noise, an anesthesiologist breathing with the vent, a scrub nurse counting tools, a monitor beeping like a metronome for risk. I like the metronome because it does not care what I did last night, it only cares whether this man stays alive. Under the microscope, the tumor looks like a typo, slightly off color and texture against normal cortex.

When I say bipolar, it is in Lila's hand before the word finishes leaving my mouth. The tool settles between my fingers like a thought I have had a thousand times, and my hands switch into the old certainty. Cut, coagulate, suction, irrigate, because the body prefers sequences. The work is exact and almost spare, nothing sexy, no shine, just training and tiny choices that can ruin a life. It is clean work, and clean work is the only kind I can tolerate when my head is not clean.

And yet another room keeps trying to leak through, low ceiling, blue light, bass in my bones, Clara's fingers on my wrist like she was reading a pulse that was not hers. Not here, not now, I tell myself, and the thought lands like a clamp. This room is territorial, and I am too, and I refuse to let the club borrow my focus. My jaw tightens once, then releases, and I push the thought back down where it belongs.

I call language check and anesthesia brings him up, the soft shift of gases and drips that turns a body from object back into person. His lashes flutter and he makes a muffled sound that the tape turns into something animal. Mr Alvarez, I say, can you hear me, and he answers yeah like he is annoyed by being alive. How are you feeling, I ask, and he says like half a truck, and soft laughter moves around the table because people cannot help themselves. Humor is cheaper than midazolam, and sometimes it works better.

We run mapping, pictures to name, numbers to count, phrases to repeat. We put objects in his hand with eyes covered so he has to find the word by touch, because language is not only sight, it is the whole body trying to label the world. His voice is slow but accurate, and I feel the quiet relief that comes with a clean test. Perfect, I tell him, we are going to let you rest again, and he mumbles do not screw up, doc, like he is joking but not really. That's the plan, I say, and anesthesia takes him back down.

As he drifts and I go back in, time changes the way it always does in surgery. It stretches around a vessel and collapses into one clean plane, minutes widening and an hour disappearing, until my shoulders creep up and my jaw locks and my breath gets small. It is fine, I tell myself, and I know the lie hiding inside that phrase. I am not talking about the tumor, I am talking about the way my mind keeps trying to lay the club over the OR, Clara's gaze framed in the microscope light, her thumb pressed where my radial pulse beats under latex.

This room does not share. It does not share attention, it does not share memory, it does not share me, and I lean into that like doctrine. When I say specimen, Lila takes the tissue and hands it to pathology, and the tumor mass recedes as borders sharpen. Normal tissue starts to re open like air entering a room sealed too long, and the metaphor is uninvited but accurate. I smooth the plane and check the margins because margins are where patients lose their lives without dying.

We close, layer by layer, with the calm that comes from repetition. When the last staple bites and the drapes come down, fatigue hits in the familiar way after long precision, not drama but a full body sense of having spent myself down to a safe minimum. For a few seconds, I am nothing but hands that did what they were trained to do, and the emptiness is almost restful. Then we move him to recovery and the day keeps moving because it always does.

A resident falls into step beside me, bright and unbruised, and tells me it was beautiful. I tell him we will see how beautiful when he can name a carrot tomorrow, because outcomes are never as cinematic as people want. He flushes but keeps grinning, and then stalls about watching me, stumbling into his own hero worship. It's normal, that is how this job copies itself, you watch someone's hands long enough and yours learn the same moves. Still, the word watch drags across my nerves in a way that has nothing to do with teaching.

I tell him I will have my assistant add him on one condition, and he straightens like he is about to be tested. Stop trying to seduce me with adverbs, I say, because it is easier to make it a joke than to admit the word hit wrong. He laughs too loud and too relieved, yes, Dr Nile, and the sound is safe again. I keep walking, because if I stop, I will start thinking.

In the scrub room I peel off my gloves, one snap then the other, and underneath my fingers are pale and wrinkled, smelling of soap and chlorhexidine. Clean, for now, sterile for minutes, and I wash again because that is what we do. Fingers laced, palms, thumbs, nails, motions so ingrained my joints could do them without me, because ritual is how hospitals pretend control is possible. Halfway through, bare skin under warm water, Clara's touch flashes across my wrist like an overlay, absurd to think of that here, though the brain does not care what I call absurd.

I brace my wet hands on the sink edge, the metal cool as the faucet hisses, and tell my reflection in the stainless panel that I am fine and not one of my own cases. My reflection looks tired, the muscles around my eyes sitting between fatigue and alarm, and the distinction matters. Fatigue is normal, alarm is information, and I do not like the information I am getting. I rinse longer than needed, because need is not the point.

The rest of the day takes the shape it always does when my inside life will not behave, flawless on paper and messy in my head. Second surgery goes smooth, because my hands do not care about my personal failures. I check a post aneurysm patient who is irritable and alive, my favorite mix, because alive patients can be mean and mean means function. I sign a discharge and talk an internist out of a CT angiogram on a patient whose worst headache of my life is dehydration, three margaritas, and bad choices, because not every emergency is real.

I sound sharp and look calm while in my head last night replays in clips, the bench, Clara saying my name like it already belonged to her. The way my body reacted when she spoke about the dock and the water, like she named a place I have never let myself visit, keeps trying to become a pattern. By late afternoon a tight ache lives behind my eyes, fatigue plus fear plus misdirected want, a common mix in this job. I could go home and no one would question it, but going home is where the quiet is, and the quiet is not safe.

So I go to my office instead, and the door shuts with a soft click that feels too final. My office is bigger than some residents' flats, because success comes with square footage and expectations. One wall is books, neuro texts, journals, a few monographs with my name on the spine, and my diplomas sit in tidy frames like proof I stayed obedient to the right system. A framed fMRI behind my desk looks pretty, which is why it is there, because the hospital likes pretty representations of suffering.

Outside the window the city is a grid of other people's problems, and I sit and open a chart pretending to read. The words blur by line three, and I close it because pretending is work and I have no extra capacity. I open a folder on my desktop of teaching cases, cleaned of names and turned into data and warnings, because data feels safer than stories. A title catches my eye, Case 47 Childhood Memory Distortion Religious Trauma, and my heart thumps once too hard even though it is not me.

It isn't me, wrong place and wrong details, and I tell myself that twice because repetition can be an anchor. It reads like my sibling anyway, female, thirty four, high performing, raised in a strict church setting, presenting with sex that feels out of line with her stated values and self image. The case language is clinical, careful, and clean, like it is describing someone else's body. My mind supplies the lake even though the word is not on the screen, and my body puts it there anyway, unasked.

I scroll and the notes get worse, vivid, pleasant memories from early teens tied to one place, no clear recall of force, no clean story of harm. The memory is coded as chosen, close, special, and the phrasing makes my mouth go dry because I know that code. Attempts to reframe as non consent meet a wall, she agrees in logic and rejects it in feeling, refuses the victim label and insists on blame, and her moral frame calls the behavior dirty while her nervous system calls it relief. It feels like reading an MRI of my own skull, the kind where you see the lesion and pretend you do not.

Halfway down I snap the laptop shut too hard, the room going too quiet. Outside, a nurse laughs, a cart squeaks, someone calls for a neuro consult, and the ordinary sounds feel obscene because they do not know what is happening in here. Inside, it is HVAC and my pulse, steady but loud, like the building has no choice but to keep me alive. I pick up my phone and my thumb hovers, because the impulse to reach for someone is a primitive thing, and I have trained myself out of it.

There is no Clara contact and no number labeled woman who knows too much, nothing to call but the usual names. Even if I had her number I would not know what to write, because how do you ask someone to explain your own nervous system. Hi, I would write, you seem to know more than I do, can you add footnotes, and the thought is so absurd it almost becomes humor. The phone buzzes and for one sick second my body expects an unknown number and one word, Clara, but it is only email.

Subject, Follow Up Board Presentation Slide Deck, and the timing feels personal. The Chief's assistant wants just a couple of slides on outcomes and stories for donors, before and after bullets, clean miracles with rounded corners. I type a smooth reply, of course, happy to, I will have it by Monday, because that is what I do when I am cornered. Life changing, I write, about a program that reshapes trauma traces while my own mind refuses to behave, and irony tastes like metal.

The door clicks and I look up ready to remove whoever ignored basic cues, but it is Lena. Of course it is, because Lena has never treated my cues as binding. She says wow, that is a murder face, and her tone is casual while her eyes stay sharp, assessing. I ask what face, and she tells me the one that says if anyone says patient story near me I will remove their frontal lobe with a spoon, then she nudges the door shut with her hip like she owns it.

She is still in scrubs, mask line on her cheeks, eyeliner smudged in a way that only looks cute if you have never done a sixteen hour shift. I say I am fine, which is the closest thing we have to prayer in this place. She says sure, that is why I am sitting in the dark at four p m glaring at my laptop like it stole my ex, and I glance out because the light has turned blue without asking me. I flick on the desk lamp and ask better, and she says worse, now she can see my eye twitch.

I should deflect, blame post op fatigue, admin, life, but instead I ask do I look like someone who remembers everything. She pauses mid sit, then lowers herself slowly like she heard something she did not expect. Okay, she says, not the opening I expected, and I tell her humor me because I do not want to explain why I asked. She leans back and laces her fingers behind her head, then puts her feet on my desk like she pays rent, because she likes to provoke order into revealing itself.

Do you look like someone who remembers everything, she repeats, and answers her own question, no. You look like someone who keeps what's useful and deletes the rest out of spite, and the phrasing makes me laugh before I can stop it. Out of spite, I ask, because the humor gives my throat room. You have that vibe, she says, like your hippocampus has a bouncer, and I hate how accurate that feels.

She asks whether I am going to tell her what set this off or if she starts guessing and gets mean. I consider telling her the truth, then feel the familiar internal clamp. Lena is the closest thing I have to a friend here, and that closeness is exactly why the truth is dangerous. I tell her I ran into a case file that got under my skin, and she says it must be some file because I eat mental horror for breakfast.

I tell her I do not eat breakfast and she rolls her eyes, because she knows that is true and hates it anyway. Do not dodge, she says, what made this one different, and I answer church, sex, split self, the usual, because broad categories feel safer than specifics. She lets out a low whistle and names it the God hates me but my body did not get the memo pack. It should sting, but it makes it easier to breathe, because naming the thing takes away a fraction of its power.

Clinically, I say, she is a clean case, she gets it in her head and her body will not join. Lena says and you hate the plan, and I pause because that is the simplest version of a complicated truth. On paper, I say, it is fine, reframe, integrate, build a story she can live with instead of one that kills her. But, Lena says, because she knows there is always a but.

Some days, I say, it sounds like telling people to forgive what they only survived by acting like they chose it. Lena watches me with that steady look that makes her a good anesthesiologist and a risky friend. New question, she says, when was the last time you slept more than four hours in a row, and I answer I am fine because it is reflex. She says she did not ask if I am fine, she asked if I am human, and I tell her that is unclear.

Exactly, she says, so she is here with a bold plan. I lift a brow and tell her I do not need rehab, and she tells me to relax because she is not doing that paperwork, she meant dinner. Dinner is bold now, I ask, because sarcasm is easier than gratitude. Dinner with carbs and no residents, she says, low risk, and I feel my body loosen at the word carbs like it recognizes a rescue.

I say I have work, by reflex, and her eyes flick to the shut laptop. Sure, she says, you look buried in it, and I try again with notes to dictate. Dictate from your phone while I am in the bathroom, she says, come on, Jax, you keep running like this and one day you will be half a millimeter off. Then I am on the stand saying you were under pressure, and I do not want that role.

The image lands too clean and my fingers tighten on the chair arms. Too far, she asks, and I admit a bit because honesty buys goodwill. Okay, she says, then let us lower the odds and feed you, because her form of care is logistics. I have a dozen reasons to say no, but there is one reason to say yes, and it is not hunger. If I am with Lena, I am not walking toward a black awning and a stairwell.

Somewhere quiet, I say, and she grins because she already won. I know a place, she says, and of course she does, because Lena has always collected exits. We walk out together, and the hallway feels less sharp with her beside me, like the building cannot swallow me whole if someone is watching. It is not safety, but it is friction against the slide.

The restaurant is three blocks from the hospital, wedged between a dry cleaner and a chemist. White tablecloths and no screens, staff who know Lena's name and treat our wrinkled scrubs like a uniform, not a warning. Back table, the host asks, and Lena says always, then slides into the seat like she belongs anywhere. Warm light and low talk, the kind of room where you can say things and the walls keep them.

We order fast, pasta, salad, wine for her, water for me, because I am not going to add alcohol to a mind already looking for holes. You know, she says, rolling the stem of her glass, sometimes I try to picture you doing something else, ortho, skin, hedge fund. I tell her I would be dead, and she tells me that is dramatic. It is true, I say, I only work when failure has teeth, anything less and I would get bored and walk into traffic, and she laughs like she recognizes herself in the pathology.

Self knowledge looks good on you, she says, and the line almost sounds like affection. The pasta arrives slick with oil and garlic, the greens biting with vinegar, and I take a mouthful and feel my body light up like it forgot food can be more than fuel. Lena watches me over the rim of her glass, amused and satisfied. What, I ask, because I do not like being observed when I am not in control of the angle.

It is funny, she says, you light up more over a clean resection than over sex. That is because a clean resection is rarer, I say, and she snorts debatable. I have seen how some attendings look at you, she says, and I roll my eyes because the idea is both ridiculous and irritating. I will not take blame for their taste, I say, and she smiles like she likes the edge in me.

For a small moment, the air shifts, and a line appears, one you cross once or never. We have not crossed it, and the fact that we could is the problem. There have been hands on shoulders that stayed too long, jokes with edges, nights where I could have leaned in and called it a mistake, and I did not. I have slept with people who know far less about me than she does, because that is the point, they are rooms I can leave.

Lena is not a room. She is a load bearing wall, the kind you do not notice until you imagine it gone. If I bring her into the mess in my head, it will not add a story, it will test the whole frame. She catches the change in me, because Lena misses very little. Hey, she says, quiet, where are you right now.

Here, I say, dinner, and she narrows her eyes like she is watching a monitor. Thirty percent, she says, the rest is where, that file, some other place. The club flashes in my mind, the corridor, the black door, Clara's fingers on my wrist right where Lena checks a pulse. Other place, I say, and she nods like that matches the chart.

You want to talk about it, she asks, and I say no because the answer has to be clean. She nods again, then switches tracks the way she switches drips, controlled and decisive. Then we will talk about something else, she says, like why half the residents fear you and the other half want to yell at them more. I tell her I am not taking that consult, and she laughs, and the sound breaks the tension.

We talk about the hospital, the new attending whose hands do not match his talk, the patient who tried to tip anesthesia in cash after a smooth tube, the rumor the board wants to name a wing after a tech man whose top skill is remembering his own passwords. For stretches, the dock fades and the lake turns into a metaphor again, and I almost believe I am fine. I am just a woman eating pasta with someone who has seen me elbow deep in gray matter and still thinks I deserve more bread. The normalcy feels borrowed, but I take it anyway.

When we step outside, it is fully dark and the air has that thin bite that makes the city feel sharper. Come home with me, Lena says, and she says it casual, but her eyes do not move away. I mean sleep, she adds, guest room, real bed, I will take your phone, and if you try to sneak out at four a m I will sedate you and bill it to your unit. The offer hits harder than it should, because it is care without conditions, which is rare.

For a moment, I picture it, a bed I do not link to the ceiling above it, sheets that do not know what I dream about. Maybe the lake does not know her address, and the thought is almost superstition. I say I have to be in early, and she says so do I, we will set alarms, you can sleep in your work clothes if you want to lean into the tragic surgeon look. I smile despite myself, because she has always been good at turning survival into logistics.

I tell her I get it and I will be fine, because the lie is my default. She studies me for a long beat and then says okay, but the okay is not belief, it is a pause. Then promise me something, she says, and I say depends, because I do not like promises. Promise me that if you are over a brain and you cannot tell if you are saving a life or chasing a high, you step back.

The words hit harder than Case 47, because she named the fear cleanly. Lena, I start, and she cuts me off with her eyes. I am serious, she says, you live on a knife edge, it makes you good, it also makes you risky, and if whatever this is starts leaking into the field I will drag you in front of the board myself. She is not joking, and the lack of joke is what makes it care.

I say I know the line, because I have lived by lines my whole life. Good, she says, keep knowing it, and for a second I want to tell her that the problem is the line moved. We stand there another moment, night pressed close around us, and then she says goodnight, Nile. I answer goodnight, Hart, and watch her walk away with shoulders set like she is carrying more than a pager and a stethoscope.

My car pulls up and the driver asks home, and I say yes. I keep my eyes forward as the city slides past, no reflections and no dark glass for my mind to paint ghosts on. Streetlights cut the windshield into brief flashes, on, off, on, off, like someone testing my attention. I do not look to the side, because the side is where the memories like to sit.

At home, I run my night checklist like I am prepping for a case. A few emails, because leaving them unanswered feels like leaving an instrument uncounted. A paper abstract on brain change after trauma work, because I like to pretend I am working when I am really avoiding myself. Toothbrush, floss, locks twice, because ritual is how anxious brains bargain with the world. In bed, I focus on breathing the way I coach anxious patients, in, out, in, out, until sleep does not arrive so much as catch me mid count.

When it comes, it does not come alone. I am in the OR, but the light is wrong, soft, dim, no harsh overheads, and the absence of harshness makes it worse. No drapes, no team, just a table and a body without a face, and my hands are already inside an opening that does not match any line I know. My gloves are wet, not red, black, and the wrongness is immediate.

Water runs down my fingers, pooling where a tumor should be, and the monitors do not beep, they gurgle like they are drowning. Across from me, where Lila should be, Clara stands instead, wearing the black dress from the club with bare arms under lights that belong on a stage, not in an OR. You're contaminating the field, I say, but it comes out muffled like my mask covers my mouth and my nose and the part of my brain that edits. You did that a long time ago, she says, and her voice is too calm.

She reaches across the table and touches my wrist, thumb pressing where my pulse should anchor me. The opening does not reveal tissue, it opens into a vertical slice of lake, and black water rises swallowing the wound, the table, the lights, and then. I wake with my breath stuck high in my chest and my heart slamming like it is trying to escape. The room is dark and still, no gurgles, no water, just my breathing, loud and uneven, like I am the only machine in the room.

It takes a full minute for my body to accept I am not holding a scalpel. Another thirty seconds before my hands stop feeling wet, even though they are dry, and the phantom sensation makes me want to scrub them raw. I switch on the lamp and stare at my wrist like evidence will appear if I punish it long enough. Dry skin, normal color, no mark, just the faint indent where a watch sometimes sits, as if the body refuses to cooperate with the story.

My phone buzzes on the nightstand and every muscle goes tight. For one beat, my brain expects an unknown number and an unknown name, because that is what fear does, it rehearses the worst. It is an auto alert, Meridian Neurosurgical, new imaging upload, Alvarez, M, and the relief is sharp enough to be anger. I open it and scroll through post op scans, sagittal, coronal, axial, clean bed, no bleed, no edema out of line, textbook if textbooks had smell and noise.

A plain success sits in my palm like proof I still know where not to cut. My hands are steady now and for the first time since the club my breath drops all the way down. Sterile hands, dirty mind, and as long as it stays in that order, field clean and thoughts boxed, I might get through this intact. I set the phone face down because I do not want to see the light again.

In the quiet, I hear my own line from a slide I have said too many times, we are not the sum of what happened to us, we are the sum of what our brains let us keep. The problem is my brain has stopped throwing things away, and it is letting something back in. Not a flood, not yet, just drops, like water finding the smallest crack in glass and worrying at it, slow and sure. Somewhere under a black awning across town, Clara might be sitting on a bench watching people bargain with their own stories, and somewhere deeper in my head a dock waits.

For now my hands still know what to cut. They still know what to leave alone. That knowledge is the only thing between me and the water.

Chapter Five

The Club

I told myself I went back to prove I was not hooked, which is what denial sounds like in my head when it is dressed up to feel neat, logical, and calm, and I told myself it was not want but curiosity, that I simply wanted to understand why I wanted what I wanted in the first place, a logic that sounded convincing enough to pass inspection even though it was already bending around the truth. I asked the car to drop me half a block away because distance creates the illusion of choice, and I have always needed to feel like I could still turn back, even though I did not turn back and the idea of doing so only hovered in me like a polite suggestion that was never going to be followed.

Rain earlier left the street slick, and the pavement shone like scrubbed steel under the reflected glow of neon, red, blue, and sick yellow bleeding into shallow puddles that turned the sidewalk into something that looked more like a warning than a path. In the glass wall of a closed shop, my shape slid beside me, warped slightly by the curve of the window as if I were walking next to someone else, and for a second it looked like another woman keeping pace, close enough to touch if I had reached out. The club itself looked like nothing at all, which is always how the most deliberate places choose to present themselves.

There was no sign and no name, only a black awning and a dark door set back from the street, with people slipping in and out so quickly that the warm interior light showed itself only for a breath before vanishing again, and you do not find a place like this by accident no matter how much you pretend you did because it requires intention even to recognize it. People come here because they are looking for something specific even if they refuse to admit what it is, and I pressed my palm to the stone beside the door so that I could feel something cold and real before crossing the threshold, then stepped inside knowing that whatever happened next would not be something I could undo.

The first thing that hit me was the heat, just a few degrees warmer than the street outside and calibrated that way for a reason, while the air was thick with breath and perfume layered with a faint metallic note that smelled like coins warmed in a closed fist. Then the sound caught up to me, a low and steady bass built into the bones of the building so that it vibrated through my chest rather than through my ears, with voices floating above it, controlled and measured, never loud enough to blur into chaos. Loudness belongs to places where people want to forget, but here people want to be noticed by exactly one person, or by the right one.

"Welcome back," the host said even though I had never told him my name and never would, because the entry system knew who I was and that was enough, with names staying pocketed and unspoken inside this building as part of the contract everyone agreed to. He stood behind a small podium in a dark suit with a smooth, neutral face that could have belonged to someone who ran a bank lobby just as easily as this door, and when I asked whether he remembered everyone or just the ones with malpractice cover, humor serving as the only way to test a boundary without declaring one, his mouth shifted only slightly as he replied that they remembered patterns, Dr Nile, which landed like praise and also like a warning.

I handed over my coat, and the small tag he gave me felt much heavier in my palm than something so light should have, as past the door the club opened in layers designed to ease people in rather than overwhelm them all at once. The outer ring was almost polite with a smoked glass bar, backlit bottles, and low tables set in soft light that showed faces while hiding regret, where couples and tight trios leaned close over drinks that cost too much, speaking in voices meant only for each other. I stayed near the bar with one hand on its cool edge, aware that my throat was bare, my hair was down, and that I had left my badge, my watch, and both of my usual markers of identity behind.

That last detail felt wrong in a way I could not immediately name as the bartender stepped in with quiet, practiced skill and asked what he could get me, making me weigh the meanings of each possible choice. Wine felt too much like donor dinners and whiskey felt too much like a confession I was not ready to make, so I asked for something bitter with citrus and no sweet, which he acknowledged as if I had told him exactly what kind of person I was. When he set the drink in front of me in a short, heavy glass, it smelled like grapefruit and a bad choice, and I watched my fingers wrap around it, noticing they were shaking not with fear but with anticipation that made my pulse feel louder than it should have.

I told myself this was just watching, that I was here to study the pattern and did not have to repeat it in order to understand it, and that voice sounded sane and house trained the way all of my most dangerous thoughts usually do. Another part of me hummed underneath the words, remembering a bench, a touch, and a name that had been said as if it were already known, with Clara unspoken but present, rising in me like a note I could not pretend not to hear. My eyes drifted across the room as I did what I have always done best, which is read bodies before I let myself read anything else.

Once you spend years in clinics, you learn to read bodies before you ever bother to listen to what people say, and a woman in the corner kept tugging at the hem of her dress, marking her as someone who had not been here long enough to feel at ease. A man in a sharp suit checked his phone between glances at the door, waiting for someone whose lateness meant they mattered, while a couple sat pressed together but faced outward as if the room itself were a stage they were meant to watch rather than participate in. All of them were performing something whether they knew it or not, and I was no different.

In the mirror behind the bar, my face floated over the bottles in a way that made it look almost disconnected from the rest of me, appearing calm and blank with just a trace of fatigue, the expression I wear between crises when I am still pretending to be functional. Nothing about it suggested that I spent nights in a basement built on rules and silence or that I measured intimacy in controlled increments, and yet I was standing there watching myself watch them, which felt like a warning I chose not to hear. The host made a small signal, just a tilt of his chin, and a server peeled off from the bar as if pulled by an invisible thread.

They were built to be hard to place with a slim frame, a black shirt, tailored pants, and short hair cut neatly at the sides, while small silver earrings caught the light and vanished again when they moved, making their face seem to change with each step. Their mouth did not smile unless it meant it, which made every expression feel deliberate, and the lack of clear gender presentation read like a choice rather than an accident, a choice that made them easy to project onto. When their eyes met mine as they passed, it felt like being measured by something that knew more than it should.

The bartender asked if I wanted another drink and I slid the glass away because I needed my head clear if I was going to survive what I was doing, telling him I was waiting for someone as he replied that we all were, which sounded too close to truth to be comforting. I told myself I was not here for Clara and then told myself that I did not even know whether she would come, repeating the thought until it almost held like a bandage applied with more hope than skill. Then the room shifted around a point across the space, and the lie broke before I had time to catch it.

She was there, not making an entrance and not posing, but simply existing in a way that made everything else feel less stable, sitting along the inner curve of the room with one arm stretched along the back of the banquette. She wore dark trousers, a sleeveless black top, and boots that did not try to impress anyone, which only made the effect stronger because nothing about her was asking for attention. The strange thing was how little she tried, because people turned toward her without meaning to, like bodies turning toward heat.

Her gaze slid across the room and landed on me with a sense of inevitability rather than choice, and of course it did, because the moment had already been decided by something neither of us controlled. She did not wave or call me over, but held my eyes one beat too long, like pressing a finger to a bruise to see how much it would hurt, before turning back to the woman in the red dress across from her. The nervous laugh and tight hands on that woman's glass told me more than any introduction could have.

I told myself I was not going over there because saying it made me feel like I still had agency, even though my body had already leaned in her direction. The server appeared at my elbow so quietly that I only noticed when they spoke my name, and I let out a slow breath I had not realized I was holding. When I asked whether they all enjoyed saying Dr Nile or whether it was just a bonus, a thin edge of amusement touched their face before they replied that they used what was in the file.

They asked me to come with them and I said I had not booked a room, because part of me still wanted to pretend that this was an accident rather than a choice. When they told me that she had, my pulse kicked once in a way that made my body feel briefly untrustworthy, because it was already reacting before I could decide how to feel. I could have said no, since nothing in their tone forced me to go, but choice is real in a way that does not always change where you end up, and I told them to lead the way.

They guided me through the outer ring without taking me past Clara's table, which felt deliberate in a way that let me save face while still moving forward. If I had crossed directly in front of her, I would have felt chased, but this route let me pretend I was simply obeying staff instead of being drawn in. We passed through heavy curtains that swallowed sound with each layer, as if the building had ears and wanted to keep secrets for us.

The bass faded into a deep internal throb that felt more like a pulse than music, and the light turned warmer as the walls became padded with dark fabric that reflected nothing back. There were no mirrors and no shine, which made it impossible to use the room to check yourself or anchor your identity. Doors sat close together with brass numbers and no names, and the lack of labels made them feel interchangeable in a way that was meant to be calming.

The server stopped at one of the doors and told me to go inside, and I asked about rules with a half joke that did not hide how much I needed to hear them. They studied me before saying that I could leave at any time if something felt wrong, which was a gentler boundary than

I had expected to be given. When I asked whether that was for me or for her, they told me it was for me, because she already knew her line.

That answer stayed with me as the door opened and low music hummed from hidden speakers, wrapping the space in something that felt almost private. The room was smaller than I had imagined, which made it harder to hide in or pretend I was somewhere else. There was no bed and no chains, just a deep couch along one wall, a round glass table, and a single armchair opposite that was angled with intention rather than comfort.

Clara sat in the armchair as if she had been placed there by design, already occupying the position of someone who was meant to be waited for. She did not stand when I entered, because standing would have made us equal, and she was not offering me that kind of symmetry. She watched me cross the threshold alone, then thanked the server, who nodded once before leaving and letting the door close with a soft, final click.

For a moment my breathing was the loudest thing in the room, and the awareness of it made me feel exposed in a way that had nothing to do with skin. When she said hello, her voice sounded the same as it had the night before, but without the edge, as if we had met somewhere ordinary instead of in a space built for controlled transgression. I stayed near the door with one hand on the frame, because I needed to feel the boundary to believe it was still there.

I told her she had booked me like a scan slot, fast and neat, and she replied that she had booked a room and guessed I would decide whether to fill it. Her eyes moved over me, not in a slow sweep and not with hunger, but with the focused attention of someone taking a measurement. She noted my breath, my posture, the tension at my shoulders, and the set of my jaw in a way that made me feel cataloged.

When she said I had dressed differently, I glanced down at the black trousers, the silk blouse, the blazer, and the small dip at the collar I would never wear to work. I told her I had come from home, and she corrected me by saying I had come from the version of myself that I liked rather than the one everyone else preferred. The distinction felt sharper than it should have, and I did not know which part of me it was meant to flatter.

When I told her I had not come to be picked apart, she answered calmly that I had, and the certainty in her tone made it feel less like an accusation and more like a diagnosis. I left the door and sat at the far end of the couch, as far away as I could without turning it into a challenge, angling my body in the familiar posture patients use when they insist they are fine. The heat from the upholstery crept into my spine, and I was suddenly aware of how tightly I had been holding myself together.

I asked whether she was going to tell me that we knew each other or whether we were living off suspense, and she replied that both could be true, but that she had not brought me here for drama. When I said I did not watch those, she told me softly that I did in my head all the time, which made the room feel smaller. Her words had the weight of something observed rather than something guessed, and that was what unsettled me.

I asked what she wanted, and she let the question sit long enough that it stopped being a line and started to feel like a real request. She said she wanted me to stop lying to myself about why I was there, and the directness of it made my pulse jump. I told her that sounded noble and asked if she charged by the hour, because sarcasm was easier than admitting how close the comment had landed.

She smiled, but it was not smug, and said that I turned want into theory so it could not touch me, which worked in surgery but did not work on her. When I repeated the words on you, she answered with a single word, mirror, and it cooled the room in a way I could not explain. The idea that she might be reflecting something back at me rather than inventing it was more uncomfortable than any accusation.

I asked her why I was there, and she told me I really did not know, which irritated me more than if she had been wrong. When I said I had ideas, she replied that I had stories, and that those stories kept me safe from having to feel anything I did not control. I told her I was there because she had hinted at shared history and that I did not accept unknowns tied to my name, which sounded convincing until she told me it was a line for a lawyer and to try again.

Heat rose in my face fast and sharp, and the reaction felt too exposed to hide behind theory. I admitted that maybe I liked how she had looked at me, and maybe I liked being reminded that I had a body that was not owned by my job or my parents' God. Her gaze softened at that, and she said it was closer, which made the moment feel like a test I had almost passed.

I reminded her that she had said she knew things from before, from when we were whatever we had been, and she replied that we were not what they wanted and that was enough. When I asked how old, she asked how old I had been on the dock, and my chest tightened as if the word had brushed something raw. I said I did not remember a dock, and the lie came out too easily, which was how I knew it was one.

She told me that I did, and then began talking about how I used water in my work, about flow, currents, and storms, as if she had been listening to me longer than I wanted to admit. When I accused her of watching my talks, she said she had watched two, which was enough to spot a leak. The way she said it made it sound less like an observation and more like a diagnosis.

When I asked whether she had been there, she answered quietly that she had, and the room felt smaller because of it. I asked where, even though my ribs already knew the answer, and she said it was at the lake. Vertigo nipped at the edge of my sight, not a full scene but a body memory, with cool air on bare legs, wet wood underfoot, and a smell like algae and old sun that did not belong to this room.

I told her she was mixing me up with someone else, because denial is often the first reflex of anything that threatens to become real. She said I had a bandaid on my left knee and that I had told her I fell running to catechism when I was actually running from my mother. The word that hit me was not dock or lake but ungrateful, and it dragged with it a cupboard door, yellow kitchen light, and a voice sharp with love and duty that made my stomach turn.

She said I had been scared that if I fell in, God would take it as proof, and my chest went still as if something inside had frozen. It was not a full memory, but an outline behind frosted glass that hinted at something I was not ready to see. I accused her of being committed to this story in a voice that sounded too thin and too high, and she told me she was not making it up but remembering.

She did not reach for me, keeping her hands where they were, and that restraint made the space between us feel heavier. When she asked what she remembered most, I said I did not want to know, but she told me it was the way I watched, as if seeing every angle might let me escape it later. That description felt too accurate to dismiss, even though I wanted to.

Chapter Six

The Body Keeps the Score

I used to believe nothing was more honest than a brain under surgical lights, because other organs perform in their own ways while the brain simply shows cost and shows what it cannot keep paying for. The heart flares, the gut hides, the liver forgives until it cannot, but the brain does not act so much as reveal what has been spent and what is still owed. Maybe that is why I chose it, or why it chose me, because honesty without comfort has always felt like my native language.

This morning the patient on my table is a woman in her forties, and a slow-growing tumor sits near the hippocampus where memory lives like a country with borders. It is the place between living and remembering you lived, the place where years sit in the dark tagged and filed as weddings, songs, grudges, first days of school, and last days of parents. The irony is too clean for anyone to call it an accident, and I still leave it alone because this is her life and her self and her history. I am about to change its shape with a blade, and I will do it with the precision that people mistake for mercy.

"Vitals are stable and consistent," the anesthesiologist says, keeping their voice at the professional register. I nod once, and the talking part of me slides back while the operating part steps forward and locks the door the way it always does. It has its own calm, and it does not care what follows me into the room because it only cares about the next millimeter. Under the lights her dura glows pale and thin, rising and falling with her breath like fabric in a draft that refuses to settle.

There is always a moment before the first cut when the room holds still, and it is not reverence so much as timing that everyone respects. Control is timing, not knowledge, and knowledge is never enough to save you from impatience. "Retractors, please," I say, keeping my voice low and even for the field. They land in my palm without a word, because the scrub nurse knows I do not want chatter and chatter steals attention.

Attention is how you avoid the wrong millimeter, so I set the field and widen it and fix it in place until there is a clean window into tissue. This tissue holds the woman's past and whatever future remains, and it does not care how carefully I arrange my instruments. The brain never looks like identity, because it looks like soft fruit and looks like something you could bruise with a bad grip. If you did not know better you might think you could scoop it with a spoon, which is the kind of ignorance that ruins lives quickly.

Identity does not live in the shape, because it lives in patterns and in electricity choosing paths and in circuits reinforced or left to die. Patterns change, and sometimes they change too well, which is how you get a person who functions and still vanishes. "Mapping is ready whenever you need it," the tech says behind me, and I do not turn my head. "We will not stimulate yet," I answer, keeping my hands steady, "because we will free the mass first and then map."

I breathe in and out, and the scalpel slides with a familiarity that is almost obscene in its ease. Tumor tissue has a resistance you cannot fully teach, so you have to feel it and learn it in your own hands. It yields late like damp paper, while normal cortex has spring and feels elastic and offended as if it expects to recover. This tumor does not, and it gives way slowly as if it already decided it belongs here.

A small sharp satisfaction runs through me, and I hate that I still get that even now. I grew up with rules that made pleasure suspect and made control suspect, and wanting too much meant you were near sin. Even now with my hands inside a skull I feel a thin thread of guilt when something goes clean, so I tell myself to focus as if focus can drown out history. "Micro-scissors, please," I say, and metal touches my glove with cold pressure through latex and a familiar weight.

I work the border while watching for the fine threads that tether memory to itself, because one wrong cut and she wakes up looking at her husband like he is a stranger. She hears her child's voice and cannot place it, and she walks and breathes while losing the person she was. The body forgives, but the brain keeps notes, and those notes become the only truth that matters later.

"Jax?" The word is not in the room and not aloud, but the sound slips between the ventilator's hiss and the monitor's beeps anyway. It lands in the part of me that is not fully here, recognition compressed into one syllable that feels too intimate for a sterile room. It is not real, or I decide it is not, because that is what I do when a threat tries to enter the field.

I decide what counts, and I decide what stays outside the window I have cut. The hippocampus pulses in the light slick with fluid, and the tumor clings to its curve like it is afraid to let go. I ignore the echo of my name and free the last attachment with a patience that feels practiced, and then the mass lifts out in one piece.

Balanced and clean is the way you want it to come away, and wanting that still makes me uneasy. "Specimen is ready for labeling and transfer," I say, keeping my tone clinical for everyone listening. The nurse takes it and labels it and passes it off, and someone behind me exhales like a private prayer. They should not, because we are not finished, and finishing is where mistakes hide.

"Let us close carefully and in sequence," I say, and my voice stays calm even while my heart refuses to cooperate. My hands are steady, but my heart moves with a delayed rhythm that feels doubled, like a second heartbeat repeats everything half a beat behind. Closure feels slow today, not in fact because my stitches are uniform and my pace is the same, but slow in my head where thought arrives early and echoes. I think the thought before it forms, and I feel the memory before it shows itself, and that is not failure yet.

It is reverberation, and it comes in fragments that do not ask permission. Wet wood under bare feet is there, and cold air on the backs of my calves is there, and the slick give of algae against skin is there. A voice tells me I am safe, and a different voice tells me to look, and both voices feel like they belong to the same world. I blink once hard, and the room snaps back into place with metal and drapes and light returning like a discipline.

The last staple bites shut with a dry final click, and I hold my expression steady as if nothing has shifted. We wheel her out to recovery, another ordinary miracle and another family that will hug me in a hallway and call it grace. Under my gloves my fingers feel steady, but deeper down they shake in a way I do not want to name.

At the scrub sink I let the water run too hot, and I do not turn it down because pain is grounding when memory is not. Skin over my knuckles flushes red, and pain assigns location and says you are here and not there. My reflection floats in the steel panel above the taps, hair pinned and mask loose at my throat, with shadows under my eyes that fluorescent light cannot fix. Competence sits on my face like a trained expression, and exhaustion is the line beneath it that never goes away.

Most surgeons do not look at themselves mid-shift, and maybe it is superstition or the ghost look of bright light and sharp angles. Maybe it is because seeing yourself makes it harder to pretend you are only a healer, and I have never been able to fully pretend that. I am not accused, and I am not innocent, and I am what I chose to be in the spaces where no one claps. "Dr Nile, can I have a minute?" a voice says from the doorway, and I turn with a towel in my hand.

Teasdale stands there, chief resident and sharp and fast, eager in the way that reads as devotion if you do not know what hunger looks like. "Yes, Teasdale, speak clearly and quickly," I say, because my patience is thin after the field. "She is waking up now," he says, "and the neuro checks look good with no obvious deficits." Of course they do, because we are good at this, and that is the problem because skill can make you arrogant without you noticing.

He hesitates and risks it anyway, and the risk makes him wince right after as if the words were a mistake. "You seemed distracted during the case," he says, trying to keep it respectful and failing in the middle. "Not distracted," I say, keeping my voice level, "but focused somewhere you cannot see yet." He blinks because he cannot tell if that is praise or warning, and I want him to hold uncertainty because uncertainty makes better doctors than worship does.

In recovery the patient blinks at me through anesthesia haze, and I shift my voice into the register families like. "Hi, I am here and you are safe," I say, keeping it simple without lying. Her eyes find my face and hold it, and recognition holds and language holds, and the scaffolding stays upright. "Doctor, will I remember everything after this?" she asks, and the vulnerability in it lands in my ribs.

There is a clean answer and a kind one, and I have made a career out of threading the gap between them. "You will remember what you need to remember," I say, and it soothes her because it sounds like permission. The truth of it unsettles me, because it feels like a sentence I have already served without knowing the crime.

By the time I reach my office my pulse is too loud in my throat, not racing but amplified like someone turned the gain up inside my ribs. My wrist itches under my sleeve with phantom warmth, like stitches pulled too soon and skin that still expects contact. Before I can argue myself out of it I unlock my phone and open the club's encrypted interface, because control looks like checking logs when fear looks like superstition.

There are no photos and no faces and no directory, because that would break the point of what they sell. There are only logs and time stamps and access entries, dull and exact, designed to feel like safety. One new entry is flagged, and the neatness of that flag makes me feel sick. CLARA (GUEST), approved by OWNER, date last night, and the labels stack like evidence.

Not a member, not a walk-in, invited, and the club brought her in with intention rather than chance. I should delete the log and I do not, and I should report the breach and I will not, because I do not want anyone else looking where I am now looking. Instead I open the OWNER profile, locked behind layers, with no name and no face and only a symbol waiting. A stylized wave, or a curved dock, or a shoreline bend like our mapping overlays, and I cannot tell myself it is coincidence anymore.

My thumb hovers as if the next tap will change the past, and it will not. I lock the phone and put it face down, because I can cut anything except what refuses to stay buried. The next morning I take the subway, because it feels like something sane people do and I am always performing sanity when I do not have time for truth. The car is full of grey coats and wet umbrellas, and rain streaks the windows turning the city into smears of light that never settle into a clear picture.

My reflection floats in the glass layered over tunnels and stations like a rider, and I keep my hands still in my lap. I resist touching my wrist, but the warmth is there anyway, and resistance feels like a ritual that no longer works. My stop arrives with a squeal of brakes and stale air, and bodies push me toward the platform, and I let them because motion is easier when you do not pretend you chose it.

In the lobby burnt coffee and disinfectant hit like always, and this building does not care what you carry in. It cares that you show up, and it cares that you perform, and the demand is almost comforting in its simplicity. Elevator doors slide shut around nurses, a tech, and a family member clutching a plastic bag with everything a life can become. Numbers climb, and a woman glances at my badge and then my face and then away, and I cannot tell if it is recognition or fear.

The neurosurgery floor is bright and sharp, white walls and hard light and no softness, and we say we like it like this. We say we want clarity, as if clarity is not the cruelest thing in a hospital. At briefing residents hover around the central station, and Teasdale runs through consults too loudly, and someone mentions a rupture and someone lists seizures. A stream of need flows around me constant as water, and I let it because it keeps me from listening inward.

Then a new voice cuts through it and says my title like it belongs to her mouth. "Dr Nile, could you step over here briefly," the Chief of Nursing says, holding the room with her presence. I turn, and beside her is Clara, not in black and not under bass and not behind velvet, but in hospital scrubs with hair tied back and a neutral face. The room does not feel the shift, but my skin does, and I feel it like a door opening behind me.

The Chief clears her throat and speaks in the tone that turns people into resources. "We have a transfer from Internal Medicine," she says, "and this is Nurse Clara Weiss with experience in sedation prep and neuro-recovery protocols." "She will be assigned to neurosurgery," she continues, "and primarily to your service, Dr Nile, starting immediately." Assigned, not requested, not optional, and the word lands like a clamp.

Clara meets my eyes, calm and too calm, and says, "Morning, Dr Nile, I am looking forward to supporting your list today." I nod once and say, "Welcome to the service, and keep your documentation clean," because it is safer than saying what I mean. Briefing continues with orders and assignments and schedules, and people scatter, and the machine keeps moving like it always does. Clara falls into step beside me without asking, and the lack of asking is its own kind of claim.

"Is there anything you would like me to review before I start," she asks, professional and polite and almost boring in a way that feels deliberate. My wrist burns under my sleeve, and I keep my face steady as if skin does not have memory. "Post-op protocols for hippocampal resections, because we have two more this week," I say, testing her with specificity. "I have read them already and I have flagged the risk points," she replies, and then adds, "and I reviewed mapping logs from prior cases as well."

No boast, just fact, and annoyance flickers in me alongside respect because they sit close in the body. "You will shadow me this week, and you will not improvise," I say, using authority as if it is protection. "I expected to shadow you, and I will follow the line," she replies, and her certainty makes me want to push back. We walk the rest of the hall in silence, steps in sync and heartbeat not, and the mismatch feels like a warning I cannot file away.

In OR-2 the next patient is a man in his sixties with a lesion against his temporal lobe, and the chart says he used to write music. Families think that detail will matter to us, and sometimes it does, because meaning can shape risk tolerance in ways we pretend are objective. "Ready to proceed with induction and positioning," the anesthesiologist asks, and I answer, "Yes, proceed exactly as planned and keep me updated." The ritual resets with mark and incise and retract and drill and dura, and here more than anywhere I feel normal.

Bounded violence for a reason is a kind of order I can live with, and rules are easier than feelings. "Dura exposed and field is stable," I say, and Julie hands me scissors before I ask because she knows my timing. Clara stands behind her outside the field, masked and gloved and watching, not in my way and not ornamental. She watches like a second set of eyes with no need to be seen, and that makes it worse rather than better.

I open the dura, and the brain rises gently pressing at the edges of its cage, alive and resistant in a way that still surprises me. It always surprises me how much it wants to remain itself, even when we are there to change it. We work, and minutes stretch and then collapse, and sound narrows to suction and monitors and my own voice when it needs to cut through. When we reach the hippocampal border again my nervous system tightens without permission, and my hand feels the old echo before my mind names it.

I angle the micro-scissors, and Clara says, "Be careful with that angle, because the tract is closer than it looks." Her voice is too quiet for anyone else, but it stops my hand, and I hate that it does. She should not speak, because she is not scrubbed in and this is my field, but she is right and the truth is not polite. The cut I was about to make would skim a tract, not a disaster, but enough to steal a name or a wife's face or a chord.

I adjust and cut differently and proceed, and no one notices her intervention except me. When we close and the drapes come down Julie murmurs, "Beautiful work today, Dr Nile, that was exceptionally clean." Anesthesia adds, "You saved his music, and the family will be grateful," and gratitude is not what I feel. I peel off my gloves and the skin beneath looks pale and wrinkled and clean, and Clara's eyes are on my hands.

Not admiring and not accusing, recognizing, and that word makes me want to break something. "You did not remember before," she says low enough to pass as routine, "but your hands did remember the line." Anger rises fast and clean and useful, and I start to say, "Stop implying things you cannot prove," but a crash in the hallway cuts me off. Metal on tile and someone swearing, and the usual chaos fills the doorway like a release valve.

"There is nothing to imply," she finishes, calm as if she is stating protocol, "because the body remembers and you are the one who said so." She walks out ahead of me, and I stand there a second too long in the stale air of a cooling OR. Someone else's blood dries on the drapes while my own history wakes under my skin, and I cannot scrub it out.

The imaging room is empty when I step in, and emptiness feels like permission. I wake the monitors and pull up the last three cases, MRI and contrast and navigation overlays, and the brain spins in three dimensions like a small planet. I zoom in on the hippocampus, left and right, dentate gyrus, tracts as thin as threads, and I tell myself I am checking for error. I tell myself I am proving my hands stayed clean, and I tell myself the echo did not touch the field.

What I am really looking for is a boundary, because control is the only thing I worship. I trace a curved tract with my fingertip on the glass, and it bends like shoreline and like a dock from above and like rope laid slack over water. Wet wood and bare feet and black water stitched with reflected light press at the edge of my vision. I shut the monitor off hard enough to make it click, and the sound feels like a decision I do not fully believe.

The staff lounge is empty, blessedly, and the vending machine hums while a microwave clock blinks the wrong time. A couch sags like it gave up years ago and no one resuscitated it, and I do not sit because sitting would make this feel like rest. I pull open the drawer by the sink and take out trauma shears, cheap steel meant for cutting clothes we throw away. I sit on the counter with my legs dangling and press the dull edge against my wrist, not cutting, only pressure, only calibration.

If I close my eyes it is not Clara I feel, but the waiting, and the choice that did not feel like choice. Someone once held a hand near me like that, close enough to choose and close enough to refuse, close enough that refusal felt like a sin. My grip tightens until metal digs into the skin over my pulse and it hurts, and good because pain is evidence and pain draws borders. I open my eyes and the lounge is still empty, my wrist red and unbroken, and I drop the shears into the bin and wash my hands like I contaminated them.

Neuro ICU is thick with heat and beeping machines, and the noise is a constant reminder that bodies do not care about story. The consult is a man in his fifties ventilated and pale, with a mass near the basal ganglia, and this will not steal memories first. It will steal movement and voice and the ability to scratch his own nose, and self is not only memory but motion. "What is his sedation doing right now," I ask, and Clara answers from the bedside with the precision of someone who knows the numbers matter.

"Sedation is holding and fentanyl is low, with dex steady," she says, her tone clean and reliable. It is the kind of voice you trust with a life if you do not know what else it carries. I scan images and run numbers and speak in plans, because plans are the only safe language I have. "Book him for first case tomorrow, and tell anesthesia we need monitoring," I say, and Teasdale nods and bolts.

Clara stands still with hands loose at her sides, eyes on the patient and not on me, and the restraint feels like strategy. "What are you waiting for right now," I ask, and I hate that my voice betrays interest. "A question you have not asked yet," she says, and there is a pause that feels like a hook set gently. "I did not ask one," I reply, and she answers, "No, but you will, and you know you will."

No smile, no smugness, just certainty, and certainty is a kind of threat. I turn away and give her work because work is distance. "Cooling protocol, and I want his core temp down by a degree by midnight," I say, and she nods and moves to the chart without comment. I head for the door, and I hate that walking away from her feels like leaving a case half done.

Hours blur into rounds and dictations and a consult I should have refused, and then my pager hits the emergency pattern. Back to ICU, teen girl, post-traumatic swelling, a seizure ripping through her, and the stakes strip away theatre. Clara is already there with Ativan in hand and calm in her posture, and we move in tandem with airway and monitors and orders and position changes. No talk, only action, and for a moment I can pretend this is the only truth.

The seizure breaks and the girl slackens and breath settles into an ugly but workable rhythm, and Clara and I step back at the same time. "This is not the first time we have worked together in chaos," she says quietly, and my throat tightens. "Where would that have been, if you insist on saying it," I ask, and the question tastes like weakness. She looks at me weighted and says, "You know where, and you always have," and then she walks away.

I do not follow, not because I do not want to, but because if I ask for more I am not sure I can hold a scalpel tomorrow with the same certainty. Knowledge is surgery, and you cut when the tissue is ready, and you do not force it without consequences. By the time I leave the hospital the cold outside feels like metal in my lungs, and I do not call a car at first because walking feels like control. The sidewalk is wet from earlier rain, streetlights painting themselves across puddles, and every splash looks like an X-ray of the city's bones.

My shoes make a soft sound, tap tap tap, and halfway down the block the sound changes. Tap tap hollow tap, too resonant for concrete and too close to wood, and my calves tighten. The backs of my knees pull in, and for a heartbeat my body insists I am balancing on something narrow above depth. Wet wood and cold air and black water underneath, and I look down to find cracked asphalt and shallow puddles and nothing else.

Concrete remembers nothing, I tell myself, but people do, and that is the problem. My apartment greets me with its hotel act, minimal furniture and neutral art and no photos, nowhere for memory to perch. I should shower and eat and sleep, but instead I go to the bottom shelf of my bookcase. Black binders with identical spines and white labels, journals, not teenage confession but professional notes kept when you are too honest for print and too cautious to speak.

I pull one at random, fellowship year, Stanford, early work on reconsolidation, diagrams and graphs and notes on how fast a memory can degrade if you interrupt the process. Halfway through a heading stops me, CASE VIGNETTE (COMPOSITE): "THE LAKE CHILD," and my stomach drops like an elevator starting down too fast. I do not remember naming anything that, and the fact that I do not remember does not comfort me. I read, and the tone is clinical and detached, a composite made from multiple cases to make a point, gender blurred and age vague, references to water and to a dock and to an older teen who watches rather than touches.

Then details appear that do not belong in a teaching case, and that is where my body goes cold. Feet numb from wet boards, cold air up bare thighs under a windbreaker, the feeling of being seen not child and not adult but possibility. My grip tightens on the binder until my knuckles ache, and in the margin my own handwriting slants fast and impatient. Check: why does this feel familiar, circled twice, and below it smaller, Don't be dramatic. Pattern match. That's all.

I close the binder, and the kitchen feels narrower, and the overhead light is too yellow like ICU corridors at three in the morning. My wrist pulses with phantom contact, and I slide the binder back into place, not because I am done but because I am not ready to keep reading. In the bathroom I turn the shower as hot as it will go, steam softening my reflection and erasing me in slow pieces. I undress and step in, and heat hits like a bolus and muscles unwind and hospital noise dissolves, and then I twist the tap toward cold because I need to test what I am afraid of.

The change is instant and violent, my body jerking and breath catching and every nerve shouting move. Cold water needles my skin and my feet slip a fraction, toes scrambling for grip on tile, and that is the moment my brain supplies the missing room without asking. The hollow thud of water hitting wood, the smell of algae and fuel, a rope creaking nearby, and my fingers dig into grout. "Stop, I need you to stop now," I say out loud, and my voice sounds wrong against tile, and still my body does not stop.

My heart drops its hospital rhythm and takes up another, too loud and too slow, as if each beat has to push through cold water before it reaches air. I force the tap back toward hot, warmth returns, and images sink, not gone but under, and I stay until my skin is flushed and wrinkled. I stay until the mirror shows nothing clear enough to question, and when I step out my wrist still tingles as if it is waiting for proof. No more experiments tonight, I tell myself, and the statement sounds like a lie I am using as a sedative.

In bed I open my laptop and stare at a blank document, and I type a header that feels like self-harm. PERSONAL MEMORY DISTORTION, SELF NOTES, and the words look obscene like I made myself a patient on my own service. I can dress it up as research and self-tracking, because plenty of scientists wire themselves and log sleep and measure stress, and why not this. Because data becomes proof, and proof is hard to cut out, but my fingers move anyway.

Not story, bullets, because bullets feel like control. • Body reacts to water cues (sound / smell / cold). • Body response comes before image. • Image: dock / wet wood / watcher / adult voice. • Mind line: "I don't remember." • Body line: "You do." • Trigger: Clara Weiss. Wrist contact. Shared past implied. I hover after her name, and I stop, and I save the file to an encrypted folder labelled LECTURE DRAFTS because no one looks there.

People assume polished slides arrive clean, not carved from doubt, and the assumption is useful. I close the laptop and I do not feel better, and I feel filed, and for me that is close to relief. Sleep comes, and I am standing on wet boards with bare feet and toes curled over the plank's lip. Cold air on calves, smaller body, center of gravity too high, horizon too far, dock swaying as my body believes it will throw me, and water moving beneath us black with streaks of reflected sky.

A girl stands beside me with dark hair in a messy knot and knees bare under a too-big windbreaker, hands in pockets like she is pretending she is not cold. She says my name, not Doctor and not Jax, but Jacqueline, and the sound lands low in my spine because no one says it like that now. "You are shaking, Jacqueline, and you do not have to pretend," she says, and I look at my hands and they are shaking. "I am not scared, I am only cold," my younger voice says thinly, and she answers, "I know, and you are still reacting like you are falling."

She steps closer, not touching, only near enough to choose or refuse, and the nearness is the whole point. "It is not fear, it is your body trying to remember what to do," she says, and I ask, "What is it supposed to do, if it is not fear." "Stay up and stay alive, even when you hate it," she says, and she tips her head toward the water. "You do not have to like it, you only have to know it is there," she says, and something moves further down the dock, taller and older and watching.

I try to look, and I snap awake, my bedroom ceiling staring back, and the thin line of light between blinds has shifted from streetlamp yellow to flat pre-dawn grey. My heart pounds heavy, each beat tripping the next as if afraid of being left behind, and I sit up with my hands shaking on my thighs. I remember the dream not as aftertaste but as sequence, boards and windbreaker and her voice, and I know that voice, not Clara's exactly but close. Different notes from the same instrument, and the recognition makes my mouth go dry.

"Stay up, stay alive," she said, and the words have weight like a command. I stand and go to the bathroom and open the cabinet, and two orange bottles stare back at me. Beta-blockers and short-acting benzos, neither with my name, and I close the cabinet because I am not ready to numb this. If I numb this I will not learn anything, and if I numb this I will not remember, and for the first time I am more afraid of not remembering than of what the remembering holds.

On the way to work I do not take the subway, and I call a car because I need distance from crowds and from mirrors in windows. When the driver asks where to, the hospital address rises ready, and another address surfaces instead. Not the club's, but the corner a half block away, the stretch of sidewalk where the awning is never lit, where

I always tell myself I could turn around and do not. My wrist pulses once like a metronome, and I say, "First stop, Rivington and Orchard, and then we will go to the hospital."

The driver nods and pulls into traffic, and I lean back because leaning back feels like a decision. There are two kinds of cuts a surgeon learns, the ones you plan and the ones you realise you started long ago before the blade ever touched skin, and I do not know which kind this is anymore.

Chapter Seven

———————∞———————

When She Watched Me

S ome people cut, some people forget, and some people watch, and I've always been the third. They think the watching is work, vitals, monitors, drips, the small, endless dance of other people's bodies, and they think I learned it in training, in wards and sims and night shifts, but they don't know I learned it at the lake, watching her, and now I watch her again.

From the far end of the corridor, Dr Jacqueline Nile walks toward the nurses' station, white coat open over dark scrubs, hair twisted back with the same clean intent she uses on a scalp, and she isn't tall and she isn't loud, still the hallway makes room for her. Residents fold into her wake and orderlies press to the wall, talk drops half a notch, and she doesn't ask for it because authority moves with her like weather. Teasdale, the chief resident, is already circling, tablet in one hand, coffee in the other, and he walks backward in front of her and tries not to trip.

"So for the ten a.m. resection, I was thinking" is what he starts to say, and "Stop," she says, and he stops mid-step, mid-syllable because one word and his body obeys. She doesn't reach for him, she reaches for his coffee, it's sweating onto a stack of unsigned consents close to the edge of the counter, and she nudges the cup back two centimeters, straight, parallel, out of the drip line. "Don't set fluids near charts," she says, "Ink runs," and it's nothing and it's everything.

That same hand held a scalpel an hour ago, and that same hand paused for half a beat when she almost cut too close this morning, and no one saw it, I did. Teasdale flushes and says, "Right. Sorry," and her fingers drop to her side. As they do, they brush the inside of her own wrist, not a watch check and not a habit she knows, a reflex, the same spot every time, just above the radial pulse where the skin is thin and the beat is easy, and she doesn't know she does it. She doesn't know I've seen that gesture before, on a dock, on a much smaller arm.

"Vitals on bed twelve?" she asks, already turning away, and I step in before Teasdale can scramble. "Stable," I say, "Systolic down five since last check, speech clear, no new deficits," and she looks at me quick and exact, the way she checks an instrument she didn't know was on the tray. "Good," she says, and our eyes hold for half a second too long. Her pupils narrow, no full recognition but something close, like a song she almost places, then she looks away, filed, dismissed, and she moves on.

I watch, and it isn't obsession, it's continuity. In every room she enters, she stands just far enough from the bed that a sudden hand can't catch her, she never leans on rails and she rarely sits, and when she uses a stethoscope she looks faintly annoyed by it, like hearts and lungs are side work. Her attention is somewhere else, she watches brains even when they're sealed in bone, and at the third bed a post-op patient fumbles a word. Nothing big, wrong month, corrected fast, the family laughs with relief, Teasdale smiles, and Jax doesn't.

Her eyes sharpen and she asks the same thing again with one small change, same load, new phrasing, and this time the answer lands clean. "Good," she says, and her shoulders stay tight as her hand drifts toward her wrist again, that small orbit around the spot where her body keeps a record. If they knew what I know, they wouldn't call that calm, they'd call it scar, and I adjust a drip. I correct Teasdale's dose under my breath so he doesn't get corrected by her in public, he thanks me with his eyes, and she doesn't see.

She's seeing something else, something she doesn't have words for yet, not in this life, not in this building, and not while she's awake. The smell does it, and in the med room I crack open a new bottle of chlorhexidine to refill the wall dispenser, the sharp bite hits hard, chemical clean with a fake citrus note someone thought would help. On the second breath it shifts, the citrus thins and slides sideways into something else, coconut sunscreen, cheap oil, a film on water, and under it wet wood, algae, rusted nails in boards, diesel from a small boat, something cold and old.

The hospital hum drains out of my ears and the fluorescent buzz turns into insect noise, the monitor beep becomes rope knocking against a ladder, and I close my eyes. The first day at the lake, I stood at the gravel drive with a duffel bag half my size at my feet, and I tried not to look impressed. Fourteen, too old to be "excited" about a church invite, too young to know why my mother gripped my shoulders in the car and called it a blessing, and "They're good people, Clara," she said, "Faithful, you'll learn so much, you're lucky."

Lucky, and the house was big in the newsletter way, wood siding peeling just enough to look humble, a wraparound porch with mismatched chairs arranged to look accidental, wind chimes. Too many, clinking over each other, never in time, and beyond it water, and the lake wasn't pretty. Green-black, opaque, ringed by reeds and soft mud, a long dock ran into it, narrow and warped, planks turned silver by sun and age, and it looked like a finger pointing into a private joke.

"Clara, there you are!" my mother's friend called from the porch, "Come, let me see you," and "Aunt" Elise. We weren't related, teeth too white, makeup too careful, her hug was warm on the surface and empty underneath. "You've grown," she said, "Practically a young lady, the girls are out back, go meet them," and out back, the water waited. I followed the crunch of my shoes around the house, gravel to scratchy grass, the porch fell behind me, and the air cooled under birches, the shade smelling of sap and insects.

They were on the dock, two figures, one taller, one smaller, both cut into silhouette against the lake. The older girl was around my age, maybe a year ahead, cutoffs, faded red shirt, bare feet hooked over the edge, and she moved like she trusted the boards. The smaller girl stood a step back, closer to shore, toes at the seam where earth turned to wood, blue windbreaker, bare legs, goose-bumped, arms at her sides, fingers curled with strain, and she wasn't looking at the water. She was looking at the line where it began.

"Hey," the older girl called, "You must be Clara," and her voice was easy, real, no church tilt, she turned fully and balanced on the uneven boards like it was nothing. The smaller girl didn't turn, she held the stillness of someone told not to move and afraid breathing might count, and "Come say hello," the older girl said, glancing back. "She doesn't bite," and at last the smaller one rotated, stiff, like her joints needed permission.

She scanned me with the focus of a predator in a prey-sized body, dark hair in a low ponytail, mouth set too firm for her age, and nine, I guessed, maybe ten. Old enough to know adults lied, too young to know what to do with it, and "Hi," I said, "I'm Clara," and she dipped her chin once. No smile, no name, and "This is Jackie," the older girl supplied, "Her parents call her Jacqueline, her mother calls her 'blessing' when she's listening and 'stubborn' when she's not," and Jackie's jaw tightened, a flicker, gone.

"I don't like the water," she said, and it wasn't a complaint, it was a test, a dare for me to make it a flaw. The older girl laughed softly, "You don't have to, you just have to stand on the dock and pretend you might," and light words. Tight eyes, and that was the first time I saw Jax. Small, rigid, bare legs braced on boards that splintered under grown men, facing the lake like it could remember her, and even then there was someone farther back on the shore, watching both of them.

"Clara? You okay?" a voice says, and the med room snaps back, white laminate, blue bins, under-counter fridge humming, chlorhexidine in my hand. "Fine," I say, and the nurse in the doorway accepts it because people hear what fits. "Dr Nile wants post-ops rechecked before lunch," she says, "She thinks one isn't as oriented as he looks," and of course she does, and "I'll do it," I say. I cap the bottle, wipe the tiny spill, and walk back into the present.

The dock became ritual before it became clear, and day one, they coaxed. "It's just water, sweetheart," her mother said, voice sweet and thin, "You're safe, we're right here," and she sat in a folding chair at the base of the dock, ankles crossed, Bible open and unread. She didn't look at the water when she spoke, she looked at her husband, and "I don't like it," Jackie said, "It's cold," and "It's summer," Elise chimed in, sunglasses hiding her eyes, "You'll get used to it, you girls can't sit inside reading all day, life is out there."

Out there was green-black and buzzing, out there looked less like life than like storage, and the older girl stepped onto the dock and held out a hand. "Come on," she said, "We'll just go to the start, no one's going to push you in," and she said it like a joke. Her eyes didn't agree, and I loitered under the birches, hands in my pockets, I'd been brought to be around "good families." No one asked what I thought good meant, and Jackie took one small step, then another.

Her feet stuck to the board with a faint tacky sound, like the wood didn't want to let her go, and her chin stayed high. If she didn't look down, there was no drop, and they stopped halfway. "That's enough for today," Elise called, "See? She's fine, so silly to be afraid," not: you're brave, not: thank you for saying you're scared, just: silly. Jackie turned with brittle care, fixed her eyes on a safe horizon, and walked back, and when she reached grass, the breath left her like she'd been underwater.

I said nothing, and there was nothing yet that anyone would call wrong, and day two, they didn't coax, they expected. "You did so well yesterday," her father said, carrying a folding chair down the dock, "Today we go a little further," and he was handsome in the way that makes congregations open wallets. Kind eyes, clean smile, a man built for trust, he set the chair near the end of the dock and lined it up neat, and "Stand here," he told her, "Look at the water, breathe, you're safe."

Then he walked back to shore and sat, he left her upright and alone between land and lake, and "I don't like it," she said, and "But you're doing it," her mother answered without looking up, "God doesn't give us a spirit of fear." I watched from the birches, the older girl was inside "helping" that day, I'd been offered the role, I said I preferred air, and no one asked why. Jackie stood where her father chose, knees locked, eyes fixed past the far shore, she didn't cry, she didn't beg, she obeyed.

Her stillness wasn't normal, it wasn't swim-lesson fear, it was older, animal, the stillness of something that learned movement won't help, and something in my ribs tightened. I thought about walking out to stand with her, say something dumb about how ugly the lake was, anything to change the picture, and I didn't. I was fourteen, I knew tempers, I knew how fast concern turns into "drama," my mother told me to behave here, so I made a smaller promise, quiet and hard, and if something happens, I will see it, I won't pretend I didn't.

Day three, it wasn't an event, it was liturgy, and "Go on, Jackie," Elise called, "You know where to stand." The older girl leaned against a post by the shore, arms folded, jaw tight, she didn't offer her hand, neither did I, and Jackie walked herself. Boards, bare feet, stillness, and behind us the adults talked about doctrine and summer programs and how "girls these days" needed structure. I listened sideways, the way kids listen when the real talk is the part no one admits, and Jackie looked like a lighthouse someone forgot to switch on.

Not the danger, the warning, and I didn't know words like grooming. I didn't know dissociation, I didn't know how a body can leave without moving, and I only knew this wasn't ordinary fear. And if no one else would watch, I would, and back in the hospital, two nurses talk about Jax like she's a minor saint. "She doesn't even chart late," one says, scrolling, "Notes in real time, who does that," and "She's a machine," the other says, "Complications dropped the month she started, Chief said she's the best thing to hit this unit in ten years."

"Did you see her on mapping? Ice in her veins, nothing rattles her," and I stir sugar into tea I won't drink. If they knew what she's standing on, they wouldn't call it ice, they'd call it load-bearing, and they don't know the posture they praise. Straight spine, measured breath, no shaking where anyone can see, and they don't know the script: look, don't move, and they don't know someone taught her that, and they don't know I heard it.

The day it almost cracked open, heat lay flat over the lake, sound pressed down, and the water looked metallic, not gold, not silver, a hard gray that could cut. Jackie stood at the end of the dock, windbreaker zipped to her chin though the air was thick, feet curled over damp wood, hair pulled back too tight, and beside her stood the woman. Not Elise, not her mother, the other one, introduced as a "family friend," someone from church, pretty in a way that photographed well and felt wrong in person, her voice was warm. Her eyes were not.

She'd been around all summer, hovering, helping, always near when the dock happened, watching like someone following a plan, and that evening she stood closer than usual, just behind Jackie's shoulder. Her hand hovered near the back of the girl's neck without touching, and "Look out there," she murmured, "Don't look down, focus on the reflection, not the depth," low voice. Almost kind, and "You're safe," she added. On shore, Jackie's mother sat on a blanket with a devotional open, her head angled toward the water just enough to look like watching, her eyes stayed on the page.

Her father paced the shoreline with a phone in hand, sometimes he glanced at his daughter, more often at the screen, and I stood between the house and the lake, pretending to study ants on a rock. "Good girl," the woman said, "Feet apart, hands at your sides, breathe in when I say, out when I say," and in. Out. In. Out, and Jackie's shoulders went too still. "She looks stiff," I called, louder than I meant, "She looks cold," and the woman turned her head just enough for me to catch the edge of her profile.

"She's fine," she called back, "Aren't you, sweetheart," and Jackie nodded once. Her mother didn't look up, "She's always dramatic," she said, flicking a hand, "Clara, don't interfere, you'll make it harder," and harder, and that word stayed in my mouth for years. "Let's try something," the woman murmured, softer, I had to strain to hear, "Keep looking ahead, whatever happens, don't move, you're in control, you're with God, you're safe," and control. Brave. Safe.

Jackie's fingers twitched once, then went flat, her eyes locked on a point above the horizon like looking anywhere else would break a contract, and I watched. I watched the woman tilt closer by a fraction, I watched Jackie's breath hitch, then settle into a rhythm that looked less like calm than surrender, and I didn't see a hand slide under fabric. I didn't see anything you could circle in a photo and call proof, and I only saw a child being trained to stay still while something happened just out of my line of sight, and it was enough.

It would never be enough for the people who decide what counts, and the next time I tried to name it, I chose words like a hostage negotiator. I already knew girls get heard more when they sound unsure, and "Maybe I'm overreacting," I told Elise in the kitchen while I rinsed plates, "But Jackie seems... scared out there," and Elise laughed. Distracted, not cruel, not kind, and "Kids get scared of water," she said, "It's good for her, builds character," and "She doesn't want to be there," I said.

"Are you jealous?" Elise asked, light as a joke, sharp as a blade, "You know her father is proud of her, try encouraging her instead of judging, hmm," and jealous. One clean word that turns concern into competition, anything you say after sounds dirty, and I closed my mouth. Dried a plate, listened to the faint clink of the dock ladder tapping against wood outside, and I don't know if pushing would have changed anything. Maybe they would have sent me home and kept her, and what I learned was simpler, and adults trust their story more than a girl's discomfort.

So I stopped asking them to adjust theirs, and I watched harder. The first time I found Jackie alone after, she was in the upstairs bathroom, sitting on the closed toilet lid with her knees pulled up to her chest, and the door was cracked. I thought someone left the tap running, and when I nudged it, the edge brushed her foot, and she flinched hard enough to hit the wall. "Sorry," I said fast, "I didn't know," and she didn't answer, arms locked around her legs, face pressed to her knees, the blue windbreaker lay in a damp heap on the tile.

"Should I go?" I asked, and she shook her head without lifting her face. I stepped in and left the door not quite shut, a finger's width open, enough that anyone passing could see, no secrets, not the kind that start behind a locked door, and she was shaking. Not for show, tiny tremors in her calves, her hands, and "You look cold," I said, and "I'm fine," she muttered. Her voice sounded scraped, and "We could get a towel," I said, and "I said I'm fine," and the tap hissed, thin sound, too steady.

"Okay," I said, and I sat on the edge of the tub, far enough we weren't touching, close enough she'd have to move if she wanted me gone. We stayed like that, water running, house creaks, footsteps below, and "You don't like the water," I said after a while, and she lifted her head just enough to glare. "I said that already," and "I know," I met her eyes, "I heard you," and her pupils were wide, not from crying, from adrenaline with nowhere to go.

"I don't like standing," she said, and "On the dock?" and "Anywhere," and I nodded. "What happened?" and "Nothing," she said, and the kind of nothing that hangs in the air like gas. "You're shaking," and "I'm cold," and "It's thirty degrees," and she twisted her mouth. "I'm tired, then," and "Of what?" and she dug her fingers into the skin above her ankles. "Of being told I'm safe," she said, quiet and exact, "When I'm not," and nine-year-olds shouldn't have sentences like that.

"Did someone," and "Don't." The word snapped out, clean, and "Don't what?" and "Don't ask questions you don't want answers to," she said, "You'll tell, then they'll tell me I'm dramatic, then I'll say it didn't happen so they stop looking at me like that," and like that. Like she was a problem, like she was contagious, and I swallowed. "What if I don't tell?" and she studied me like an adult, measuring risk, and "Then you'll know," she said, "And you won't do anything, and it'll be worse."

"For who?" I asked, and "For you," she said, "If I pretend I chose it, it feels less bad, if I don't think about it, it's like it didn't happen," and years later, I sat in the back row of an auditorium while Dr Jacqueline Nile spoke into a mic about reconsolidation. About how a brain can flip a story to keep agency intact, about how people recode what was done to them as what they wanted, and she didn't know she was quoting a nine-year-old version of herself.

In the bathroom, I let the water run a little longer, steam fogged the mirror, our outlines softened, and "Okay," I said, "We don't have to talk," and she unwound a fraction. Enough that I could see she'd been ready to fight me, and "But," I added, "I'm going to sit here anyway, if that's okay," and she hesitated. Then nodded once, and we stayed until the water ran lukewarm and someone knocked to say dinner was ready, and on the stairs down, she walked three steps ahead of me.

Not holding my hand, not alone either, and that was all I could do. Be there when she walked back into the room, and now, in the hospital, when she walks away from a bed with a chart tucked under her arm, spine straight, jaw set, I know the posture. Everyone else sees power, I see what comes after, and at the end of my shift, I stand at the window at the far end of the corridor. It looks over a reservoir, a concrete bowl of water with railings around it, sodium lights fracture on the surface, wind breaks them into pieces, and joggers loop the path below, circling a contained body of water, and it looks nothing like the lake.

My nervous system doesn't care, and footsteps behind me, I don't turn because I know the cadence. "Long day?" Jax says, neutral voice, professional, the tone you use for a colleague you trust with patients, not with anything else, and "Always," I say. She comes to stand beside me, close enough that I catch her in the glass, pale coat, dark hair, the shadow under her eyes no makeup wipes out, and we both look at the reservoir.

"Ugly," she says, and "The water?" I ask, and "The railing," she says, "It's meant to look safe, it isn't, if someone goes over, they don't get out alone," and it lands so clean I almost laugh. "Trust you to see that," I say, and her gaze slides to me in the reflection. "You too, apparently," and our eyes meet in the glass, not straight on, and for a blink, the overlay is perfect. Two faces, one story, split by time and edits, and I wonder what she sees when she looks at me, and I know what I see when I look at her.

A girl on a dock, a hand hovering near her neck, a promise of safety that was anything but, and she looks away first. Back to the water, and "You did a good job today," she says, "With the seizure, you stayed ahead of me," and "You taught me that," I say, and her brow tightens. "I only met you last week," and I don't correct her. In my head I answer: you met me in a bathroom, on stairs, on every dock your mind keeps calling nothing, and out loud I say, "You teach clearly, people learn fast around you," and she accepts it with a small nod, like skill is the minimum.

"I'm heading out," she says, "Try to go home at a reasonable hour, Nurse Weiss, we need your brain intact," and the irony hits hard. "Goodnight, Doctor," I say, and she turns, her fingers graze the inside of her wrist as she walks away, and I watch until she's gone. I have a choice, and I can leave this alone, let her live in the edited self she built, the surgeon, the lecturer, the club version she keeps in a sealed room, respect the walls her brain put up, so she doesn't have to name what was done in God's name and discipline.

Or I stay close, risk being read as threat, risk becoming the person her mind rejects so it can keep the old story intact, so when it breaks, she isn't standing on that dock alone. I think of the bathroom, the way she said, "If I pretend I chose it, it feels less bad," and the way she built a career cutting into other people's brains instead of looking at her own. I think of the club, her body remembering my touch before her mind allowed it, her wrist burning under my fingers while her mouth said she didn't know what I meant, and I think of the log: CLARA (GUEST), Approved by: OWNER.

I didn't have to sneak into her orbit, someone opened the door, and I don't know whose hand did it, I know what they want. The past is coming for her, with or without me, and I press my palm to the glass. The reservoir blurs under my skin, city lights smear into something unsteady, and "I couldn't stop it then," I tell the version of me that still stands by birches, "I can't erase it now," but I can do something. I can be there when she remembers, and I can hold her gaze and not look away when the worst part surfaces, the part she built her whole life around avoiding.

I take my hand back, turn toward the on-call room where I'll lie down and pretend rest is real, toward another day of watching her not remember. She always thinks she's the one doing the cutting, and she has no idea how much was done to her first. She doesn't remember the first time she stepped onto that dock, I do, and I remember exactly who told her she was safe.

Chapter Eight

———————∞◇∞———————

The Dock

I find her in the charting alcove at the end of the hall, it's one of those shallow recesses built into the wall like an apology. A desk, two terminals, a row of stools that never feel clean, fluorescent light that makes everyone look ill. Nurses cycle through like tide, coffee cups, clipboards, half-finished notes, the click of pens, the soft squeal of wheels when a cart turns too tight. Clara stands in the middle of it, she looks like she belongs here, scrubs, badge, hair tied back, hands calm. But her attention isn't on the screens, it sits underneath the noise, the way good anesthesia sits under pain, quiet, specific, ready.

She doesn't notice me at first, that irritates me more than it should. If you're going to step into my life like a ghost, you don't get to miss me. "Follow me," I say, my voice stays low, it could pass as a request, it isn't. Clara looks up, no confusion, no flinch, no false cheer. Just that small, steady nod, like she expected this turn all day.

She doesn't ask where, she doesn't glance around for cover, she falls into step beside me as if she's done it before. I take her to a consult room off the side corridor, no windows, no phone that works, one table, three chairs. A tissue box that never runs out because no one wants to be seen replacing it, the glass panel in the door is painted over for "privacy." It's where we tell people their scans are worse than they hoped, it's where we tell them it's not operable. It's where surgeons go when they don't want eyes on them.

I shut the door behind us, the latch clicks, neat, final. Clara stands in the center of the room, hands behind her back, she isn't scared. She isn't defensive, she has the posture of someone waiting for a result she already knows. That makes my throat tighten, I don't like being studied, I don't like being measured. I speak first, because silence gives her space, and I ask what exactly do you think you remember.

It comes out colder than I mean, it sounds like a question on a stand, a question meant to trap. Clara watches me for a long beat, then she says that's not the question you're afraid of. I stare at her and tell her she's been implying things you don't understand. A flicker touches the corner of her mouth, not a smile, a muscle remembering how to smile. "Jax," she says, you don't believe me, but you don't disbelieve me either.

Something pulls tight under my breastbone, and I tell her not to use my name. "I'm not using it," she says, "you're hearing it," and the words land with a dull, precise thud. Like a reflex test, no consent required, I tell her I don't remember you. Clara nods once, like I've confirmed a lab value, and she says she knows, that's the problem. I hate the calm in her voice, I hate the idea that my mind is a shared room and she has a key. I tell her she's trying to manipulate me.

"No," she answers, "I'm trying not to push you past your edge," and the nerve of that tightens my jaw. The presumption that she knows where my edge is, and I step closer without meaning to, not threat, assessment. The way I stand at a field and decide what I can cut, I tell her whatever story you're building, stop, you're not warning me, you're not saving me, you're projecting. Clara lowers her gaze, not submission, care, like someone setting a glass down so it won't shatter.

"Is that your medical view?" she asks, and I tell her it's the only one that matters.

She breathes in slowly, too controlled, too neat, like she's been trained to keep her pulse out of her face. "Then tell me," she says, "what do you remember," and my pulse jumps hard enough that I feel it at my wrist. As if someone tapped an artery, I don't answer, and Clara doesn't fill the silence with comfort. She fills it with pressure when she tells me to describe it, the dock, and the room cants. Just a few degrees, enough, and I hear myself say cold.

Clara stays motionless, and she asks what else. I say wood, wet, and she asks what else, and I swallow. I can describe brain tissue in a way that makes interns pale, I can describe a bleed with a steady voice, this is harder because it isn't "medical," it's mine. I say laughter, and her eyes sharpen when she asks whose, and silence holds. My brain throws up fragments, sound without source, a mouth without a face, and I say mine.

Clara waits, she doesn't rescue me, and I add that someone else's, and she nods once. No triumph, no pity, just a clinician hearing the symptom she expected. She asks what did it feel like, and my fingers twitch, and a flare of phantom warmth sparks where her hand touched my wrist last week. Not want, not romance, recognition, and I say good, and the word comes out thin, and I say it felt good. Something in Clara's expression cracks, not into tears, into stillness, anger and grief packed tight so nothing leaks.

"Yes," she whispers, "that's how they wanted it," and I step back before my mind catches up. I tell her she doesn't get to frame my memories for me, and she tells me then remember them yourself. I have nothing for that, not anything I'm willing to hear, so I do what I always do when I can't control an answer. I attack the premise and tell her you think there was abuse, but you don't know what you saw, you were a child.

Clara's head tilts a fraction, and she says she wasn't confused, she was late. I say late, and she says late to see how much you needed the lie, and my jaw tightens. I tell her you misread, and her eyes don't flinch when she says she misjudged how scared you were to admit pleasure. The sentence slices the wrong way, not clean, not shallow, wrong layer, and I don't decide to hit her. My hand moves, the slap lands sharp and flat, like a dropped clamp on tile.

Clara's head turns a fraction, no stumble, no raised hand, no shock that performs for me. She only whispers your mother saw, and the sentence drops straight through the room. No echo, no bounce, your mother saw, and my reaction is smaller, worse, a glitch. My palm burns, her cheek reddens slow, a handprint rising like proof that waited years. I tell her she's lying, and the words feel thin even as I speak them.

"I'm not," Clara says, and I tell her you want something from me, and she says no. I tell her you're obsessed, and she says no, and I tell her you're misremembering, and her gaze darkens. Not offended, just tired, she says I remember, you don't, and her tone isn't righteous, it's careful. Like she's talking near a sedated patient, like she's trying not to startle me into a fall, and I turn for the door. My hand reaches three inches to the right of the handle, and I stare at my fingers.

Absurd detail, a surgeon missing a handle, and then I correct the line and close on it with perfect precision. The door opens, that part still works, and I step out into the hall and don't look back. Noise hits like a curtain, ventilator hiss from a nearby bay, a page overhead, the rattle of an IV pole. Someone laughing too loud at the end of a shift, none of it is louder than that one sentence inside my skull. Your mother saw, it doesn't fit.

My mother was devout, strict, severe in the way people call "principled." She policed skirts and necklines like infection control, she used shame as if it was soap. If she saw something wrong, she would have stopped it, she would have, no. That's not what my brain is reaching for, it isn't reaching for what she would do. It's reaching for what she did, and I feel it in the way my breath turns thin.

At the charting station, I pick up a pen to countersign a transfer, and the header reads ORTHOPEDICS – HIP ARTHROSCOPY CONSENT. Wrong floor, wrong service, wrong body part, and Teasdale says gently, "Dr Nile, that's for Ortho." His voice is careful, not because he cares about Ortho, because he's scared I'll turn my eyes on him. I look at the form, then at him, and I tell him I know. I place it down with slow, deliberate care, like I'm demonstrating a point on purpose.

"Just checking you're awake," and Teasdale laughs, awkward and relieved, right, of course. He believes me, they always believe me, competence is a religion in this building, no one wants to question the priest. I slide the correct chart toward him, and my signature is smaller than usual, tighter. I walk away before he sees the tremor in the line, and in the locker room I change into fresh scrubs. The elastic snaps hard against my waist, and my hands move anyway, badge, coat, collar.

I fasten the buttons out of order, skip the middle, hook the ones above and below, fabric pulls crooked, I leave it. A small error I chose, a controlled wrongness, and the coat feels off against my skin. So does my skin, and I go to the scrub sink even though I'm not going into an OR, I need the ritual. Water, soap, nails, knuckles, forearms, every motion correct, every motion slow, and pain blooms where the water runs too hot. I don't turn it down, pain has a job, pain says you are here.

Julie passes behind me and pauses, and she asks rough morning, quiet, and I say no. She hears the lie, she doesn't challenge it, that's one of the reasons I keep her close. Rounds happen, my voice works, my hands examine, my eyes catch small shifts in face and speech. Only memory refuses to cooperate, and Clara passes me twice in the hall, she stays on task. No approach, no retreat, just presence, like water in the distance, there whether you look or not.

At 17:32, I finish dictating an op note, temporal lobe lesion, margins clean, no bleed, no new deficit. My wrist aches faintly, I don't touch it, I decide that counts as a win. My phone buzzes on the desk, private line, no caller ID, and a message appears. "You don't have to remember all at once," and ice slides down my spine. It isn't Clara's voice, not in tone, not in rhythm, and Clara wouldn't leave a trail that neat.

Another message lands before I can type, "Ask her why she didn't look away," and my pulse spikes. Who is this, I type, and there's no reply, and I delete the thread. I do not forget the words, and I leave through the east exit so I don't pass the nurses' station. Outside, the air smells like wet concrete and diesel, and the sky hangs low and heavy, as if it can't decide whether to break open. Across the street, a newsstand sells coffee and glossy magazines, and a child points at one with a surgeon on the cover.

His mother says not that one and steers him toward candy, and a bus hisses to a stop. People climb on with their umbrellas and their bags, and I don't board, I watch them disappear into a moving box. Their brains will forget this moment before it's even done, mine doesn't, and cold air lays itself on bare calves. Wet boards under small feet, a hand cupping my cheek, not a slap, not punishment, a correction, a repositioning. Not Clara's hand, older, firmer, a woman's voice behind me, look at me, don't move, good girl.

My stomach drops, and I grab the bus-stop pole as if I'm bracing for intubation. When I inhale, the air tastes wrong, lake water, old metal, algae, and two laughs overlay. Mine, high and thin, someone else's, older, pleased, and then another laugh. Farther back, not amused, knowing, my mother, and I don't cry, I don't shake. Surgeons don't break in public, we break in supply closets and scan rooms, or we don't break at all.

My knees soften anyway, just enough that I sit, and I cross my legs so it looks like choice. I fix the misaligned button on my coat, one breath, then another, it has to be enough. I stand and walk into the rain, not toward home, not toward the club, not toward the lake. Just forward, something has started cutting, and for once, it isn't me, and at home the silence feels unsafe. Silence is a scan, it shows too much, and I turn the TV on low, talking heads, a laugh track, a sports recap.

I don't take in a word, I just need sound, a hallway without blood. Coat off, bag down, bathroom, cold water over my hands, not washing, cooling, and my wrist pulses under the stream. The spot where Clara touched me prickles, not want, recognition, and I lean toward the mirror, looking for proof. Red eyes, a crack in my mouth, a tremor I can blame, and I see none. Just a face composed enough to pass, structure intact, function missing, and I cook as if it matters.

Vegetables cut too neatly, pasta boiled too long, food plated with the symmetry of an incision line, and I don't eat it. I pour a glass of wine and don't drink, and I watch the surface ripple when I set it down. As if I'm waiting for it to settle like blood, and a fork is in my hand before I notice. My grip is the grip I use for forceps, and what exactly am I remembering, not an "event." A procedure, instruction, positioning, a child guided like a patient under sedation, look at me, don't move, good girl.

My throat closes, not emotion, habit, a trained pause, and I set the fork down. I step back from the counter, don't touch anything else, and by midnight it returns, not fear, presence. Like someone standing two feet behind me, just outside touch, not watching, waiting, and I go to the window. The city glows below, smeared light on wet asphalt, and a man stands under an awning smoking. Smoke rises in slow coils, I should draw the curtains, I don't, and instead I unlock my phone. My thumb moves before intent, and I open the club's encrypted site, I don't look for Clara.

I look for the symbol, that curved line that could be a wave or a dock, and I tap it. A prompt appears, ENTER ACCESS PHRASE, and I don't think, I type good girl, and the page unlocks. My stomach drops hard, clean, and a single link appears, MEMBERSHIP ARCHIVE – CHILD ADMITTANCE RECORDS. Children weren't members, children were offered, and my finger hovers over the link. Pulse in my wrist, pulse in my throat, I don't click, not yet, and I close the phone. I breathe, and sleep comes like anesthesia, sudden, heavy, total.

I'm on wet boards, bare feet, toes curled over the lip of a plank, and the air is cold against my calves. I'm smaller, off balance, the horizon too far away, and water under us is black, streaked with light. A hand behind me adjusts my posture, not rough, not gentle, correcting, and hands flatten mine at my sides. Chin lifted, look at me, don't move, good girl, and Clara is there. Farther back, teenage, arms crossed, jaw tight, she knows something is wrong, she stands in the only place she can stand, witness, and the dock tilts. My body pitches forward, and I wake on the kitchen floor, I don't remember lying down.

A bruise throbs on my hip, pain: local, mild, clear, evidence, and I shower scalding hot until my skin blooms red. I lock the door twice, check the stove twice, compulsions stack like sutures, not panic, I tell myself. Precision, and at the hospital the next morning, the first person I see is Clara, she's at the nurses' station with a chart in hand. Coffee untouched, she looks up when I approach, no smile, no flinch, no apology, and we stand with the space between us dense. With things neither of us can claim as fact yet, and I ask when did you see her.

I don't name who, I don't have to, and Clara doesn't pretend to misunderstand. "Before you did," she says, and I ask who was she, and Clara says one question at a time. I'm asking, I begin, and she cuts in, you're remembering, and heat rises at the base of my skull. Start with the lake, she says, and I snap no, and she says then start with your mother, and my jaw locks. You don't get to, I start, and Clara sets her chart down slowly, like she's putting away something sharp. You asked me when I saw her, she says, I saw her watching first.

My chest goes tight, and Clara says before anything happened, before anyone touched you. Before anyone touched me, and the last phrase slides in like a blade, and my throat closes, and Clara's voice stays steady. Your mother stood on the shore like someone guarding a boundary, she says, but she wasn't guarding you, and my lungs don't seize. My pulse doesn't race, everything in me goes quiet instead, and Clara says you think you're angry at me. You're not, you just don't know where to put it, and a bed rolls past behind us, a monitor beeps. The floor keeps moving like nothing is happening, and I tell her you're dismissed.

I'm not your resident, she replies, and I say you're dismissed from this conversation, and she says I'm not in it. You are, and I step closer, too close, our breath mixes, and I whisper you don't know what happened. Clara holds my gaze, and she says I know what didn't, and I ask what does that mean, and her jaw tightens. No one saved you, and the sentence hits harder than the slap, and I leave without knowing which step is the first. Not retreat, escape, and a resident hands me a chart, I sign without reading the header. Someone explains a CT finding, I process it on autopilot, my hands stay steady, my voice stays clean, something under it doesn't.

In Neuro ICU, a junior asks me a textbook question, Dr Nile, Fernandez says, what if the lesion is right up against the fornix. The answer should come first, protect the fornix, keep the tract, and instead my mind supplies a phrase like a reflex. Hold still, look at me, good girl, and I blink once, and I say protect the fornix, at all costs. Fernandez nods and writes it down like scripture, I hear my own voice and feel sick, and I step into the break room for walls that aren't covered in scans. The air smells like burnt coffee and tired bodies, soup explodes in a microwave, someone swears softly, and I sit.

Half a minute later, Clara comes in, she doesn't speak at first, and she turns on the tap. She washes her hands with a surgeon's sequence, palms, backs, fingers, webbing, wrists, too thorough for a nurse between patients, and she tells me you think remembering will ruin you. I say nothing, and she says it won't, and I ask how would you know, and my voice comes out colder than I feel. Because it didn't ruin me, she says, and I tell her you weren't the one being touched, and she answers not by her. The words land like a dropped clamp, and I look up, and Clara turns the tap off, water drips in a slow line. Some of us weren't hurt, she says, we were used.

Used, and she steps closer, not threat, not comfort, unclear, and I hate that. No one believes one child, Clara says, but two, one silent, one making noise, that breaks the story, and my mouth is dry. You weren't meant to remember the lake, she says, you were meant to remember me, and my throat tightens, and I ask why. Clara's eyes shine, but she doesn't cry, and she says if you remembered me, you'd remember why I pulled you away. Her voice drops, and you'd remember who pulled you back, and the room shifts, boards, cold air, my wrist in a smaller hand. Tugging, and another hand on my other wrist, larger, stronger, pulling me into place, and a laugh behind me. A woman's voice, warm and wrong, stay here, let her watch, that's all she's good for.

Air leaves my lungs in a small, sharp gasp, and Clara lifts a hand, palm out, not touching, and she tells me to breathe. I do, one breath, then another, enough to stay upright, enough to hurt, and I ask who was she. Clara's mouth tightens, and she says you already know, and I say no, I don't, and she says then ask your mother. The words chase me out of the room, and the consult I'm called to is a seventeen-year-old in step-down. AVM behind her right eye, half her head shaved, electrodes taped down, one eye blown wide, the other bruised, and her mother sits behind her with hands knotted tight. Her face has angles that catch at me in a way I don't like, and she asks Dr Nile, and I nod.

My words feel delayed, as if they have to travel through water, and I look at the girl, and she says it hurts. Pain doesn't mean damage, I say out of habit, a lie, in its own way, and I ask how long has it been like this, and she says two days. And before that, I ask, and she says a month, and before that, and she shrugs, eyes locked on mine. Years, and her mother jumps in, she never said anything, not until she couldn't see, she didn't want to make a fuss, and the girl's mouth tightens. Pain doesn't matter, she says, flat, and a chill runs straight down my spine, and I ask why would you think that. She answers without pause, because you're meant to ignore it, and then, like she's explaining math, it's easier to stay still and wait for it to be done.

Still, wait, don't move, good girl, and my throat closes. I turn to the imaging screen so they can't read my face, and the AVM curls through her brain like wire strangling a tree. It could rupture tomorrow, or never, and surgery could blind her, or save her, or kill her, and a brain trained to suffer quietly. A brain like mine, and I tell them we'll operate, and the mother gasps with relief and gratitude, and the girl nods as if I've offered to remove a splinter. I leave before I can't breathe, and in the corridor, I lean against the wall for three seconds, and then I take out my phone. Mom, and my thumb hovers over Call, and calling is reckless. My mother doesn't answer questions, she gives rulings, but Clara's voice sits in my head, then ask your mother, and my thumb presses. Ringing, once, twice, three times, I hang up before it connects, and one part of me says coward. Another part replies surgeon, you don't cut blind.

I book the girl's case for tonight, emergency slot, override, and I request the senior anesthesiologist. No one argues, they never argue when I speak like that, and in pre-op, Julie hands me my cap, I tie it too tight, and she says you'll give yourself a headache. I already have one, I answer, and Julie doesn't push, she hands me gloves, and she says she'll scrub in with me. You don't have to, I tell her, and she says she knows, she will, and I don't realize how much that matters until she steps away. I'm alone at the sink, and water runs, soap foams, and my hands move through the ritual, palms, backs, fingers, webs, wrists, again. Again, and I tell myself compulsion isn't panic, it's a kind of prayer.

In the OR, the girl is draped and sedated, head fixed in the frame, and the mother waits outside with a paper cup of coffee. A face full of hope, incision, bone saw, craniotomy, and the steps calm me, I can orchestrate bone and blood. We expose the AVM, it throbs on its own schedule, a rogue pulse, and Julie adjusts suction, and her fingers brush my wrist. Normal OR contact, my body doesn't know that, and for a split second another scene overlays it, wet skin, cold air, a hand on my neck. Lifting my chin, not rough, not kind, correcting, good girl, and my knees threaten to soften, and the room threatens to sway. Julie murmurs Jax, and I say I'm fine, and this time it's close to true.

I isolate the nidus, clip feeders, the AVM collapses, starved, and we cauterize, irrigate, close. When the girl wakes, she will see, she will hurt, she will live, no one saved me. I saved her, and after, her mother cries into my coat, tears soak the fabric, I let her, and the girl opens both eyes and looks at me. It doesn't hurt, she whispers, and I tell her it will, tomorrow, and she nods, no child should know that timetable. At 2:11 a.m., the hospital is quiet in the way only hospitals are, machines running, bodies breathing, people behind doors, yet the halls feel empty. I walk the corridor outside Neuro ICU, and Clara is at the far end, writing notes, and she looks up as I approach.

Not surprised, not wary, she asks your patient, and I tell her she woke up, she can see. Clara nods once, and she tells me you chose pain over forgetting, and I stop, and she says that's the difference. You think forgetting keeps you clean, it doesn't, and I ask you think remembering makes me pure, and she says no, it makes you human. Silence sits between us, sharp as bone dust, and then Clara says, very quietly, your mother didn't look away because she didn't want to, and the sentence lands with hard, brutal clarity. The dock tilts in my mind, the shoreline, my mother on a blanket with her book open, head angled just enough to look like supervision, maybe she was watching, maybe that was the point. The past is coming either way, Clara says, I'm just done pretending I didn't see, and she turns to go.

Before she leaves, I ask what was she to you, and Clara pauses, and her jaw works once. Like she's deciding how much truth I can hold without falling, and she says she wasn't my mother, and her voice sharpens. She was yours, and Clara walks away, and the corridor sways under my feet, boards over water. For the first time, I understand what's opening inside me, it isn't a wound, it's a case, and I am not the one holding the knife.

Chapter Nine

---◇◇---

The Woman on the Shore

M y mother called it spiritual rest, and she said it the way other mothers said holiday or treat, as if being tired was a sin and time away was penance, and she announced it at breakfast while stirring sugar into her coffee like the decision was already locked. She said we were going to the lake for spiritual rest, no television, no phones, no distractions, and at twelve I heard no exit because the words were clean and almost holy. If you argued with them you became the problem, and I asked if I had to come because I still thought questions meant choices, even though I was already learning that in our house questions were only allowed when they matched the answer.

She lifted her eyes from the cup and told me of course I did, that it would be good for me, and good for you always meant this will hurt and you won't get to complain. She reached across the table and smoothed my hair, and it wasn't comfort so much as correction, like flattening a page that had started to curl. She said I'd been too much in my head and that we needed to get me back into my body, and I didn't know that was the point of the whole trip because I thought she was only annoyed that I liked books more than people. The sentence sat there anyway, quiet and absolute, like a plan she didn't want me to see yet.

The lake house sat at the end of a winding road that smelled like wet leaves and petrol, and when the trees opened there it was, two stories, grey siding, a porch that sagged just enough to look honest. Behind it, the lake looked like dropped sky, cracked and flat, grey-blue with thin ripples like veins, and a narrow dock pushed out like a finger. My mother stepped out of the car and breathed in slow and loud and asked if it wasn't peaceful, but the air tasted like wet wood and algae and something in it made my teeth ache. I was still staring at the water when the woman came out to greet us, and the timing felt deliberate before I had language for that.

She moved like she belonged there, no pause on the porch planks and no flinch at the creak, hair pinned up loose on purpose with strands escaping like a plan, a white shirt with sleeves rolled and faded jeans that had been worn, not bought. Evelyn, I didn't know her name yet but I knew her shape, silhouette first and then voice, and she called that I must be Jacqueline while smiling at me instead of my mother. I hated my full name, my mother refused my short one, and Evelyn reached for it like it was hers already, so I said it was Jax too fast and the correction felt like a confession. Evelyn repeated Jax like she was tasting it and called it a strong name, and my mother made a small pleased sound, the kind she made when a child behaved as expected.

She said I insisted on that and that Jacqueline was too feminine, and she made feminine sound like a diagnosis, but Evelyn kept her eyes on my face and said strong girls can have soft names and that we could talk about that later. Then she turned and hugged my mother with quick practiced warmth and said she was so glad she came and that she looked worn out, and my mother laughed short and brittle and repeated spiritual rest like it explained everything. Evelyn glanced back at me, measuring, and said we'd help her relax, and I didn't know who we was, I only knew I'd been placed inside the sentence without permission.

Inside, the house smelled like old wood and lemon oil and something sweet under it, a perfume that had outlived the person who wore it first, and crosses hung in the hall, simple wood ones my mother approved at once. She said God was everywhere, and Evelyn answered that most of all where people were willing to listen, and later I would replay that line and hear the hook inside it. At twelve, I only heard that my mother liked this woman, and that alone made me want to pass whatever test was coming. Wanting approval had always been a survival skill in our house, and I didn't know yet what it would cost me here.

The first time I saw Clara was through a window, because they gave me a small bedroom upstairs and I unpacked the way my mother liked, neat stacks, socks paired, books in a straight line. The window overlooked the shore and the glass was streaked as if someone started cleaning and gave up, and outside on the grass between the house and the dock a girl sat with her back against a rock. She was thirteen maybe fourteen, dark hair in a low messy braid, knees scabbed in three places, reading a paperback with the cover bent back, and every few seconds her eyes slid to the dock. Evelyn stood there too at the edge looking out at the water, and no one spoke, and it looked like a staged photo, woman on the dock, girl on the shore, house behind them like a witness that wouldn't talk.

My mother appeared in the doorway behind me and told me to put my things away neatly like I were flinging them around, and I said I was, and her gaze drifted past me to the glass. She said good, Clara's here, I'd have company, and she sounded pleased that I wouldn't be able to hide in my books, and I asked who she was. My mother said Evelyn's niece or cousin, she didn't recall, they brought her here in summer, and she stepped beside me so our reflections overlapped in the glass, same face shape, different eyes, hers sharper and less forgiving. She decided I'd like her and called her observant, and the word landed heavy even though I didn't know why, and I said okay because that's what I said when I didn't know the rules yet.

That afternoon we went down to the water and I wore the blue windbreaker my mother insisted on, too big, cuffs swallowing my hands, zipper pressing my throat, because she said lake wind was tricky and modesty wasn't seasonal. Clara was already on the dock sitting cross-legged with toes over the edge and shoes in a heap behind her, and Evelyn stood a few feet away with her hands in her pockets, relaxed in a way that felt planned. Evelyn called Jax and told me to come meet Clara, and Clara looked over her shoulder with eyes sharper than I expected, not cruel, just awake like she'd seen more than kids should. I said hi and stopped where grass ended and wet boards began, and she said hi and turned back to the lake like she wanted to show she didn't need me, and that alone made me want her attention.

My mother told me not to hover because it was unbecoming, and she stayed where the grass ended with arms folded and ankles crossed like a person running a test, not watching play, so I stepped onto the dock. The boards flexed under my weight like walking on someone else's held breath, water slapped the sides, and the smell of algae and damp rope climbed my throat. Evelyn told me to be careful because wet wood lies, and her voice wasn't a warning so much as an invitation, and Clara watched me come closer with her eyes flicking once to my windbreaker. She asked if I was hot and I said a bit, and my mother called that I'd be fine and that I said I was cold more than I was, and heat rose in my cheeks because it was the familiar move, my own experience edited out loud.

Evelyn said it was too warm for that and that I could take it off if I wanted, and if you want was an adult's favourite test, a phrase they used while watching to see if your want matched theirs. I hesitated because my mother's gaze pressed between my shoulder blades, and I said I was fine, and Evelyn tilted her head and studied me, then told me suit yourself and that we had time. That was how it always started, as permission dressed as patience, as if the only thing being tested was my choice. I didn't know yet that the real test was whether I would call it my idea.

We fell into a routine and I didn't know it was training because kids mistake repeats for safety, and you don't see the trap until the pattern feels like the only calm thing. Mornings were chores and prayers and long kitchen talk about faith and discipline and building character, and their voices blurred into a steady hum like the kind I would later hear in hospitals. Afternoons were the dock, always the dock, always framed as care, and Evelyn would guide me into place near the edge and talk about balance and strong posture and chin up and not looking at my feet, looking out. I obeyed because I was good at directions and better at praise, and when she murmured good girl the words sank deeper each time, as if the dock were writing them into me.

Clara was there most days, on the shore at first and then on the dock, sometimes beside me and sometimes a step away, and she didn't talk much because she didn't need to, her presence carried weight. Once, when the wind picked up and the boards felt slick, Clara asked if I had to stand there, and my mother answered from the grass without lifting her eyes from the Bible that I needed to learn not to fear falling. Clara said I could learn that closer to shore, and Evelyn laughed soft and said I wasn't a toddler, I was capable, wasn't I, and they both looked at me. At twelve I understood capable meant chosen and chosen meant safe, so I said yes and that I was fine, and my mother smiled without warmth and said I knew what I wanted, and Clara's jaw tightened as she stared back at the water.

Some moments looked like normal summer, skimming stones and splashes at the edge and Evelyn pointing out constellations, and my mother correcting my posture even when we were standing still, but under that the script thickened. Evelyn would shift me half a step and tell me to stand here, no here, hands at my sides, don't fidget, look at me, and her eyes stayed on my face, and she would tell me to breathe slow, in, out, and I did it. Then she would whisper good girl and the words would land like instruction, not comfort, and Clara watched, sometimes trying to crack the scene open with humour by asking if we were training me to be a lighthouse and that I was going to start blinking in code. I laughed because I needed the release, but Evelyn didn't smile, she told Clara to mind her tongue and said some of us were trying to help her, and my mother looked up and told Clara that if she didn't have something useful to add she shouldn't interfere, and interfere sounded like medicine, like procedure, like consent already signed.

Clara flushed and looked at me with urgency and murmured that I didn't have to stay there and that I could come sit with her, and for half a second my weight shifted toward her. Then my mother's voice cut across the water and said Jacqueline, hold still, full name, command, and my body froze as if the sound had hands. Evelyn's fingers brushed my shoulder, light and neat, and she said good girl, and the choice vanished, and Clara stepped back just far enough to show she had tried. That day I learned a rule without naming it, that if you refuse rescue hard enough people stop offering it, and I understood that in the way kids understand weather, as something you cannot argue with.

The horror wasn't only what happened, it was how it was named, because Evelyn would call me mature and different and say most girls my age were silly, and my mother echoed it in her own key by calling me serious and disciplined and saying that's why we trusted her with more. More meant pain and rules and secrets, and every shiver got called courage and every pause became a chance to prove I wasn't weak, and doctrine drowned out the instinct that kept trying to speak. You wanted this, you're strong, good girls adapt, and I wanted to be good, I wanted my mother to look at me the way she looked at Evelyn, so when Evelyn adjusted my chin with two fingers I stayed still. When she stepped too close under the reason of balance I didn't flinch, and when she said trust me I did, because my mother was watching and not stopping it, and in a child's logic that meant nothing terrible was happening.

I remember one afternoon with sharp edges because the light had shifted late and the sun hit the water sideways and turned it into broken glass, and the air carried a chill that didn't match the day. My mother called it a blessing and said it was perfect weather for reflection and that the lake reveals things, and she said it like she was ordering a scan, and Evelyn was already on the dock barefoot with sleeves rolled like she'd been waiting. Clara sat on the grass with her arms wrapped around her knees watching the water like she was trying to make it behave, and Evelyn called me over and said today we work on stillness as if that wasn't always the job. I kicked off my shoes and stepped onto the boards and the wood was cold in the way that climbs into bone, and Evelyn told me jacket off, I didn't need it, and I glanced at my mother and she nodded once, so I slid the windbreaker off and air met my arms like exposure.

Evelyn placed me at the edge with my toes just shy of the drop and told me hands at my sides, chin up, eyes on me, and I obeyed, and the world narrowed to Evelyn in front of me, water behind her, my mother on shore a blur at the edge of vision. Evelyn told me to breathe slowly, in, out, and I inhaled and exhaled and the air scraped, and she told me I was doing so well and that most girls giggle or squirm and I didn't, I understood, and the praise burned. She pressed me to say I did, and I said yes, and she asked why, and I searched for the right answer like it was a scripture prompt, and I said because it makes me strong, and Evelyn smiled as if I had spoken the password.

From the shore my mother's voice floated over the water saying I'd always been strong and she told her, and you'd think that would feel safe but it didn't, it felt like permission. Not protect her, she can take it, push more, and Clara stepped forward and called that maybe I was tired and we'd been doing this a lot, and my mother said I hadn't complained, and Clara said I wouldn't, and Evelyn's eyes cut to Clara and told her that if watching makes her uneasy she should go inside. If watching makes you uneasy, not if this is wrong, and Clara's hands clenched and she muttered she wasn't the one she was worried about, and Evelyn turned back to me and told me to ignore her because she doesn't get the work, and work was my mother's favourite word for pain.

My memory smears there like a thumb across wet paint, and I know more happened, touches dressed up as correction and skin learning to obey the wrong voice, panic and pleasure braided into the same spike, and that belongs to another chapter. This one is about who refused to see, because what I recall with clean clarity is not Evelyn's hands, it's my mother's eyes, because she didn't look away, not once. She didn't look unsure, she watched like someone timing a test she had approved, and Clara's gaze kept snapping between us, me at the edge, Evelyn in front, my mother on shore, and at one point I saw Clara's mouth form stop and no sound came out. I didn't say it either because I was busy trying to be the girl they wanted, still, composed, chosen, and chosen is a drug at twelve when worth is measured by how well adults praise your pain.

The trip ended the way trips do, car packed and house tidy and thanks spoken, and my mother walked with Evelyn toward the porch while I stood by the car hugging myself inside the blue windbreaker even though the day was warm. Clara lingered a few metres away with arms crossed and a face set older than both of them, and my mother told me to say goodbye and I asked to whom and she snapped not to be rude, to Evelyn, to Clara, they'd been very good to me. Good turned my stomach, and I went to Clara first and said bye, and she looked at me like she wanted to say ten things and trusted none of them. She blurted that if I ever feel weird about this later I could call her, and I asked weird how, and she swallowed and said just weird, like a bruise you can't see, and my mother cut across us and told Clara that's enough, and Clara flinched like she'd been struck by a rule.

Evelyn laughed and smoothed the moment like a hand over a wrinkle and said teenagers, always dramatic, and then she turned to my mother and stepped close enough that if you weren't watching you'd miss the angle. Her hand settled on my mother's arm like affection with a purpose, her mouth moved near my mother's ear, and I shouldn't have heard it but the lake was quiet and the wind shifted and the words floated back clear. Evelyn said she's ready, and my mother answered with a soft hum of approval, and she didn't ask ready for what and she didn't say stop, she only nodded and smiled at me like I'd passed. Like something had been achieved, like the ache in my teeth was proof of growth, not warning.

On the drive home my mother called the week life-changing and told me I grew up and it was good for me, and trees blurred past the window like vertical lines on a scan and the lake fell behind us. I asked what if I didn't like it, and she made a small sharp sound and told me not to be ungrateful because most girls never get a chance like that, and chance is what you call harm when you need it to sound like generosity.

When the person meant to save you calls it a chance, you rewrite your own story to survive, because the other option is to admit the lifeguard wasn't there to pull you out, she was there to time how long you could stay under. Halfway back we stopped for petrol, my mother went inside, and I stayed in the car and watched the station life, a child crying for sweets, a woman arguing over a receipt, a teen scrolling a phone bored and safe, and I pressed my thumbnail into the soft skin of my wrist until it hurt because if I made my own pain maybe it would cover the other.

We didn't talk about the lake after that, not straight, we talked around it like people talk around a tumour they aren't ready to name, and at church my mother called it a blessing and told anyone who would listen that the Lord gave us a place to rest. She said Jacqueline needed shaping and she came back steadier, and steadier and shaped and grounded sound good if you don't know what they cover, and women patted my shoulder and called it good for me and said girls are too soft now. People asked if it was fun and I opened my mouth and saw wet wood and praise like a leash and Clara's tense face and my mother on shore still as stone, and I said yeah it was different, and they laughed. My mother shook her head like she found me cute and said always in her head but we're working on it, we, as if the lake and the dock were part of a plan we all agreed to.

The first time I tried to talk about it I was fifteen, and I chose my words like I was handling a blade, and my mother sat at the kitchen table marking Bible study pages with a red pen, the same focus she used on my report cards. I asked if she still talked to Evelyn and she didn't look up, she said at times, why, and I said I was thinking about that trip, and she told me I should be grateful because not many people open their home like that. I said I knew and then the sentence jammed, and I said I felt strange sometimes about what she was doing with me, and my mother set down the pen and her face didn't soften, it sharpened. She repeated doing like it was obscene, and she asked what I was saying, and my body told me to back away, and I said I didn't know and that some of it felt off, and she snorted and told me I was twelve and everything feels off at twelve.

She cut in and asked if it was hard or helpful or a lesson, and her voice went cold, and she said I never complained, not once, I never asked to stop, I never said I felt bad, and I remembered standing on the dock with my throat locked around words I didn't have. I said I didn't know how, and she snapped know how to speak, that I never had trouble speaking, that I wanted to impress her and I did, and now I wanted to act like I was forced, like a victim, and victim was the word she refused to allow. I told her I wasn't saying I was forced, and it was a lie I told to stay safe, and I said I was trying to make sense of it, and she picked up her pen again and said there was nothing to make sense of. She said I went, I learned, I grew, end of story, and she underlined a line so hard the paper tore, and she told me to pray if I was upset but not to turn her choices into my teen drama because she did what was best for me.

I went upstairs and stared at myself in the bathroom mirror and I looked like someone who had been believed all her life, and that was the trick. People believed my mother, I did too, because the other option was to admit I'd been hurt while she watched, and at fifteen that truth was too heavy. So I shoved it into a closet and leaned my back against the door, and years later I built a life on that door, med school and residency and fellowship, a career built from control and clean hands and the ability to stand in catastrophe without shaking. People praised my calm and told me I didn't rattle, residents whispered like I was made of steel, patients called me cold and meant it like respect, and anything that might have cracked me got renamed strength.

I told a safe version of the lake story when I had to, strict faith and character summers and a hard mother, and people nodded and some looked shocked and most looked impressed, and they asked if I came out of that and became this and called it rare. I let them keep that story, I told myself grit was the point, and when the dock surfaced I called it a lesson and filed it away because I needed it to be harmless. If it wasn't harmless then my mother wasn't only the woman on the shore, she was part of the water, and that was the conclusion my brain would not allow. Now, sitting in a hospital hall years later, the scene runs again with a different cut, and in the first cut the dock was centre and Evelyn was the threat and I was the test and my mother was background.

Now the frame shifts and I see her folded arms and the tilt of her head and the way she never once said no, and the nod when Evelyn whispered she's ready, and the question ready for what opens like a wound. Ready to be offered, ready to be shaped, ready to be hurt and called strong after, and Clara's words sit under my skin like grit, your mother saw, and she didn't give me new facts. She gave me the meaning I refused, because there is a gap between not knowing and not wanting to know, and kids don't get that gap, adults do, and my mother chose not to know in a way that helped her. A daughter who didn't collapse, a daughter who didn't ask for comfort, a daughter who learned early that if she renamed harm she had to own the outcome, and that's the terror, not only the woman on the dock, the woman on the shore.

Clara was a kid too, she didn't have power, she had eyes, and she watched me at the edge and watched Evelyn step closer and call it work and watched my mother nod like she was approving a plan, and Clara learned early what I refused to learn, that no help was coming. I wasn't only hurt, I was left there in plain sight, and you can forgive what someone does in the dark, it's harder to forgive the person who stood in full light and called it needed. Even now with a scalpel and a clean name and awards long enough to please the kind of people my mother chased, there is still a twelve-year-old me on that dock, feet cold, chin up, hands at my sides. Eyes locked on Evelyn because turning around means seeing my mother, arms folded, gaze steady, timing my endurance.

Evelyn says good girl and my mother says she's ready, and for a long time I believed them, and I called it discipline and then grit and then a big summer when I needed it safe to say out loud. Now, with Clara's words lodged in me, the image clears, and Evelyn isn't the only one in focus, and my mother isn't a bystander. She chose the scene, she set the terms, she signed the consent form with silence, and I wasn't ready, I was available, and she was the one who opened the door.

Chapter Ten

---∞---

Reconstructed Desire

There's a question we don't ask in medicine because we pretend we've solved it, where does desire come from, biology, we say, hormones, dopamine, oxytocin, reward loops, old drives dressed up as romance and impulse. We talk about scans and signal, we point to bright spots on fMRI when subjects look at someone they say they love, and we avoid the harder question, who taught you what to want. Because if desire is learned it can be examined, if it can be examined it can be altered, and if it can be altered then half the choices you swear are yours might be trained reflex. We don't like that, we prefer chemistry, chemistry can't be blamed.

The morning after the call with my mother, I wake before my alarm, I don't feel rested, I feel braced, like I spent the night holding my own ribs apart so nothing could close. For a few seconds, there's that blank moment in the dark, breathing, no labels, then the stack returns, neat and fast, Jacqueline, Doctor, Surgeon, today's cases, and under it the word my mother used like a blessing, ready. "She's ready," I used to hear it as praise, ready for adulthood, ready for weight, ready to be the kind of daughter people point to, now it lands different, ready to be shaped, ready to be placed, ready to perform.

In the shower, I catch myself standing the way Evelyn taught me, feet apart, knees loose, weight even, spine tall, chin lifted just enough. It's not comfort, it's posture you keep when someone is watching, "Don't hunch," she used to murmur, "They won't see your face," and they were never named, that was part of it, an unseen crowd you serve without consent, God, adults, men, everyone. I force my shoulders to drop, I turn my back to the spray and let the water hit the knots at my neck, it splashes messy, it runs where it wants, not in clean lines, and it feels wrong, ungraceful, untrained. I stay like that anyway, a small rebellion on white tile, I scrub too hard, skin turns pink, like I can make my body pick a side, memory or function.

I stare at my wrist, clean, pale veins, no mark, nothing to prove contact except the way my nerves insist there should be fingerprints. "It's nothing," I tell the tile, "I'm tired, that's all," and the tile never argues. On the subway, my reflection floats in the window over the city sliding past, scaffold, brick, a cyclist cutting too close to traffic, a taxi horn that sounds like a warning no one obeys, my face sits over it all, faint and misaligned, like two images layered wrong. I watch myself the way I read scans, detached, exact, how much of this body is mine, the way my ankles cross, the way my knees angle to take space but avoid touch, hands on thighs, relaxed but ready, the calm face people call cold, when it's just focus. I think of Evelyn on the dock, one hip set, arms loose, never limp, head tilted like she was inviting you and judging you at once, she could make you feel chosen without saying your name.

I shift on the plastic seat, straighten, then soften, tiny changes, like I'm testing a new tool. If someone filmed me and traced each motion, would I know which gestures are mine and which are repeats, probably not, wear something long enough and you stop seeing the seams. The hospital is aggressively normal, an aneurysm consult that's a migraine, a follow-up where the family wants a guarantee I can't give, an admin meeting flagged "time-sensitive," which means "this could hurt you later." Morning conference is packed, residents shoulder-to-shoulder around the screen, I stand at the front with a frontal lobe case on display, eloquent-adjacent, ugly vessels, the kind that makes trainees fall in love and makes admin fear my stats. "This region," I say, circling it with the laser, "non-dominant cortex, near-motor, low eloquence, we can be generous here."

I shift the pointer, "But here, no," I tap a smaller zone near language tracts, "One millimetre too far and she can't name her children." The room tightens, someone inhales like it costs them, I keep going, steady, "We'll do awake mapping, max safe resection, no hero work, preserve function before pride." And as I speak, I hear my voice like it belongs to someone else, slow cadence, clean consonants, reassurance with just enough lift to pull the room with me, I know that rhythm, not my mother's, Evelyn's, the tone she used on wet wood, chin up, hold still, good. I slow down a fraction, not for them, for me, to hear the shape of what I'm doing, I'm talking about taking language from a living person, and my voice says this is fine if you stay inside my lines.

When I finish, there's soft, polite applause, people scatter into their own lists, I stay to coil a cable. My hands move with neat grace, turn, pull, loop, no waste, I didn't learn that first in an OR, I learned it on a dock, where poise was a test and being watched was the point. Some people stumble into being desired, I was trained. In OR-3, the patient is a woman in her fifties, lesion pressing into orbitofrontal cortex, the part we blame for bad choices when we don't want to admit we're guessing, awake craniotomy. I like awake cases, they force truth, you can't treat someone as an object when you need them to speak while you're inside their skull, they also force performance from me, control as comfort, charm as anaesthetic.

"Good morning, Ava," I say while we prep her scalp, "How are you feeling," she gives a thin smile, "Terrified," and I say, "Good, fear means you grasp the stakes, sociopaths aren't scared." The nurses laugh, Ava lets out a shaky sound that almost counts as a laugh, then flinches as the local burns, humour as incision, pressure release. "We'll talk through it," I tell her, "I won't do anything without warning, if something feels wrong, you say so, you're on the team." Her husband stands to the side with a foam coffee cup crushed in his hand, he looks like he'd rather fight the tumour himself than hand her over to a stranger with a title. "We'll bring her back," I say, meeting his eyes, he nods too fast, "Thank you, Doctor," they always thank you before they know if you earned it.

Once the bone flap is off and the dura opened, the air shifts, sound drops a half-step, light turns harsh, a brain exposed is not holy, it's pink and pulsing and obscene in its need. "Ready," I ask, "Ready," anaesthesia says, "Mapping online," the tech replies, "Okay," I say, soft, "Let's go," and the same cadence slides in again, not on purpose, never on purpose. "Ava," I say, "I'll stimulate parts of your brain, I'll ask you to speak, tell me anything, breakfast, weather, how much you hate me, deal," she whispers, "Deal." "You're doing well," I tell her, "If something feels wrong, say so, you're not here to impress me," and that last line comes out sharp, like a sudden pivot to avoid a vessel, in my head my mother overlaps it, you wanted to impress her.

"Stim," the tech says, I touch the probe to cortex at the lesion's edge. "Ava, favourite place," she exhales, "The ocean, on a boat, far enough you can't see shore," "Why," "Because no one needs you," she says, "You're just there, small, it's a relief." I smile under my mask, "I think you and I handle not being needed very differently," and a small laugh moves through the room like a valve opening. We keep going, stim, test, answer, stim, test, answer, and my voice stays steady, hold still, breathe, good, the way Evelyn taught me to talk to myself. I am echoing the woman who shaped me into something useful, only now I'm shaping other people, reenactment in scrubs.

Halfway through, Fernandez hands me a micro set, her grip is wrong, I feel it before I see it, a tiny wobble where her hand meets the tool. "Relax," I say, she tenses, knuckles pale under gloves, and an old impulse rises, pure muscle memory, touch her wrist, guide her fingers, fix the angle, not harsh, intimate. The way Evelyn corrected me, the way a "small touch" becomes a lesson your body keeps, my hand lifts, hovers a few centimetres from her skin, then some inner camera pulls back, woman with rank, younger woman trying to please, a touch framed as help. I drop my hand, "Again," I say, "Grip from the side, not the top, you're crowding the tip," she adjusts, "Sorry," and I say, "Don't apologise," too sharp, "Learn," and she blinks.

My chest tightens, that line isn't mine, not at the root, I've heard it on wet wood under a grey sky, don't fuss, don't pout, learn. Desire isn't only what you reach for, it's also what you expect others to do when you speak. The case ends well, we take what we can without stealing function, Ava sings a line when we stim near language and the words come out clear, on pitch. "Beautiful," I tell her, "That's a lawsuit avoided," she gives a weak laugh, then they deepen sedation for closure. As she drifts, she murmurs, "You kept telling me what to do, it made it easy," and later, at the scrub sink, I stare at my foamy hands while that line repeats, you told me what to do, it made it easy.

In the club, that's the whole structure, you hand someone a script, you call it freedom because you agreed to the script, you call it desire because your body cooperates. On the dock, it was the same, hold still, don't move, good girl, obedience can feel like safety when the other option is chaos. What if my whole erotic language is built on that equation, attention + control = want, no wonder the club fits, no wonder Clara unsettles me. She won't play the role I offer, she won't let me run the old scene clean, she keeps insisting I have choices, people like me don't like choices, we like tests.

Between cases I hide in my office, I tell myself it's charts, it's not. Behind textbooks on my shelf, there's a cheap spiral notebook I keep because it looks harmless, to anyone else it's doodles and vessel lines, today I write something else. Differential: Desire, I treat it like a consult, Signs: – Pull toward controlled surrender, – Arousal linked to being watched and graded, – Shame when I start; ease when I obey, – My tone and stance in power roles echo old ones. History: – Church: obedience as virtue, – Lake: "lessons" in stillness and praise, – Mother: approval tied to performance, Working idea: Desire as a trained response to authority, then I write one question under it, What do I want without instruction.

My pen hovers and nothing comes, not quiet like peace, quiet like a blank scan when symptoms say something is there. I can recite vascular maps in my sleep, I can cut a tumour with my hands calm, I cannot name a want that isn't a reaction to someone else, and the thought is so unsteady it forces me to stand. I pace to the window and back, like a caged thing counting bars, outside traffic moves, people cross streets, the city keeps breathing. In here, I'm arguing with a notebook.

That night, I sit in my living room with the lights off, my apartment is neat, white and grey, clean lines, the kind of calm you buy when you don't trust your own mind. My phone lies face-down, the club app sits a thumbprint away, the access phrase I typed to open the archive, good girl. I still haven't opened it, instead I run my life like surgical footage, I'm not hunting for drama, I'm hunting for technique. First kiss, I can't picture the boy's face, I can picture the angle, the timing, the moment to part my lips because I'd watched enough to learn the cue. His surprised sound landed right where it should, I felt proud, not I want this, I did it right.

The first time I had sex was the same, old enough to pretend it was choice, young enough that it barely was, I remember the mechanics, the right sounds, the right pace, none of it was instinct, it was learned. I'd been given a role years earlier and never stopped playing it, partners changed, script stayed, and every partner since has told me the same thing, "You're confident," "You're responsive," "You're so good at this." What they mean is you perform desire with no visible shame, they never ask where I learned it, neither did I, "Experienced" is easier than "trained."

At the club, roles are named, Top, Bottom, Control, Service, people think labels make things safe. You tick boxes, you name limits, you call it consent, you declare it clean, sometimes it is, in my case it isn't. The first time I let someone restrain my wrists, my body answered fast, heart, heat, flood, I called it want because the other option was calling it fear. The dominant's fingers rested on my pulse, "Colour," she asked, "Green," I said at once, she smiled, "Then you like it," and I did, that's the problem. Pleasure doesn't wipe the past, it only tangles it.

A child can laugh on a dock, a teen can lean in because leaning away is worse, an adult can consent to a scene that mirrors the old one almost perfectly. Enjoyment doesn't cancel power, it just muddies the proof, I flip the phone over, the icon looks harmless. I don't tap it, not yet. The next day, I watch myself more than my patients, it's not ideal, it is true, and in a hallway glass panel I catch my posture when I'm being watched. Weight shifted just enough to look relaxed, spine long, eyes direct, and in conference, before I speak, I feel my gaze sweep the table, who will obey, who will resist, who will need to be pulled, and in the OR I hear the words I use when a resident gets it right.

"Good," I say, "Like that," I could change the words, I don't, not yet, I need to hear them long enough to decide if they belong to me. Late afternoon, I'm in the skills lab with med students around a mannequin, we run neuro checks, pupils, grip, simple questions, and I tell them to remember they're not only collecting data. Repetition teaches the brain what matters, what you check first is what the system learns to protect, they nod, pens ready, like I'm handing them a key, not basics. I point to a student with wrinkled scrubs and a badge that still squeaks, "Test her arm strength," he fumbles at the mannequin's wrist like he's afraid he'll break it. "No," I say, "Not like that, you're apologising with your hands, patients don't need apology, they need certainty."

I step closer and the old urge rises again, touch his wrist, fix the angle, I shut it down. "Stand here," I say, shifting him with my voice, not my hand, "Feet apart, shoulders loose, you're not asking, you're checking," and he adjusts to mirror me. "Better, now: firm grip, clear voice, 'Push up against my hand,'" he does it, stronger, cleaner, the others copy, one after another, a row of small repeats. I watch them and something opens under my ribs, if I'm not careful, I become what hurt me, not as a symbol, as a person. A woman who teaches obedience as safety, a voice others adopt as their inner script.

"Doctor," a student asks, "Like this," and she's standing almost how I stood at twelve, chin up, hands at sides, waiting for approval like air. Something in me recoils, "Drop your shoulders," I say fast, "You look like you're waiting for a verdict," they laugh and she relaxes. They don't know why my voice shook, I do. That night I open the notebook again, New heading: Who benefits, – Club owners, – People who like compliant partners, – Admin who reward doctors who never say "I can't," – My mother, who can point at my life and say, "See? It worked," – Me. My pen pauses on the last one, Do I benefit, and I think of the rush of being wanted, the high of being the calmest person in any room, the way shoulders drop when I give orders in a crisis.

These aren't ideas, they're rewards, reinforcement, each reenactment is another note in my brain. This works, this keeps you safe, do it again, and wanting to tear it out feels like betrayal of the only methods that ever kept me functional, but if I don't change it I never find out what's under it. Not pure, nothing is pure, just mine. Two days later, in the locker room, I catch another repeat forming, Julie argues with a new nurse over the instrument table, "You can't leave the micro set there," Julie says, "She prefers it on the left," "She always prefers it on the left," the nurse mutters. I step in and they snap upright like I just called a code, "Problem," I ask, Julie's "No" is too quick, "Just organising," and I look at the table, perfect, the layout my hands expect, of course it is.

They've learned my script, "You can change it," I say, and both women stare like I've lost it. "The layout," I add, "Put it where it makes sense to you, I'll adapt," Julie frowns, "But you always," "I know," I cut in, "Try it," and no one trusts softness from someone known for control. In the OR, it throws me, the scalpel is where my hand expects forceps, suction lives on the other side, every reach is half a beat late. My heart ticks up, not from danger, from being off-script, this is what happens when you move the dock one metre over, the body screams wrong, it isn't wrong, it's just not trained. We finish without errors, patient leaves with what matters intact, and after, Julie looks at me, cautious, "How was that," she asks, I peel off gloves and air hits damp skin, "Awful," I say, "Do it again tomorrow."

Her mouth lifts, slow and startled, "Yes, Doctor," and small moves, tiny edits, you don't rip out the whole problem, you change the steps and see what survives. Later that week I pass the nurses' station and see Clara, she adjusts an oxygen line on a restless patient, fingers steady, voice low, the patient's breath slows, not because Clara orders it, because she stays. She doesn't see me, I watch how she stands, close enough to help, far enough not to crowd, shoulders soft, weight grounded, nothing staged. Nothing seductive, it's care, and my chest tightens with an urge to touch her that isn't about the club and isn't about a test, it's about the fact that she knows the first script and refuses to pretend I wrote it.

My hand lifts on reflex, then I stop, who taught me to reach with my body before my mind checks in, not Clara. Evelyn, my mother, the church, the club, every place that taught me anticipate what they want and become it before they ask, I tuck my hand in my pocket. "Jax," Clara says, sensing me before she turns, I stand just out of reach, "Nothing," I say, "I was just watching," and she reads my face like a chart. "You look like you're about to cut into something," she says, "I am," I reply, her eyes drop to my empty hands. "No tools," she says, soft, "Not yet," and I walk away before I can ask her to tell me what to want.

That night, in bed, I list the day's small breaks, the tray moved, the wrist I didn't touch, the words I almost changed, tiny shifts. But in neurosurgery, a millimetre can be the gap between speech and silence, between walking and a chair, between a person intact and a stranger wearing their face, maybe desire works like that. Maybe you reroute a circuit one reflex at a time, I don't know, we build whole labs to help people forget. We fund almost nothing on how to remember and still live, and as my eyes start to burn with fatigue, one question rises, plain and sharp, who taught me to want like this, and the next one, harder, what happens if I stop learning from them. I turn onto my side, my hand rests on the inside of my wrist, where her fingers were, my pulse taps steady against my fingertips, and for the first time, I try to hear it as if it belongs to someone who might answer, mine.

Chapter Eleven

Not Clara

The first thing I notice is that Clara doesn't move the way she does in my head, because in my head she is all clean angles, wrist turned just so, eyes sliding sideways, a mouth that tilts at the exact moment you want it to, a pattern I've replayed so many times it feels stored, not made up. In the hall she's just a nurse, she walks fast and she doesn't glide, she gets places, and at the station she holds a pen in her teeth when both hands are full, she laughs with her whole face when Teasdale makes a joke so bad it should be written up, she bumps her hip on a cart and keeps moving, she swears when the screen freezes, and sleep debt sits under her eyes like faint bruises that won't heal. Watching her work is like seeing your own memory as a collage, because the woman I want isn't here, not the way I built her.

I stand at the far end of the corridor and pretend to read a chart while Clara argues with a junior resident about doses, her voice is firm, not soft, not teasing, and the sharp edge I remember from the dock is there but it's aimed outward, not at me. "You can't just bump her up because the number looks low," Clara says, and she points at the labs like she's holding the line for the patient, "Look at her creatinine, we're not trying to blow out her kidneys," and the resident mutters something as if muttering counts as medicine. Clara holds his gaze until he fixes the order, and it's the stare that hits me, not because it turns me on, because I know it. I've seen it before, on someone else, on the dock, on Evelyn, and the thought lands so lightly I almost miss it, like a hairline crack you only see when the light shifts.

Clara walks away and she passes close enough that her shoulder brushes mine, it feels like an accident and she doesn't look back, her scent is barely there, soap, detergent, clean cotton, nothing planned. My pulse still jumps anyway, and my brain supplies the wrong face, not Clara, pinned hair, sleeves rolled, a smile that sat between comfort and command, Evelyn. I close my eyes for half a beat and I taste lake air, and I understand the wrong person has been haunting me, not wrong as in false, wrong as in filed in the wrong place. Clara is the one my body answers now, but the template came from somewhere else, an older frame, an earlier scan, someone my mother called kind.

After rounds I lock myself in my office and tell myself I'm catching up on notes, but the room feels too small for what's inside it, and Harrow's paper lies open on my desk like an accusation. Pleasure recoded as agency, coercion turned into choice, and I shove the journal aside and open a blank page instead, because I can't keep thinking in circles. At the top I type two names, Clara, Evelyn, and I set them into two columns like I'm pretending this is clean. It's a stupid exercise, the kind of thing a therapist hands you with a cup of tea and a box of tissues, and I do it like a consult because that's the only way I know how to touch a wound without flinching.

Under Clara, I write what my body reacts to, wrist touch, exact pressure, quiet force in a crowded room, the way she says my name like it's a memory not a title, eyes that watch more than they talk, and I stop because my throat tightens around the list. Under Evelyn, I write what my mind pretends is history, wrist set on the dock, "Hold still" said like praise, the way she used my name like she knew I'd give it to her, eyes that watched both of us. My chest tightens as if the lists are pulling on the same tendon, and somewhere along the line my brain spliced them, because the traits I've pinned on Clara, guidance, control, instruction, being seen by someone who already knows what you can take, those belonged to Evelyn first. Clara was there, but she wasn't the imprint, she was the part of the frame I used so I wouldn't have to stare at the center.

I find Clara in the one place you're not meant to talk about anything that matters, the staff stairwell, no cameras, no patients, bad paint, dead light, and the smell of cleaner that never quite fades. She's between floors leaning on the rail and staring down through the gap like it's a drop not a couple of metres, her badge is flipped and her hair has slipped loose, and she speaks without turning. "You're avoiding me," she says, and I tell her I'm busy because I'm still pretending those are opposites. She answers, "Those aren't opposites," and I step down until we're level while the stairwell hums with the building, the low grind of a place that never sleeps, and I feel the shame of being alive inside the noise.

"I watched you today," I say, and her mouth twists like she's deciding whether to make it easy for me. "Lucky me," she says, and I snap, "Not like that," then catch myself because I'm hearing my own tone harden, "Not only like that." She looks at me quick and sharp, like she's reading a monitor, and I feel the ridiculous urge to pass a test I didn't consent to. "I thought you were the one," I say, and she doesn't play dumb, she only asks, "The one what," as if she's already tired of being cast. "The one who taught me," I say, and the words come out ugly, "How to want what I want, how to stand, how to obey," and she looks back over the rail.

"I didn't teach you any of that," she says, quiet and flat, "I tried to stop it," and my jaw locks because that isn't what I remember. "That's not what I remember," I say, and she answers, "I know, that's the point," and I sit on the step across from her so I stop towering, because the surgeon costume is not helping. "Tell me your version," I say, and she breathes out like she's bracing for a needle. "You want the whole thing," she asks, "No edits," and Harrow's line flashes through me, removal is never neutral, so I say yes, give me the closest you've got, and she gives a short dry laugh like she hates that I'm asking her to carry this again.

"There is no uncut footage," she says, "but I can give you what I remember," and she shifts her shoulder against the cold wall and fixes her eyes on a point I can't see. "I was twelve that first summer, maybe thirteen," she says, and her voice stays steady the way people talk when they've practised saying the truth without bleeding, "Old enough to know adults lie, young enough to think they lie for you." I don't speak, I let her have the space, and she tells me her parents sent her to Evelyn like it was a gift, church-adjacent trust dressed up as faith, matching decor and the right lines and a lake house that looked like proof. My throat tightens because my mother trusted crosses more than people, and Clara says the phrase, spiritual rest, and it hits like a slap because it's mine too.

"Did you believe her," I ask, and Clara's mouth goes hard, "I believed the part where I got to be somewhere else," she says, and she talks about posture, tone, face, and whether she smiled enough when she served dessert, the same drill in a different house. "The first time I saw you," she says, "you were in that ugly blue jacket, staring at the dock like it was a test," and my chest flares because she remembers. "How could I not," she says, "It was like your mother wrapped you in a statement," and then she says something that makes my stomach drop in a new way, "You think I seduced you."

I blink because the word feels too big, and she doesn't soften it. "You made me that," she says, "In your head you turned me into the one who taught you where to put your hands, when to hold still, you put me where Evelyn stood," and air leaves my chest. "You weren't on the dock," I ask, and she says sometimes, when she was made to be, but most of the time she was on the shore or the porch or in a doorway, close enough to see and not close enough to stop it without making it worse. I ask how it could get worse, and she looks at me like I'm missing the obvious wound. "She told me," Clara says, "'If you scare her, she'll tell her mother, then your family will pay,'" and my stomach drops again because the system underneath the lake shows itself.

"Money," I ask, and Clara says everything, mortgage, work, leverage, comfort worn like a coat, and I hear the mechanism click. "So you weren't pulling me toward her," I say, and Clara nods once, "I was pulling you away," and my palms go slick. "I remember your hand," I say, then stop, "On my wrist, on the dock, pulling," and she answers immediately, "Backwards, toward the house," and my head fights it because my remembered version is cleaner. "That's not how it feels," I whisper, and she says it was guiding, just not where you've put it, and the stairwell tilts for a second into wet boards and held breath and a body caught between two pulls.

"And Evelyn," I ask, because I need to name her or I keep naming Clara. Clara's mouth tightens, "Smiling," she says, "Telling you you were brave, telling your mother you were a natural, making it sound like a gift," and brave and natural sit in my mouth like old medals that turn to rust. "Why didn't I hate her," I say, and I don't finish the sentence, and Clara does not let me dodge it. "The one you want," she says, and I stare at the stairs below her shoes because yes, that is what I mean, why isn't it her face I see, why you, and Clara shrugs tight. "Because I was safe to blame," she says, and she holds my gaze while she tells me the truth I keep circling, if I made Evelyn the monster my whole world cracked, but Clara was near my age and quiet and watching, and it was easier to turn a peer into a temptress than to admit my mother handed me over to someone she admired.

The sentence cuts clean and I try to protest, and she stops me with the only verb that matters. "You lived," Clara says, and her voice stays even because she's done the maths years ago, "You turned it into something you could stand, you told yourself you wanted it because you were special, chosen, you told yourself I was jealous and I didn't get it." My throat burns because I can see it, I can see my own camera work, the way my mind moved the anger to a safer target. "She looked like she hated me," I say, and Clara answers without hesitation, "I hated what she was doing to you, I hated what she made me watch," and a memory rises sharp as cut glass.

I'm twelve and the lake stinks like algae and metal and wet rope, Evelyn stands behind me with hands on my shoulders pressing down and lining up my spine like I'm a mannequin, "Chin up," she says, "You can't see the horizon if you stare at your feet," and my mother laughs from the shore with folded arms and bright eyes. "She reads too much," she calls, "Always in her head, this will be good for her," and good for her lands in my gut like a stamp, because it isn't protection, it's permission. Clara stands near the start of the dock with one foot on wood and one on grass like she's split down the middle, and she says maybe I'm cold, careful, and I answer I'm fine before I can feel anything, because the right answer comes faster than the body.

Evelyn's hands tighten for a beat and she says see, she's brave, aren't you, Jax, and praise hits like warmth, brave, strong, chosen, and I want my mother to hear it and store it as proof. Clara steps closer and says maybe we should go inside, a storm's coming, and the sky is clear, and my mother calls her dramatic, says she always imagines danger, and

Evelyn laughs softly and says Clara is protective, it's sweet, but Jax needs to learn to hold still. Her hands slide down my arms to my wrists and she sets them at my sides like she's placing tools on a tray, "Like this," she says, "You're safe, we're right here, aren't we, Clara," and Clara's jaw jumps and she says I'm here like it's a warning pointed the wrong way.

Evelyn murmurs near my ear about two women watching over me, very spiritual, and I don't know the word but I know the feeling, being seen, being measured, being allowed. I straighten and I obey and the phrase lands in my chest like a burn, hold still, look at me, good girl, and on the shore my mother looks proud. "She's ready," Evelyn says, not loud, a private note meant for my mother, and my twelve-year-old brain records the scene with the wrong lead because later, when I replay it, I shift the camera. Clara becomes the one I watch, Clara becomes the one I want, Clara becomes the one I blame, because I can't afford to put it on my mother or on Evelyn.

The stairwell comes back in pieces, concrete, rail, hospital air, and my palms are cold. "I don't remember her saying that," I whisper, and Clara nods once, "I do," and I ask why she didn't tell me sooner as if sooner was a real option. "Because you weren't ready to hear it," she says, "You had to decide someone else was dangerous first, Harrow, the club, me, anyone but the woman your mother trusted with your soul," and trusted twists in my gut. I look at Clara properly and she is my age, worn down by nights and old grief, her gaze steady but tired, no shine, no hunt, no plan, and she doesn't look like the version I rehearsed. She looks like what she always was, a witness, a kid on the shore who saw too much.

"You weren't who I wanted," I say, and the truth forms as I speak it, "You watched me want her," and Clara's face softens in a way that's worse than anger. "That's what scared me," she says, "How much you needed her to approve of you, you lit up when she praised you, it was like watching dye go into a vein, I could see it spread." I swallow and I line up the images in my head, Evelyn's face in lake light, her hands on my shoulders, her voice low and amused wrapping brave and strong around me like a coat, and then the club owner's gaze overlays it, the way she told me to stand, the way my body answered when someone said good girl. Same script, different woman, and no wonder my brain cast Clara in the wrong role, she was the safest stand-in.

"I keep thinking about Harrow's paper," I say, and Clara grimaces, "Of course you do," and I tell her what it says in the only terms I can hold, when the brain can't take the truth it doesn't erase it, it rewrites who the villain is. Clara lifts a brow and asks who I picked, and I say you, me, anyone but Evelyn, anyone but my mother, and the words feel like bone through soft tissue. "Replay," Clara says, quiet, "You turned the wound into a job," and I think of the OR and the ritual and the control and the rush of being the one who decides where the blade goes, and I think of the club and the roles and the way I let strangers step into a shape I refused to name. Not Clara, not really, and I say it out loud because the sentence needs air, I thought I was obsessed with you, and Clara tilts her head and says I was obsessed with what she meant.

"What's that," I ask, and she smiles with no warmth in it. "Proof it happened," she says, and silence settles between us like silt because she's right, she always was. For the first time I let myself picture Evelyn without turning away, pinned hair like she was always headed somewhere, the small line at the corner of her mouth when she was pleased, her eyes flicking between my mother and me checking the setup like we were two parts of a study. I feel sick at how well I remember her, sharp, kept, not blurred, not faded, like I carried her face on purpose, not because I loved her, because my body learned that loving her was how I survived her.

Who taught me to want like this, not Clara, the woman on the dock, the one who called me brave, the one who told my mother she's ready, the one whose voice I still hear when someone says good girl in the dark. I open my eyes and Clara is watching me, and I admit the part that tastes like betrayal and relief at once, I remember her too clearly, too tender. "Good," Clara says, and her voice stays clean, "Now stop punishing the wrong person," and she pushes off the rail and starts up. I ask where she's going because I'm not ready to be left with the center of the frame, and she says back to work, some of us still have patients, and then she stops on the next landing and looks down.

"Jax," she says, and she doesn't let me turn the truth into shame, "Wanting her doesn't make what she did okay," and my throat tightens because I know that is the fight inside me. "But it does mean," she adds, softer, "the part of you that thinks you chose it will fight hard before it lets go," and then she's gone. I sit alone in the stairwell and behind my eyes the dock rises again, Evelyn's face, my mother on the shore, Clara small and furious watching, and Evelyn whispering she's ready. This time I don't move the camera, I keep it where it belongs, on Evelyn, not Clara, never Clara, and the imprint was always Evelyn, and now that I've named her I don't know what that makes me.

The stairwell feels smaller after Clara leaves, like the walls were waiting for her absence, and I should stand and go upstairs and act normal and cut into someone's skull and remind myself that whatever was done to me didn't stop me from being good at this. But I don't move, because I've worked for thirty-six hours straight without food or water or sleep and I've never had my body refuse an order, and now it does, because a memory does what bleeds and tumours never managed. It steals my motion, and when I force myself up my knees protest and my spine feels wrong in its own setup, my palm slick on the rail, and the thought hits like a blunt tool, you wanted her, not a teen crush, not a mix-up, something deeper, admire dressed up as want, obey dressed up as choice.

Above me a door opens and spits out hospital sound, monitors, voices, scrubs brushing past, normal chaos, my place, and I wipe my hands on my coat and step through. In the hallway my body runs on habit, I nod at a nurse, sign a form, offer a soft look to a patient's wife who hasn't slept since her son seized, and I perform care without my brain because the performance is reliable. When I reach my office I shut the door and sit in the dark, not full dark, a slice of light leaking under the blind like a thin cut, and I pull my phone out and type her name into a search bar like I'm trying to intubate my own panic. Evelyn, dock, lake house, abuse, grooming, witness, trauma, and the results are cold, papers, studies, cases, and the headings taste like metal in my mouth.

I skim a section about scaffolds and praise and how a predator builds a ring around a child until giving in feels chosen, and acceptance becomes tied to obeying, and the child starts to call it part of herself. Participation, that word sits in my gut like a stone, because kids don't know the gap between choice and permission and no one tells them that feeling special isn't safety. My memories weren't sex, I made them sex later to survive them, because if I wanted it then I wasn't powerless, if I wasn't powerless then I wasn't harmed, and if I wasn't harmed then my mother wasn't part of it, and it's a loop with the shape of want. I snap the laptop shut because the silence is too loud, and I don't know what else to do with the fact that the defence is built from the same material as my desire.

I don't see Clara again until close to midnight, she's charting outside ICU2 cross-legged on a stool like a kid on a curb, her shoes off, socked toes wiggling now and then like she's proving they're still hers. I tell her she never goes home and she tells me I'm still here, and fair is the only thing we have left. I lean on the wall and cross my arms to hold myself steady, and I tell her what she said is ringing, that Evelyn was teaching me, teaching us, and Clara nods once and calls them lessons we didn't need. I ask what Evelyn taught her, and Clara looks like she knew this was coming and hated that she was right. "She taught me how to disappear," she says, and I frown because she never disappears, she's sharp and direct and present, and she cuts me off because she knows exactly what I'm trying to praise.

"Sharp is cover," she says, and her voice stays flat, "If I'm useful, I can't vanish," and she taps her pen against the chart like a metronome that keeps her from falling. "You were her prodigy," she says, "I was her context, the before shot that made the after look like magic," and my stomach dips because I can see the structure, contrast, proof, theatre dressed as care. "You think she was showing my mother," I ask, and Clara shakes her head, "She wanted your mother to admire her, to see what she could shape, and your mother admired discipline more than protection," and the line hits the same place every time. I whisper that I was smiling, and Clara answers with a precision that makes it worse, I lit up, and that's how I lived through her.

I ask if Evelyn touched Clara and for a beat I think I've crossed a line, but Clara looks at me and says no, she didn't need to, and when I ask why not she smiles with no joy. "Because I didn't need shaping," she says, "I was already obedient, already scared, she didn't want two broken prodigies, she wanted contrast, she wanted someone to watch the change and envy it," and the words land heavy. Evelyn didn't need to touch Clara, she needed Clara to watch me being shaped, to watch me go back, to watch me glow when I was praised, to watch me call it a gift, a good girl, and my throat burns and my hand goes there on its own like it's checking for a pulse.

I tell Clara I thought the lake was a game and she says so did I until it wasn't, and we sit without talking while ICU hums behind us, machines breathing, families whispering, a steady ache of work and fear. Clara says I wasn't stupid, I was twelve, lonely, taught that being chosen meant being strong, that wanting approval made me rare, not at risk, and I hate how correct it sounds because it makes my adult defences look childish. Clara says she was taught silence is loyalty, that seeing makes you guilty, and she folds her hands like she's holding that guilt where it can't spill. "We learned opposite things from the same harm," she says, and I hear the shape of our lives in that one sentence, my hunger for control, her refusal of influence, my craving for tests, her watchfulness like armour.

When Clara leaves to check a post-op patient, I stay on the stool, and a nurse walks by and gives me a soft look like she thinks someone died. In a way someone did, the version of me that could keep Clara in the wrong role and call it desire. I pull my phone out again and scroll old club messages, instructions dressed up as checks, and every line sounds like Evelyn's praise. Your posture is perfect, you're so responsive, a natural submissive, and I feel the mechanism with sick clarity, I wasn't replaying sex, I was replaying a coping move, not craving control, craving worth, not arousal, approval, and Evelyn built the frame and the club just rents it.

I grip the phone until my fingers ache and the fear moves under my ribs, because if Evelyn is the start then pulling her out might strip away the person I've built. Who am I without the wants she trained into me, what's left if I cut out the thing that shaped the whole brain, and in surgery I know what happens when you take too much, the patient lives but not as themselves. Harrow's line hits again, removal is never neutral, and I feel the question as a physical threat, am I about to ruin myself, and the fact that I'm asking means I already know the cut is underway.

It's close to 3 a.m. when I walk toward the exit, night staff barely look up, after midnight surgeons are just another kind of ghost, and outside it's rain with fog lifting off the street under the lamps like pale gas. My phone buzzes, unknown number, one line, remember correctly, no flirt, no cue, just a demand for clean recall, and my job is built on that demand. I type back stop contacting me, and three dots appear, then the reply comes, I'm not contacting you, you're contacting yourself, and I freeze because the sentence is too neat. Another message follows, Evelyn didn't want your body, she wanted your loyalty, you need to decide if you're still giving it to her, and loyalty lands harder than desire because it names the bargain.

I stare until rain blurs the screen and I feel the truth settle in, not love, not desire, loyalty, the promise of being strong and unbreakable and the kind of girl my mother could finally be proud of. I learned it too well, and now I have to unlearn it without losing myself, and that's the surgery, not a clean cut, a rebuild. I slide the phone into my pocket and my hands shake from cold and from naming it, and behind me the hospital rises white and hard in fog like a church built for second chances. Ahead is the club, the archive, the truth, not Clara, not desire, Evelyn, the woman who taught me what to want, and now I will learn want without her or I will lose myself trying, and I step into the rain because the cut is already made and there's no going back.

Chapter Twelve

---∞---

The Lake's Lesson

There's a point, halfway through a craniotomy, when the map stops helping, because you've done what you always do and it works until it doesn't. You trace the known roads, you mark the sulci, you find the vessels you can name in your sleep, and you move with the calm you earned the hard way, then you reach the place where the tumour has changed the land. The brain no longer matches the book, edges blur, planes tug out of shape, a familiar landmark shifts three millimetres and suddenly you're not sure what you're looking at, and this is the part no one romanticises because there is no perfect map for damaged tissue. You decide whether to keep trusting the page you brought in, or admit it's out of date and work off what you see, off colour, off pulse, off small cues you can't fully justify to anyone watching, and that is where I am with my memory.

I lived most of my life with one version of the lake and it was clean and usable, the kind of story you can carry into adulthood without choking on it, I was chosen, I was strong, I was learning, and now I can see that was never the lake. That was the map, and tonight I'm going back to the tumour because I'm done operating from a diagram that only works if I keep lying.

I don't go to the club, not yet, and I leave the hospital through the side exit that smells like disinfectant and damp coats. The air is cold enough to sting the thin skin under my eyes, the rain has stopped but the city still shines slick with leftover water, streetlights smearing across puddles like someone dragged paint with a thumb, and my shoes make a soft wet sound on the sidewalk as I walk without a plan. That is unusual for me because my life is lists and time blocks and clean checkmarks, even my breaks are scheduled and even my pleasure comes with a form, consent boxes and limits and colours that pretend a system can make a body safe. Tonight I have none of that, I pass the subway steps and don't go down, I pass the coffee place where the barista knows my order but not my name, "Large black," he calls like it's a title, and he's closed now with chairs upside down on tables and the smell of old grounds and bleach drifting out when a staff member opens the door.

My scrubs cling under my coat and the fabric at my knees holds damp like the day refuses to let go, and my body wants home, bed, silence, a shower hot enough to burn the shape of the hours off my skin. I don't give it that, I keep walking, and there's a rhythm to night walking that feels like anaesthesia at the edge, not sleep and not rest, only a thinning of thought, a small numbness that can look like peace if you're desperate. I turn a corner and the reservoir appears, not natural, an oval of black held in by concrete with a low metal rail to keep joggers from slipping in and dying in a way no one wants to clean up, and a few trees line the path bare enough to look like veins.

The surface of the water is flat and dark, it doesn't reflect cleanly, it holds light and ruins it, and it is a cheap copy of the lake that is still good enough. I walk to the rail and rest my forearms on the cold metal and it bites through my sleeves, the chill running straight into bone, and my body responds before my mind does, shoulders rising and breath going shallow. I close my eyes and I don't force memory because brains don't respond to orders, they respond to conditions, so you create the right setting, give the right cue, and wait.

The damp smell comes first, wet stone with a faint algae note, not the lake but close enough that my nervous system leans toward it, then sound, water slapping against an edge, a drain gurgling somewhere, distant tyres hissing on wet road. Then cold, the kind that finds the backs of your legs, the kind you don't notice until you stop moving, and I let my body go first because my body remembers what my story edited. Cold at my calves, wind under a loose jacket, bare feet on rough boards, adult voices low and close, pulse slowing, and the map opens.

In the version I kept, the lake trip was spiritual rest, that's what my mother called it, a change of scenery, a break from your head, a chance to be in God's presence, and she said it like a prescription as if a week away could fix a child. She turned everything into a virtue if it served her point, discomfort, fear, shame, and the house itself didn't match the horror I later tried to feel, because it wasn't gothic or rotten or a cabin from a cautionary tale. It was normal, grey siding and a porch that creaked, deck chairs with faded stripes and a grill with old grease in the tray, a stack of plastic cups on the counter like someone had hosted a party and cleaned up badly, and that normality helped because it made everything harder to name. Evil doesn't need a costume, it only needs cover that looks ordinary.

The dock was the only thing that mattered, long and narrow and old enough that the boards had gone soft from weather, and if you stepped in the wrong place the wood flexed like it wanted to give. Green algae feathered the edges, the water dark enough to look deep even where it wasn't, even where your feet could touch bottom, and in my old story I wasn't afraid. I was careful, I tested the board with my toes, watched how it moved under weight, measured risk like a small adult, and fear was for other kids, loud kids, kids who cried when they scraped a knee, kids who ran to their mother for comfort, and I didn't do that. I stood at the end of the dock because I wanted to, because Evelyn asked, because Evelyn invited, and that was the first lie I built into a fact.

"Chin up," she said, "Hands at your sides," and her voice was low and smooth and sure, not sweet and not fake, not the careful tone adults used when they were scared of breaking me with the wrong word. Adults spoke to me like I was a test they hadn't prepared for, nervous and stiff and cautious, as if one mistake would crack me, and Evelyn didn't act careful. She spoke like she assumed I could follow, like she had already decided I was capable, and it felt like respect because respect is the easiest mask for control when you're twelve and hungry to be seen.

The first time she positioned me she didn't touch me, she used her voice, "Feet apart," and I obeyed, "Good, look straight ahead, not at me, at the water," and I did. Then, like it was nothing, she said, "Picture walking on it," and it was absurd and impossible and my chest lifted anyway because she wasn't talking to me like a child, she was giving me a task, an image, a thing to hold. Behind me my mother stood on the shore with arms folded and a calm face, supervising, I told myself, protecting, and I needed to believe that because if my mother was there and calm then nothing terrible could be happening. "There," Evelyn murmured, "Perfect, see, you don't need to be afraid of falling, you only fall if you look down," and I said I wasn't afraid because that was part of the game, and then she said it, "I know, you're a good girl," and back then the words landed clean, like a grade, like a mark on a paper, a reward you could earn again if you did it right.

That was my version, the polished file I kept because it made the memory usable, and day after day there were small exercises, balance and stillness and holding a pose and trusting instruction. Sometimes she stood close enough that I could feel her breath near my ear, sometimes she stepped back and let the wind do the work for her, and sometimes she made a small sound of approval that I learned to chase the way you chase a drug. My mother never stepped in, of course she didn't, because there were no raised voices and no bruises and no obvious harm, only a woman teaching a girl to be composed, and once I glanced back toward shore and my mother's face held something I stored as pride. Approval, approval for my stillness and control, approval that finally matched my grades and prizes and relentless proving, and not just good at things, her look seemed to say, a good girl.

She wasn't ignoring me, she was seeing me, and being seen felt like safety, being placed felt like belonging, being chosen felt like power, so I turned the story into a rule. If I want it, it can't be done to me, if I'm watched I'm not prey, I'm the main act, if I'm chosen I'm not weak, I'm rare, and desire equals autonomy, mine, and it was a beautiful equation because it made betrayal feel like triumph.

I open my eyes at the reservoir and the water has shifted, a thin gust moving over the surface, streetlights smearing in long broken lines, the reflection refusing to hold, bending, snapping apart, and so did my memory. I kept the outline and changed the shade, I kept the dock and the orders and my mother's proud face and the thrill of being the focus, and I cut everything that made those details sick, not cleanly because brains don't erase, they edit. They cut moral threat, not sensory fact, and now I remember the laughter, not just mine, not just Evelyn's, my mother's too, soft and thin, a sound that can pass as joy if you need it to, and a sound that can also pass as a blade if you stop lying.

Back then I told myself they were laughing because I was doing well, because I held still, because I followed orders without whining that my legs ached or my toes were numb, and adults laugh around kids for other reasons. Sometimes they laugh so they don't have to say stop, sometimes they laugh because saying stop would mean admitting they knew it was wrong, and sometimes they laugh because it keeps the air light, and light air lets harm pass as nothing. I remember Clara now too, because in my old file she was background, another kid, older and awkward, hovering between friend and stranger, a blur, and now she is sharp. Arms crossed, mouth tight, eyes fixed on me with a look I used to call envy, and it wasn't envy, it was alarm, and she was trying to hold the scene in her head like proof.

It wasn't every day, and that matters because intermittence is how a trap dresses itself as privilege. The dock lessons were special, framed as more, "Just you and me," Evelyn would say, "The others can play by shore, you're ready for more," and ready for more became one of my favourite phrases because it fit everything after. Residency, fellowship, promotion, hard cases, anything that singles you out, anything that makes you feel chosen, and it all echoed the lake.

The day my brain built the final version around comes back in layers now, and layer one is the story I lived. My mother called that afternoon a test, "You say you want to be a surgeon," she said while she zipped my windbreaker up to my chin, "Surgeons don't flail, they don't panic when it gets hard, they hold still, they focus," and her hands were brisk and efficient, not warm. "Today you'll practice," she said, and I nodded full of that smug heat only a gifted child can carry, the heat of being sure you can win if you just try hard enough. "I can do that," I said, and she replied, "Prove it," and on the dock Evelyn waited with her hair pulled back that day, no flyaways and no softness, a clean line of intent.

"Feet apart," she said, "Good, hands at your sides, shoulders back, head up, try not to shiver," and the wind was sharp and the water darker, clouds moving over it like something pacing, and I swallowed discomfort whole. "Look at me," she said, and I did, and her eyes were bright and focused but not fully on my face, as if she was looking at the shape of me rather than the person. She stepped closer, "You learn fast," she murmured, "You have no idea how rare that is, most girls collapse, they cry, they ask to stop," and she said it with mild disdain, like weakness was a choice. "You don't," she added, "You want to see how far you can go," and pride surged through me hot and clean and addictive because she saw me, she understood what my teachers took months to catch, pushing me wasn't cruelty, it was respect, and that was what I needed to believe.

"Good girl," she said, "Stay very still, no matter what," and in layer one that is where the memory used to end, me on the dock holding still, happy with the test, drunk on being noticed. Layer two starts where layer one used to fade to static, and I didn't remember the distance between us, but now I do. She wasn't an arm's length away calling orders like a coach, she was right behind me, and I can feel it as phantom pressure, heat at my back, the shape of her body lining up with mine, breath near my ear, and at first her hands hovered, not touching, waiting to see if I'd flinch. I didn't, because I thought any reaction would disqualify me, make me ordinary, make me breakable, then her hand closed around my wrists, not harsh, certain, and she brought my arms in and set my hands against my thighs.

"Here," she said, "Better line, always think about the line," and my mind supplied meaning like it always does, dancer, surgeon, stage, anything but the obvious. From shore my mother called out, "She admires your control, don't disappoint her," and that sentence is the blade because it splits the whole story open. She admires your control, don't disappoint her, and I wasn't obeying Evelyn alone, I was performing for my mother, and that performance is what made the scene survivable. If my mother saw it, it must be fine, if she wasn't afraid then my discomfort wasn't danger, it was growth, and if she allowed it then it wasn't violation, it was permission, and the hand on my wrists became teaching, the breath at my ear became guidance, and the rush in my chest became proof. Proof I was strong, not harmed, strong, and that is what my brain filed under lesson.

I remember the moment Evelyn moved my foot, a small nudge with her arch against my heel, widening my stance by a few centimetres, and it felt like care because I needed it to feel like care. "Feel how stable you are," she murmured, and I nodded, and she said it again, "Good girl," and the phrase ran through me like current. Somewhere off to the side I heard Clara, "Can I come out there," and my eyelids fluttered like sleep, like shock, and Evelyn called back, "Not now, this is advanced, you'll distract her," as if I was balancing on a ledge and Clara's presence could make me fall. My mother laughed that thin laugh again, "She's doing so well, aren't you, Jax," and I said yes, of course I did, because there was no safe answer except yes.

At the reservoir my body slips into the old pose without asking me, feet slightly apart, shoulders back, chin up, hands at my sides, and I've done this in the club a thousand times with strangers and rope and eyes on me and a safeword I never wanted to use. I called it want, I called it kink, I called it freedom, and now I can see where it began, a child on a dock, a woman behind her, a mother on the shore, and a script about worth. If being watched means being valued then wanting to be watched feels like choice, if stillness under pressure earns praise then craving pressure feels like agency, and I didn't grow into this, I was trained.

My erotic brain didn't form in a quiet room, it grew around this moment like tissue around shrapnel, it built itself around harm and called it structure, and the first time someone at the club called me a natural I felt the same rush I felt at twelve. Not because I loved serving, because I loved being special, because I loved being seen with focus, the way my mother never looked at me when I aced exams or won prizes, alert, impressed, fully there, and somewhere deep in my nervous system surrender fused to approval. Desire equals autonomy, if I choose to kneel no one can make me, if I choose to obey no one is using me, if I choose the rules then what happens inside them is mine, and the horror isn't only that I was hurt. The horror is that I renamed the hurt as proof of power, then built my adult self on that lie.

In neurosurgery we talk about eloquent cortex, areas you can't touch without cost, remove the wrong millimetre and you take speech, movement, the person's sense of self, and a child's moral wiring is eloquent. Shift the wrong piece and everything after misfires, and my mother's face on that shore was eloquent, smiling, laughing, approving, never saying stop, never saying this is wrong, never saying come here and stay with me, you're a child and you owe no one this. She said, "She admires your control," she said, "She's helping you," she said, "You're such a good girl," and she allowed Evelyn and I processed it as safety.

I didn't think if my mother allows this then maybe she doesn't care what happens to me, I thought if my mother allows it then it must be safe, it must matter, it must be a mark of trust, and I learned a rule that wrecked my life. If a trusted adult doesn't object then what's happening is fine, so when a senior surgeon screamed at me in residency and then clapped my shoulder for not crying I called it training. When a lover set rules that left me shaking and empty then praised me for taking it I called it intimacy, and when the club owner traced a hand down my spine and said, "I can tell you've been trained," I smiled because I thought it proved I was strong, and I never called it harm. The act at the lake ended and the misread didn't.

People talk about blocked memory like a film locked in a vault, and it wasn't like that, because my brain didn't hide the lake, it filed it, scheduled it, labeled it. Origin, not trauma, stamped with neat conclusions, I am tough, I can take discomfort, being chosen means I am better, adults test me because I can handle it, pain means I'm doing it right, and those aren't thoughts. They're rules, protocols, and survival doesn't care about nuance, it cares that you make it through with enough function to keep moving, so it rewrote the event to keep my identity intact. It didn't erase fear, it renamed fear as excitement, it didn't erase coercion, it renamed it as challenge, it didn't erase my mother's betrayal, it renamed it as endorsement, and every time I replayed the memory I reinforced the edit, not the raw scene, and the groove got deeper. I was strong, I passed, I was never a victim, and now beside an artificial lake under city lights I can finally see the raw cut.

It isn't graphic and it isn't theatrical and that makes it worse, because it is almost plain. A woman uses a child to feel powerful, a mother uses a child to prove a belief, and a child turns terror into triumph because the other story would kill her, and the horror isn't hidden hands, it's the logic. I realise with dull shock that the lake's real lesson was never about grit, it was about story, because Evelyn taught me to stand still, my mother taught me to call that stillness strength, and my brain taught me to crave it. After that any scene that echoed the dock lit up the old path, someone gives orders while someone else watches, someone praises me for taking it, someone makes my body the site of their test, and my nervous system goes, this one, this is where we win.

No wonder the club felt like home, no wonder Clara felt like danger, because she was the only person on that shore who wasn't playing along. She saw the setup and refused to call it discipline, refused to call it growth, refused to rename exploitation as teaching, and she didn't polish the memory into a prize, she kept it as what it was, a wound. I did the opposite, I framed it, I admired myself for how well I handled it, and that might be the worst part because I have praised myself for surviving what someone else should have stopped. I have turned endurance into romance, I have loved the scar more than I hated the blade, and I have called that desire.

The reservoir ripples again, a dog barks behind me, a jogger's shoes slap the path, a car door shuts, someone laughs too loud near a bench, and life keeps moving because it always does. I stand at the rail and feel cold soak through my shoes and I can see the plain timeline with a clarity that makes me sick, the lake ended, the dock rotted, algae thickened, the house changed hands, Evelyn moved on, my mother moved on to fresh reasons, Clara moved on with her own damage, and my story kept going. Every time I chose a scene that matched that day I wasn't replaying the act, I was replaying the meaning, and I wasn't only surviving, I was keeping the script alive, and that is what turns my stomach.

Not only that a woman used a child with my mother's quiet nod, not only that my body did what a child's body does when praise and fear get tangled, the horror is that my brain, smart and loyal, turned it into a manual. You are strong because you endured, you are special because you were chosen, you are free because you keep choosing it, a sealed equation until now, because now I can admit the thing I called desire might not be mine. What I called autonomy might be choreography built by a woman whispering good girl while my mother watched, and what I carried as proof of power might be proof of how well I was shaped.

Abuse is awful, but a false story can be worse, because abuse ends when the abuser leaves the room and a false story follows you into every room after. It chooses your lovers, picks your bosses, tells you what praise tastes like, trains you to call fear focus, and it stands beside you at a city reservoir decades later and tells you what you're allowed to call trauma. I tighten my grip on the cold rail and I understand the lake's lesson was never about standing still, it was about what story I would tell myself so I could keep standing, and I have told the wrong one for twenty years.

It's time to rewrite it, and rewrites are surgery, careful and bloody, with no promise you keep everything you want, and if the cost of keeping Evelyn's version of me is hearing her voice every time someone says good girl, then I'm ready to risk becoming someone I don't yet know. Someone who wants without a script, someone who doesn't confuse being watched with being safe, someone who doesn't call freezing consent, and the lake is gone but the lesson remains. For the first time I'm not sure I want it, and that doubt, clean and sharp and real, might be the first sign I can heal.

Chapter Thirteen

———————— ∞◇∞ ————————

Unlearning Seduction

There is a sharp kind of shame in learning your breathing is borrowed, that the small things you thought were you, your pauses, your stillness, the way you hold a stare, aren't taste or grit or style. They're steps, a set routine, and someone else wrote it: Evelyn, my mother, the dock. I don't know how to live without putting on power first, which means I've never owned it.

So I wake early, before sunrise, before I can brace, before the mask slides on by habit. I stand in front of the bathroom mirror and tell myself, out loud, that today, I won't seduce anyone. It sounds stupid the moment it leaves my mouth, like a dare no one asked for, like a line from a bad play. I turn on the tap and run cold water over my wrists, not washing, not cleansing, proof, skin, pulse, here.

Seduction was never sex, it's focus and pull, it's how I make rooms bend toward me. I've done it so long it feels like breathing, and today, I will try to breathe wrong. I dress without choosing, no fitted blouse, no hard seams, no jacket that makes my shoulders look like command. Scrubs, pulled on fast, left alone, and I don't tug the waistband flat, I don't smooth the collar, I don't fix the strand of hair that sits off-kilter near my ear. I look like someone who didn't try, someone who doesn't need to, and it feels like leaving the house with two different shoes, like I've stepped out without armor.

The elevator doors close, and the mirror inside shows me back to myself, plain, dull. My body tries to correct, chin up, shoulders back, a clean line, and I don't let it. I ride up with a slouch I can't stop noticing, my hair is wrong, my stance is wrong, and it hurts. Not my bones, my name, the pain of pulling down a frame you mistook for skeleton.

When I step into the surgical wing, Clara is the first person I see, corner desk, charts, tea she won't drink, that tired set to her mouth that reads like too many nights in a row. I walk toward her without timing it, without the slow pace that says I know what I do to people, just walking, and I have no idea what "normal" looks like on me. She glances up and her eyes search for the hook, and I open my mouth and hear myself picking a tone, not sharp, not soft, not knowing, and I land on flat. "Morning," I say, and Clara blinks once, like she's checking she heard right, then says, "Morning."

Silence sits between us and it is not charged and not tense, it is awkward, and awkward feels like skin with no bandage, raw, alive. I don't know what to do with it, because my old move is to add weight, a cutting joke, a clean remark, a look that turns the space into mine, and I don't. I stand there with nothing in my hands, and Clara waits a beat, then asks, gentle but direct, "Are you okay?" "I'm fine," I say too fast, too clipped, old voice, the one I wear like gloves, and her brows lift. I try again, slower, "I mean... yes, I'm fine, just tired, it's early," and she says, "That's not why you're different," with no sting and no blame, just an observation.

I swallow and I shrug, trying for casual, and it feels like copying a person I've only watched from afar. "I'm unlearning things," I say, and Clara studies me a moment, then says, "You don't have to say that like you're confessing." "It feels like one," I tell her, and her mouth softens, "Most cuts do." I don't tell her I feel like I'm doing this on myself, awake, no numbing.

At the morning brief, I do something else I've never done, and I sit with the residents. I don't stand apart with that slight space that keeps me safe and sets them on edge, I take an empty chair at the center of the table, and they freeze. I see backs straighten as one, hands stop fidgeting, eyes turn careful, and they don't know what to do with me this close. I don't know what to do with their fear, so I say, keeping my voice even, "This morning's case, walk me through your plan, not mine, yours." Silence answers, because they're waiting for the show, they're waiting for me to take the room the way I always do, clean, hard, neat. "Who wants to lead?" I ask, and there are blank stares, a cough, and Julie, my scrub nurse, hides a smile behind her coffee cup.

Fernandez lifts her hand like it might get her punished and says, "I... I can," and I nod. I lean back and I let her stand, I let her own the board, and she talks through mapping, bleed risk, where the vessels will fight us, where the brain will lie. I don't cut in, I don't correct, I don't guide with a throat clear or a tilt of my head, and it feels like letting someone walk across traffic with no hand to hold. But she does fine, not perfect, fine, and when she finishes, the room waits for my verdict, because that's the ritual, they want the stamp. I don't give them theatre, I don't give them dread, I say, "Good," just good, and they don't know what to do with plain praise, no sparkle, no threat, no hunger under it.

I stand and say, "Let's prep," and they follow, a little off-balance, like birds that have flown behind a storm so long they forgot what calm air feels like. In the OR, I usually hold the room without trying, I lead through tight focus, through pressure, through the sharp pull of my attention. Today, I lead through function, not allure, not fear, work, and during drape, a resident shifts and blocks my line of sight. Old me would fix him with two fingers at the elbow, a small touch, exact, a quiet claim, and today I use words. "Step left, please," I say, and he shifts, and it takes more effort than it should not to touch him.

Touch has always been my tool outside the cut, a way to close space, a way to make people feel my hand even when I'm not there. Without it, I feel blunt, like a knife without an edge, and halfway through the cranial opening, I notice my grip on the drill. Too tight, too hard, and I'm acting control with my hands instead of having it, so I loosen my fingers. The tool steadies, and Clara stands behind Julie, watching, not the bone, not the field, me. She's not judging skill, she's watching restraint, like she's keeping score of my choices, and I hate that my first thought is to win. I force my jaw to relax and say, "Retractors," calm, not crisp, not sharp, not staged.

Julie passes them, and we expose the mass, a pale, uneven lesion close to the parietal cortex, tucked like a secret no one wanted to name. I guide the team through the steps without raising stakes into drama, without turning the room into an altar, and we debulk, we irrigate, we close. Clean, plain, done, and when I strip my gloves, I don't do it with that small flourish I've never admitted I do. I remove them, and the room feels odd, and I can't tell if they're let down or relieved, maybe both. In the hall after, a resident stops me, he looks unsettled, like the floor moved, and he asks, "Are you... changing your process?" "No," I say, "Just how I speak," and he nods, slow, "It's weird." I almost laugh, "It is," and then he adds, softer, "It's good, just weird," and I tell him, "Most change is."

He walks off looking strangely proud, like being treated without performance made him feel like a person, not a prop, and maybe that's the point. At lunch I avoid the lounge where power passes between chairs like a virus, I join the public line, I buy a plain sandwich and a plastic cup of water. No art, no ritual, no curated meal that says: look at me, even when I'm eating, and I don't scan the room for eyes. I don't hold court, I don't draw people in or push them away, I exist, and it's awful.

After rounds, Clara finds me in a staff corridor, not close, not far, and she looks at me without hunger and without distrust, recognition. "You're trying," she says, and I admit, "I don't know how," and she replies, "That's what trying looks like." I exhale and say, "I feel wrong," and she says, "You feel like a patient, most healing does," and healing lands like a diagnosis I don't want in my chart. Then she says, quiet, like she's placing a bandage where it won't be seen, "You don't have to impress anyone to deserve attention." I don't answer because I don't know how, I nod once, small, not staged, and then I walk away.

That night I stand in front of the mirror again, and I don't set my feet, I don't lift my chin, I don't angle my face to find the version of me that looks like command. I just look, and something strange happens, I don't know her, because the woman in the glass exists without performance, without an audience, without pull. She is a body and a face and a person in cheap light, and it terrifies me. I brace my hands on the counter and my fingers twitch, once, twice, then again, and a tremor starts. Not from fatigue, not from a long case, from emotion with nowhere to go, and my hands start to shake, not big and not loud and not a scene, a small, stubborn quake that won't stop, the body refusing the pose it has held for years.

I stare at my hands and understand, with sick clarity, that without seduction, I don't know how to hold anything, not a tool, not a room, not a memory, not myself. I whisper to the mirror, "I don't know how to be," and it comes out small, unplanned, honest. For the first time, honesty shakes me more than fear ever did.

The next day I get a consult I shouldn't have, a thirty-eight-year-old woman with trigeminal neuropathic pain. The chart is thick, the pain has a long tail, the meds list reads like slow surrender, and she wears expensive shoes, nails done, poise like armor. She reminds me of me, and when I walk in, she straightens, as if she expects a game, because people like her treat weakness like an audition. She smiles with care, like dignity is something you can arrange, and I don't answer with charm. "How long?" I ask, and she blinks, "I'm sorry?" "The pain, how long," I say, and she answers, "Oh, three years," then crosses her legs and waits for my eyes to land where hers want them. I don't, and I ask, "Triggers?"

Her smile thins and she says, "I thought you'd... introduce yourself first," and I tell her, flat, "I'm Dr. Nile, triggers?" It's the first time I've watched someone get hurt by a lack of performance, because she expected warmth that is really control, the tone I use like a blade: I see you, you matter, I will decide what you get. Instead she gets: you are here for care, and her face tightens, not grief, insult, and she mutters, "You don't have to be rude." Neutral feels like an insult to people who survive by being compelling, so I soften my voice a notch, not a lure and not an apology, human. "I'm not being rude," I say, "I'm listening," and she stills, and it disarms her more than charm would.

She answers the questions without flirting with the room, without bargaining for my interest, her voice shrinks into truth, less smooth, and by the time I finish the exam, she's crying. Quiet, no show, and her mask slips because mine never arrived, and power without seduction isn't cruel, it's relief. She covers her face and says, "I don't like being seen like this," and I tell her, "You're not being seen, you're being treated." Her breath shakes, and for a moment, I almost fall into the old habit, touch her hand, murmur comfort, offer a neat little line that sounds like care but acts like claim. I don't, I hand her tissues, useful, plain, and I say, "I'll help you with the pain, not the performance." It's the kindest thing I've said in a consult and the coldest, and she whispers, "Thank you," not for warmth, for clarity.

Later, Levin corners me outside Radiology, his mouth tight, like he's holding back an argument he thinks he should win. "You were... different," he says, and different, to him, means softer, less sharp, less feared, and he goes on, "You delegated, you didn't... command." "That's on purpose," I say, and Levin scoffs, "You think leadership is some group talk, we don't have time, residents need direction." "I gave direction," I say, and he throws back, "You gave them rope," and I answer, "And they didn't hang themselves." He looks truly confused and says, "They're meant to admire you, fear you a bit, that's how you control them," and I tell him, "I don't want control, I want skill."

His jaw ticks and he says, "If you don't dominate them, they stop listening," and I give him a small smile, not sharp, not playful, not bait, just a fact on my face. "If their respect needs my show," I say, "they're not surgeons, they're followers, I don't need followers," and he blinks, caught off guard, because he wanted a duel and he wanted me to meet him on the old field. "You're losing your edge," he says, low and mean, and I answer, "No, I'm losing my crutch." He doesn't get it, but he fears it, and he walks away, because you can't fight someone who won't perform the war.

After that, maybe because of it, I do something that feels like swallowing glass. I find Clara in the break room, yogurt, tablet, her shoulders still set like she's braced for bad news, and I sit across from her. Not close, not staged, just there, and I ask, "What are you reading?" She lifts a brow and says, "A paper on nurse-led neuro checks," and I say, "That sounds... useful," and she answers, "That wasn't praise." "It wasn't an attack," I tell her, and we watch each other like two animals testing distance. I try another line without weight and ask, "Do you like your job?" "Yes," she says, then frowns, "Why are you talking like someone taught you how humans work?" "Because I'm trying not to use you," I say, and it is the truth, ugly, clean.

Clara blinks twice, then she laughs, not bitter and not sharp, real, and she says, "I never thought I'd hear you say that." "I never thought I'd need to," I tell her, and she asks, "Do you?" "Yes," I say, "Turns out," and she sets her spoon down. "So what do you want from me right now?" she asks, and nothing is the answer, nothing is the first honest answer I've ever had, and I say, "Nothing." She narrows her eyes, searching for the hook, for the ask hidden under the line, and there is none, and it unsettles her the same way my plain voice unsettled the patient. People don't trust honesty that doesn't come with a performance of virtue, and she says slow, "So, you want nothing," and I say, "Yes."

She studies me and says, "That's the first time you've looked at me without trying to pull something out of me," and it hurts because it's true. We sit in silence, not charged, not tense, silence, and it's unbearable and new, and after a while, Clara says, "This is awful, it's like watching you learn to walk." "I know," I say, "I hate it," and she answers, softer, "I don't, it means you're letting yourself exist."

At home, I face the mirror again, and this time I try not to see stance or power, I see form, bone, skin, small flaws, and no one is watching. I expect disgust or shame or empty space, and what I feel is worse, nothing, because without seduction, the mirror doesn't tell me who I am. It tells me nothing at all, and if seduction gave me a self, what is left without it, a face, a body, a person with tired eyes. Not chosen, not rare, not special, real, and that truth is colder than Evelyn's hands ever were.

The tremor returns while I brush my teeth, a small shake at the fingertips, then the wrist, a protest, and I set the toothbrush down. My reflection wavers, not a trick of sight, a trick of self, the fear of seeing myself with no armor, and my hands shake harder. Not weakness, lack of script, and when you live by performance, truth is clumsy, and when you live by control, consent feels like falling. I sit on the bathroom floor and I let the tremor run, I let my body panic without making it pretty, without turning it into a scene with a lesson. I'm not fine, I'm learning, and learning hurts more than any memory on that dock, because this pain has no villain, only absence, only truth.

I press my shaking hands to my knees and breathe, not elegant, not steady, air, in and out. For the first time, I wonder if my want was ever mine, and for the first time, I see how often I touched people with an aim, a result, a pull, a proof. For the first time, I let my hands shake without trying to look strong, and I whisper into the quiet apartment, "I don't know how to want without being watched." It's the most bare sentence I've ever said, and no one is here to praise me for it, which means it might be real.

The morning after, I test my hands before I test my mind, and I wake before the alarm, my body braced, like it remembers pain ahead of time and tries to meet it early. Under the covers, I flex my fingers, open, close, thumb to each fingertip, and there is no tremor. Hope is stupid and it comes anyway, and in the bathroom I pick up the toothbrush. Halfway through the top row, the tremor starts, small, insistent, and foam gathers at the corner of my mouth like I'm the one seizing. I freeze and set the brush down with care, and the shaking stops, and I murmur, "So you like an audience," to my nervous system, because of course it does.

This isn't failure, it's timing, it waits for stakes, it arrives when I might be seen. I rinse my mouth, pat my face dry, and look at my reflection, no pose, no lure, and I tell myself, "This is not okay, you have work." The mirror doesn't argue, and I don't go to pre-op, I go to the skills lab. A whole floor of fake heads and silicone brains meant for training, plastic skulls, practice drills, tools lined up like toys made for adults, and I haven't needed this place in years. I used to come here for fun, and now I come for triage, and I lock the door.

"Privacy" is what I would call it, and the truth is simpler, I can't let anyone see this yet. I pull on gloves, pick up micro-scissors, and stand over a dummy head like it's a stand-in for my own, no audience, no eyes, just my hands. "Incision," I say under my breath, out of habit, and the first cut is clean. The fake dura parts with a soft give, I place tiny retractors, I expose the mock cortex, and I pick up bipolar cautery for no reason other than comfort. My hand holds steady, and of course it does, because nothing here is alive and nothing here can die because of me, and I make it harder.

Microscope on, zoom in until the field fills my sight with pale folds and painted vessels, and I line up a practice aneurysm clip. My fingers tremble, a hair, enough, and I pull back and my jaw locks. The old urge rises, snap at someone, blame them, build a wall of rank around myself, because that persona always steadied me, power as a sedative, and I refuse it. I don't pace, I don't swear, I don't invent an audience so the tremor will behave, and I stand there with the tool and the shake. I take one breath, then another, and I let the tremor show itself instead of strangling it, and it spikes, then, absurdly, eases. "Oh," I whisper, "You don't like being alone either."

It lands as a fact, my hands shake when they're allowed to be just hands, when there's no role to hold them in place. Surgery has always come with an alibi, and when the alibi fades, the act has nowhere to hide, so I reset the dummy and I try again. This time, I narrate, not to impress and not to teach, to anchor, and I murmur, "Find the neck, protect the small branches, respect the angle." Simple, boring, and the tremor lessens, and I tell my fingers, "This is work, not theatre," and they listen, for now.

On the ward, I almost undo my whole day in one second, because a med student, wide-eyed, underfed, buzzing with need, backs toward a mobile CT scanner. I see it before he does, and reflex takes my hand and my fingers close around his forearm, warm skin, thin bone, and he inhales, shocked. His eyes fly to mine, ready to be chosen, ready to be marked by either praise or shame, because he'll take either and call it worth, and it's the old script. I could seal it with one move, thumb press, held gaze, half-smile, a line that sounds like advice but is really claim, and he would remember it forever.

I release him like his skin burns and say, "Watch your space," neutral, no purr, no edge, just warning. He flushes, nods, steps away, "Yes, Doctor, sorry," and I keep walking, heart pounding. That tiny moment, touch first, then words, tells me how deep this runs, because my body went straight to the same move I learned on a dock. Adjust, correct, own, and I didn't even want to, and that's the worst part.

At midday I try again with Clara, and it goes badly, in the best way. I find her near the desk and ask, "Do you have fifteen minutes, coffee," and her brow lifts. "Is this social or clinical?" she asks, and I say, "Social," aware of how strange the word feels in my mouth, and she checks the clock. "I get a break, fine," she says, and we sit in a corner of the cafeteria, away from residents, away from eyes that would turn this into gossip. I don't take the chair with a view, I sit with my back partly exposed, and it feels like walking into an OR without checking the power. Clara stirs sugar into her coffee and I hold mine and do nothing.

"How long have you worked nights?" I ask, and she shrugs. "Years, you don't notice unless you need something," she says, and it's true and it stings. "I notice now," I say, and she gives me a small, dry smile. "Do you, or do you notice that I notice you?" she asks, and there it is, and I breathe. "I'm trying to learn how to relate to you without... taking," I say, and she corrects, "Without seducing," and I say, "Yes." She leans back and studies me and asks, "And what does 'relate' look like to you?"

My mind offers scenes with weight, charged looks, meaningful touches, a confession shaped like a blade, power as currency, and I say, "I don't know." "That's not an answer you like," she says, and I admit, "It's becoming common," and we sit in that, heavy and plain. Clara sets her cup down with care and says, "Jax, hear this," and I say, "Okay," and she says, "I am not your rehab." The words land clean, no cruelty, boundary, and she keeps going. "I won't be your practice dummy for ethical touch and non-seductive talk, I'm not a lab, I'm not the place you test new habits, I already paid for this story once, I'm not paying again."

Heat rises behind my ribs, shame and anger, both looking for a target, and I start, "I wasn't," and she says, "You were, not on purpose, which is the whole problem." I close my mouth, and the urge to win her back flares, to charm, to turn the moment, to make her soften with the right line, and I don't. Today, I won't seduce anyone, and I ask, too sharp, "So what can you be, if not that," and Clara's face softens a fraction. "I can be someone who tells you the truth, someone who won't play the old part, someone who steps in if you try to cut into yourself without backup," she says, and I say, "A colleague." "A witness," she replies, "Colleagues don't sit on docks."

My throat tightens and she sighs. "Practice on mannequins, practice on residents, practice on your mirror, but with me, you show up as you are, no hidden aim," she says, and I tell her, "I don't know how to promise that." "Then we keep space until you can," she answers, and it hurts more than any rejection, which is stupid because it's not romance. It's rarer, someone refusing to be used, and I nod because it's all I can do without reaching for her hand, and I say, "Understood." Her gaze eases and she says, "That doesn't mean I don't care if you fall apart, it means I won't be your cushion," and I ask, "You think I'll fall apart?" "I think you already are," she says, "You're just doing it slowly."

That night I don't go to the mirror, I sit on the floor by my bed, hands loose on my thighs, and they shake. Less than before, more than I want, and I say out loud, "I'm not being watched," and it's both true and not, because no one is here, but my body still expects eyes. It still hunts for approval like a dog hunting scent, and I add, "I'm not seducing anyone," and that one is true, and my hands twitch, small and lost, like they're still waiting for music. I let them, and I don't steady them by summoning rank, I don't picture a room leaning in, I don't imagine a lover waiting for a line. I picture nothing and let the shaking exist without turning it into a story.

I've always handled feeling with words, reframe, rename, make it clean, and now my body takes the hit because my mind has stopped doing the edit. My hands panic for every feeling I refused, and they shake and shake, and I tell them, "I see you." Not tools, not weapons, not bait, mine, and the tremor doesn't stop, but for the first time, it doesn't feel like a threat. It feels like the start of a new script, one where agency isn't a costume, one where desire isn't a show, one where I might touch someone without needing an audience to feel real. For now, I sit on the floor and let my hands shake, because unlearning seduction hurts more than any cut I've ever made. But this time, I choose where the blade goes, and I am finally willing to bleed for it.

Chapter Fourteen

———————— ∞ ————————

When Memory Fights Back

There are only two places I've ever trusted my body, on the dock and in the OR, and one of those nearly destroyed me while the other I turned into religion. Now they're starting to look the same, and it's meant to be a routine miracle, an elective case, a fifty-one-year-old woman with a left frontal meningioma, broad base, compressing but not invading, mass effect more than malice. Her symptoms are mild, headaches, flattened affect, the subtle executive dysfunction that makes families reach for euphemisms because truth feels like betrayal, and she tells me in pre-op with a weary half-smile pulling at one corner of her mouth that her husband says she is blunt now. She used to be nice, she says, now she sounds like her mother, and I give her my usual line, balanced, lightly reassuring, faintly sharp, that she may like herself better after we get this out.

She laughs in that desperate way patients laugh when they are about to hand you their skull, her husband squeezes her hand, and she says she trusts me, and I feel the familiar shift in the room, the subtle tilt of gravity toward me. Once that steadied me, now something under my sternum flinches like an animal that knows the shape of a trap even when it cannot name it. Clara stands at the back of the bay, not charting and not half-present in paperwork the way she usually is when she is trying not to be visible, and she says she wanted to see the case from beginning to end. We both know that isn't true, because she is here to see me, and I pretend not to notice because noticing is intimacy and intimacy is a currency I no longer know how to spend without taking something with it.

Surgery is scheduled for ten, and at 08:30 I am in my office staring at my hands over a keyboard I am not typing on. They are calm, no tremor and no flutter at the edges, no betrayal, and I tell them they are fine like they are uncooperative residents, and they do not answer. A knock comes and Teasdale leans in with an expression a little too careful, like a man approaching a wild animal he has been praising for years, and he tells me everything is set for OR-4 with anesthesia ready and radiology having sent the fusion data with updated DTI just in case. I tell him overcompensating is a love language in this building, and he chuckles dutifully, then lingers, waiting for the rest of me, the part that gives him a role, a script, an orbit, and I don't.

When he leaves, my body slides into the familiar sequence, coat, badge, mask shoved into pocket, and it is not thought, it is liturgy, a ritual designed to make the self disappear behind competence. In the scrub room I catch Clara's eyes once only in the steel reflection and not directly, and she asks if I slept. I say yes, which is a lie, and she asks about my hands, and I flex them and say fine, which is a half-truth, and she tells me that if anything feels off I say it out loud. I mutter that we have been through this, and she replies that we have been through me pretending it isn't happening, and water runs on skin with soap in the lines of my palms while ritual overrides reality.

I scrub until my hands are raw and clean and obedient, and then I step into the OR, bright and cold and humming gently with machines that keep people alive while we violate them in the approved way. Julie is already there laying out trays, residents hover like satellites, and anesthesia is mid-lecture to a new fellow about blood pressure control with a voice cheerful in the way only someone who does not touch brains can afford. When I enter the energy shifts, it always does, even when I am trying to be neutral, because the role drags awe behind it like a comet tail. Someone says good morning, and I nod without identifying who, because eye contact is intimacy and I ration it now.

The patient is prepped and draped, sedated into stillness, her skull waiting beneath iodine-yellowed skin like a secret smoothed into silence, and this field is the one place where nothing touches me unless I cut it open first. Fernandez asks about a burr hole on the frontal line on navigation, and I confirm, my voice authoritative without seduction and clean without cruelty, and she steadies the drill. I guide her by speaking instead of touching, telling her to lift her wrist and let the machine do the pressure, and she does it perfectly, and when she withdraws I take the tool.

The moment my fingers close around the drill something jolts through my hand, not tremor and not slip but recognition, like a nerve firing in an old scar. Bare feet on wet wood, pressure at my wrist, a voice coaxing posture, good girl, and my thumb tightens involuntarily so the drill angle shifts three degrees. Three degrees is the difference between a clean entry and a dural tear, the distance between competence and catastrophe, and Julie sees it while Clara sees it and the room does not speak because it has been trained not to. I force my hand still and bore through the skull with precise, artificial slowness like I am puppeteering my own body with a delay between intent and movement, and bone dust rises pale and grainy as if I am scraping frost from a window.

Irrigation, suction, retractor placement, choreography covers me like a surgical drape, and for a while, minutes and then an hour, routine holds. The bone flap comes off and the dura is opened in a clean curve, and the brain pulses gently against our intrusion, indifferent to our myth of mastery, while vessels arc and branch like a map of a city I have memorized in another life. I trace them with the calm of someone who has built her identity on precision, and then we approach the tumor margin. I request the microdissector, it is placed into my hand, and it fits against my fingers like a memory of someone else's palm against the back of my hand, steadying and instructive and claiming.

A tool is supposed to be neutral, but I have never held anything neutrally, because other hands shaped my body and my body kept the instruction. I insert the microdissector and my fingers spasm, a tremor that is small and violent and insistent like a current and a warning and a refusal, and I say quickly to retract here, converting the shake into motion and disguising loss of control as decision. Fernandez adjusts the retractors, assuming intent and assuming I am still the god she trained herself to obey, and Clara's voice cuts through the room low but firm telling me to pause. I say no, she says I need to pause, I say I am fine, and she says I am not, and silence shreds the air while everyone freezes.

The anesthesiologist looks up sensing danger but not knowing where it sits, Julie murmurs that vitals are stable as if stability in one body offsets collapse in another, and I repeat that I am fine with a voice almost gentle, which frightens me more than anger ever could. The tremor spreads through my fingers like a small thunder and my hand becomes a lie threatening to become truth, and if I keep going I know I can do this, but if I keep going I might rupture the ACA and kill this woman. Not today, so I withdraw the dissector and say that someone else needs to close.

The room reacts as though the earth tilted, because a surgeon stepping aside mid-operation is not humility but scandal and failure and blood in the water, and Fernandez starts to object that the resection is not complete. I cut her off and tell her to switch and call Levin, and under surgical masks the collective inhale is nearly inaudible, because this is not how legends behave. Clara touches my arm, not corrective and not dominant but human, the contact brief and precise, a boundary rather than a claim, and she tells me softly that I do not have to choose between pain and performance.

Performance pulls the dock and my mother and Evelyn whispering into the room, choice disguised as obedience and grace used as a leash, and I step away from the table. I tell them to finish it again, and then I leave the OR, and when the door closes behind me my body nearly vomits. My legs do not buckle, because a surgeon does not collapse where it can be seen, and the nausea spikes and then drops sharp as a cut, and I lean against the wall with palms pressed flat to cold plaster while my hands will not stop shaking.

This is not tremor but revolt, not a flashback but an aftershock, my body remembering instruction like muscle memory telling me to hold still and be chosen and that good girls make it look easy. I slide down until I am sitting on the floor like a child in time-out, and a janitor steps around me quietly pretending not to notice, and that kindness is worse than pity. If I cannot operate, what am I, and if my hands betray me, how do I exist, and there are no answers, so I rest my forehead on my knees and breathe into the ache behind my ribs, knowing I did not fail the surgery but failed the performance.

Clara comes into the hallway without urgency and without alarm, just presence, and she does not crouch over me like a rescuer or loom like an authority, she sits beside me mirroring my posture so we look stupid together and equal. She says I stopped, and I tell her I had to, and she says that is the first time I have ever chosen safety over image, and I let out a laugh that tastes like salt. She tells me my reputation is still there and that it just looks human now, and humans are terrifying because humans bleed and humans are unsafe, and my voice cracks in a direction that is not quite sadness when I say I might have to quit surgery.

Clara does not argue and does not soothe and does not give me false hope, she says I do not have to decide right now, and I look at her, actually at her, the person who saw me then and sees me now, her gaze steady and not seductive and not pitying. Witness, nothing more and nothing less, and for the first time I understand that witnessing can save someone and watching can break them, and both happened on the dock while only one is happening here. As the tremor eases my chest tightens with a certainty worse than fear, that if I stop performing I might finally see what was done to me, and I do not know if I can survive knowing it.

There is no protocol for this and no procedure for a neurosurgeon losing the temperament that makes her a neurosurgeon, and while we run simulations for intraoperative stroke and aneurysm rupture and malignant hyperthermia there is no drill for when the surgeon is the complication. Clara does not leave until I stand, and even then she does not touch me or guide me or offer the gentle pressure at the forearm that people call support, because I would mistake it for control anyway. We walk back toward the locker room together in silence, and I realize how much I have relied on tone, mine and other people's, to tell me who I am and what I am allowed to be when the ground shifts.

The locker room hums with fluorescent indifference and the bench is cold, and I sit while my coat feels like lead. I pull off my surgical cap and hair falls messily with strands sticking to my forehead with sweat, and Clara stands near the sinks telling me I need a break. I ask if she means fifteen minutes, and she says no, longer, and when I say I do not take time off she tells me I need to, and when I say I need to operate she replies that that is not true right now. Her words are not sharp but diagnostic, and she adds that my brain and hands are fine and that my body is not malfunctioning, it is remembering.

I whisper that that is worse, and she tells me it is only because I built my entire identity on forgetting, and I stare at her through the mirror at this woman I once thought was seducing me and who was never the cause of anything but only the witness. There is a wound at the center of who I am, and she is the only person alive who knows where it is, and she tells me I think I am losing control when I am actually gaining it. I say I do not feel in control, and she agrees that for the first time I am not performing it, and then she leaves me with that, no hand on my shoulder and no pull, because real life is not staged like seduction.

I am alone and I hate it, and hospitals never punish competence directly because they smother it with concern, and by noon three emails wait from the Chief of Surgery and Risk Management and a blankly titled message from Wellness Support Liaison. The words patient safety appear four times, and they are using the language of care the way we use antiseptic, enough to keep liability from infecting the building, and I reply to none. Teasdale knocks again looking oddly pale, and he tells me he heard they pulled me from OR scheduling, and I confirm it, and when he asks if I am okay the question is too intimate in too casual a mouth so I deflect it by asking about the pathology courier.

He nods relieved and flees, and language becomes safety while routine is anesthesia, and I stay in my office until I cannot breathe in it anymore. I go to the cafeteria because it is where normal people go when their lives are falling apart and they want to be seen as functional, and I sit at a plastic table near the vending machines where the air tastes like fatigue. Conversations around me are too loud and too mundane, and my name travels like a contagion, and I stab a piece of chicken while my hand trembles once and then stops, and I do not know if that is improvement or suppression.

I chew slowly and it tastes like nothing, because food is fuel now and pleasure is suspect, and a chair scrapes across from me as Clara sits without asking. She tells me I am being discussed, and I say I assumed, and she says I am not the villain, and that is not new. We eat in silence while she sips tea and I force myself not to correct my posture, letting my shoulders slump the slightest bit because it feels like peeling skin off in public. She tells me quietly that I am allowed not to be perfect, and I reply that perfection is not the problem but how I learned it, and she nods slow and says that is why it is dangerous.

They schedule it like a colonoscopy, routine and invasive, in a beige office with diplomas and a plant that wants to die, and Dr. Becker offers a practiced smile. She says they want to ensure my well-being and that surgical tremor can have many causes, and I tell her I have had no tremor outside surgery. She asks if I noticed it only when operating and under stress, and I say it is not stress but memory, which I did not mean to say, and she pauses with her pen hovering. She says they have to follow protocol with neurological and psych evaluation, and the word psych lands like a net.

I tell her that what I believed about control matters, not the shaking, and she blinks because she was trained for liability and not poets, and she repeats that they need to ensure patient safety. I tell her I withdrew to protect patient safety, and she says they want to acknowledge that and that I did the right thing, and six months ago I would have sculpted this into admiration, but today I do not perform. I sit in the truth and tell her it did not feel like the right thing, and she says it will, and she believes that, which scares me.

By late afternoon I wander with no cases and no calendar dictating where I stand, and I pass OR-4 where Levin is dictating my surgery with flat triumph. He sees me and his tone falters, and he tells me he finished, and I say I know, and when he tells me I left at the right time something in his voice is almost grateful. I tell him he did well, and he does not know what to do with praise that is not manipulative, and he finally asks if I am okay. I say no, and he nods once like a man who has just heard truth, and he tells me I will figure it out, not comfort and not dismissal but a fact.

At home I cannot open a drawer without noticing how I reach for the handle with a wrist flick that does not feel like mine, and I brush my hair with a cadence I did not invent. I uncork a bottle of wine and then stop, because even the motion looks like seduction, and I set the bottle down without drinking, not because I need control but because I have never met myself sober without performance. I sit on the kitchen floor with my back against the cabinet and lift my hands as the tremor returns like a protest and a pulse of rebellion, not weakness but memory refusing anesthesia.

I feel it in my wrists where Evelyn held me still and where my mother watched, the mother who did not pull me away or say no or even look away, who let someone shape me, and memory is not trauma revisiting but the body saying I survived by copying and now I must un-copy. My hands will not stop shaking, and at midnight I whisper that I do not know if I ever wanted to be a surgeon, not because I did not love the work or was not good at it but because I mistook precision for choice and authority for autonomy. I correct myself and say I do not know what I want, and maybe that is the terror, losing the script I mistook for identity.

My hands tremble harder and I let them, and in the quaking of those fingers something breaks, not my career or competence but a leash I never knew I was wearing. I try to sleep but my body stays awake like a guard posted at the edge of a battlefield that has not been attacked yet, and the bed feels too permissive while breath catches without rhythm. At 2:21 a.m. I give up and sit on the edge of the bed with my spine curved forward in a posture that resembles a child on a dock waiting for instruction, and I straighten instantly, nauseated by my own body language.

Exhausted but lit, I splash water on my face and stare into harsh bathroom light, telling myself this is the body that learned silence before language and seduction before choice. I whisper that I do not know what I want again, slower, and the mirror gives me nothing but a witness, and that frightens me more than any villain ever did. I end up in the emergency psych clinic at 03:12 a.m. not for admission but because I cannot bear the stillness at home, and the receptionist looks baffled when I give my name because surgeons do not come here voluntarily.

A psych resident appears and introduces himself, and when he asks what is going on I almost laugh because the question is too small for the answer. I tell him I had a tremor and that it was both movement and panic, and when he asks what triggered it I say a memory that was not mine until recently, meaning I lived it but did not remember it correctly. He names it reconstructed, and the word lands like an incision, and when he asks if the body remembers differently than the mind I tell him he has no idea. He says I am scared of what my body knows, and I reply that I am scared of who taught it to know, and something like empathy flickers over his face.

He offers medication and I refuse, because if I sedate myself I will lose the only honest information I have left, and he suggests daily check-ins as observations rather than evaluations. He writes in my chart that trauma response with occupational risk is present and that surgical clearance is withheld, and it feels like a sentence but also a starting point. As I leave he tells me memory is not the enemy but interpretation is, and he does not know he just rewired the last twenty years of my life.

The next morning I arrive at the hospital with no plan to operate and the hallways look unfamiliar while whispers scatter behind me about my case and my absence, because they think brilliance is armor when it can be bait. I stand in the observation booth above OR-2 watching a vascular aneurysm case unfold with disciplined intimacy, and I could do it half-asleep, but I am not down there. I watch someone else embody the choreography I mistook for personality, and I do not feel jealousy but grief, because from here I can see how seductive the work is and how mastery is mistaken for autonomy. I whisper that it is not power but obedience, and Clara appears beside me, telling me I miss who I thought I was, and she is right.

In the afternoon they send me to physical therapy to prove my body is intact, and I pass every test with no tremor, and the therapist says I look fine, which is the problem. I look fine and sound fine until the field resembles a boundary I did not choose, and then my body refuses, because the last time I held still under pressure it was obedience to harm. The form says neurological integrity intact and recommends return to OR when cleared by Psych, as if trauma is not motor learning, and at 19:47 I go to the hospital library for property records.

The lake house and the dock come up with a deed signed E. Rowan, not Evelyn, and recognition hits like blunt force because the microdissector I used yesterday is a Rowan-brand instrument. The page blurs as I realize technique may have been passed through coercion and mentorship twisted into inheritance, and I call my mother who does not answer. I sit with the truth until pain becomes fact, wondering if I became a surgeon not to save people but because someone taught me being handled was the only way to matter, and maybe precision was not passion but survival made beautiful.

Near midnight I walk into an empty OR and step to the table without picking up a scalpel, placing my bare shaking hands on the drape and letting them tremble. Control was never strength, it was symptom, and my body shakes because it is telling the truth, which is panic and defiance and refusal to be steady on command anymore. I whisper to the empty table and to the child I was that I am not holding still for you, and my hands shake harder while for the first time I do not try to fix them.

Chapter Fifteen

---∞∞---

Reclaiming Agency

T here is a difference between being controlled and being decisive. One is done to you, you do the other. Most of my life, I confused the two, if I could anticipate control, if I could lean into it before it landed, I told myself I was choosing. That was the lie that kept me upright, that was the lie that kept me unbroken, at least in the version of unbroken I learned to perform.

Now the lie is cracking, so I do what I have always done when faced with something I do not know how to feel about. I study it, not from the inside of my nervous system, but from the outside. From the data, from her, from Evelyn, from the woman on the shore.

My mother used to call it spiritual rest. "You come back so much calmer," my father would say, never quite looking closely at anything. "It's good for Jax," she'd answer. "She needs environments where she isn't the smartest person in the room." Translation, places where I could be broken down into something more manageable. Places where intelligence could be reframed as arrogance, competence as defiance, agency as a problem to be corrected. I used to hate those trips the way children hate vegetables, with irritation, not understanding, and I told myself I hated the boredom, the wet shoes, the sermons that smelled like mildew and authority.

I told myself I hated the way the adults spoke in riddles so they never had to say anything clearly. Now I understand what I actually hated, I hated the feeling of being handled, not physically at first and not in ways that would have made a decent villain in a courtroom, but in ways that were deniable and portable, the kind of handling you can baptize as guidance. They did not start by taking my body, they started by taking my interpretation. They taught me the most dangerous thing you can teach a child, that discomfort is not a signal, it is a test, and that failing the test is not pain, it is shame.

I am in my office between consults, blinds half-closed and fluorescent light buzzing like an irritated insect, while the hospital does what it always does, humming on, indifferent to human thresholds, and my inbox refills as my pager sleeps and wakes. A cleaner's cart rolls past my door like a slow prayer, and my fingers hover over the keyboard for a moment, reluctant, as if searching her outside my own skull is a betrayal, then I remember the dock and I type, first her maiden name, then the married one, then both together, plus the word that always hovered around those trips like incense, retreat.

At first it is boring and predictable, alumni newsletters, a published letter to the editor about "maintaining moral standards in public schools," a church fundraiser photo where everyone's teeth are too white and their eyes are too tired, and a short profile praising her "community service" and "ability to guide young women into purpose," purpose being another word that tastes like rope as I scroll anyway because the thing about control is that it always leaves paperwork and people who believe they are righteous are careless, they do not hide, they advertise, and then I see it, a cached PDF, and I click.

The file opens with a wheeze, as if the server itself is embarrassed by the contents, and the design is old, sepia-toned and faux-handmade, the aesthetic of people who want their control to look organic, like it was grown from soil rather than engineered in boardrooms. On the cover is a lake at dusk, a dock extending into dark water, and a slender figure at the end of it with her arms open and her hair blown back. My lungs seize, it is not me, not literally, but it could be, and that is the point, the dock is not a place, it is a template, a posture you can transport.

Below the image a tagline curls in cursive, where obedience becomes freedom, and being seen becomes healing. Obedience, freedom, seen, healing, four words that have done more violence to me than any scalpel ever could. I scroll, and the founder introduction appears in the same syrupy cadence my mother used when she wanted something to sound inevitable, announcing that Evelyn Stone leads The Restored Vessel, a community for women seeking to reclaim their bodies from shame and passivity, and that through guided spiritual praxis and somatic devotion they cultivate daughters who know the holy power of being chosen, holy power of being chosen being the phrase they used on the dock when they called my terror a calling.

My hand tightens on the mouse and the cursor shakes slightly, not because my hand tremors now but because the screen is suddenly too close and my body is doing that subtle recoil it learned to do silently. There is a grainy photo on page two, a group of women standing at the edge of a lake, linen clothing and bare feet in grass, smiles calibrated between serene and smug, and in the center a woman with sharp eyes and soft hands, Evelyn, with another woman to her right, arms folded and chin lifted just far enough to suggest that everything around her is a test she has already passed, my mother.

I lean in until my forehead nearly touches the screen because I have seen her in family photos and corporate shots and church directories, always polished and managed and professional, and this version of her is different because here she does not look like someone obeying doctrine, she looks like someone enforcing it. My stomach rolls, slow and clinical, as if my body is trying to expel a narrative it can no longer digest, and I print the page before I fully decide to, evidence, not memory, evidence.

The printer hums and spits the paper like a reluctant witness, and the photo lands in my hand warm, still carrying the heat of the machine, which feels obscene because evidence should be cold and inert and not make my throat tighten the way this does, but it does anyway, because it proves something I have spent twenty years trying not to prove, this was real, and it was not an accident.

I am halfway through scanning the rest of the document when a line at the bottom of the last page catches my eye, the generosity of Meridian Integrated Wellness Foundation and other partners supports the Restored Vessel, Meridian of course, the name sitting there in clean sans serif like it has not already threaded itself through my professional life in logos on research grants, quiet plaques in the hospital wing, and the letterhead on Harrow's drafts about trauma-induced memory excision, Meridian having always been a neutral word to me, a donor, a benefactor, a line in a budget, a name you thank in acknowledgments because that is how science works, you take the money and pretend it does not have fingerprints.

Now the name tastes like lake water and metal railings as I scroll to the footer and see a small logo I have never bothered to notice before, a stylized curve suggesting horizon or shoreline or, if you have stood there barefoot and shivering, a dock, the same curve that glows in neon above the club bar, and I pull up the club's encrypted site on my phone, the one my hand unlocks with muscle memory and that loads after my thumb gives it permission, where the stylized wave appears, minimal, elegant, expensive.

I set my phone beside the printed brochure, not identical but intimately related, iterations on a shape that has been following me longer than I have been old enough to vote, Meridian funds Harrow, Meridian funded The Restored Vessel, The Restored Vessel became Evelyn's lakeside retreats, the dock became doctrine, doctrine became the club, and it is not a thread but a circulatory system that I have spent my entire career operating on at its end-stage consequences while calling it neutral science.

The realization should shatter me, but instead it sharpens me, because at least now I know what kind of tumor I am dealing with. I could keep this to myself, because it is what I am built for, solitary analysis and control through secrecy, treating it like a private diagnosis, something I hold and manage and never let reach the surface where it might ruin me, which is precisely how they kept us compliant, so I do the opposite.

I print more copies, the brochure, the donor acknowledgments, the leadership photo with Evelyn and my mother standing at the lake's edge, and a screenshot of the Meridian logo on the footer, assembling it like a board pack or a clinical file, a chart for a patient named my past admitted under false pretenses.

I tuck everything into a manila folder, and it makes my hands feel steadier and my mind feel like it has a grip, because paper is an old kind of control, a kind I trust more than memory.

Then I find Clara. She is in Post-Op adjusting a patient's PCA settings, her movements efficient and unromantic in the way real care always is, because real care looks like a pump dose shifted by two milligrams rather than a grand gesture, and her eyes flick up when she feels me watching, that familiar hypervigilance now aimed with more precision than fear. I ask if she has five minutes, and she says it depends, whether this is neurosurgery or me, to which I answer both, watching her finish what she is doing, check the patient monitor one more time, and nod toward the end of the corridor where a half-empty family room sits with the lights half-off, smelling faintly of old coffee and worry as we step inside together and I close the door behind us.

I do not sit because it feels too much like a consult, and instead I hand her the folder, telling her to start with the photo, and she opens it, pulls the picture free, and reacts instantly, shoulders locking, breath catching, fingers tightening on the edges of the paper as if it might bite her while she says that it is her, not asking who or wondering if, just stating it, Evelyn, before her thumb drifts to the right side of the group and stops and she adds quietly that the other woman is my mother.

My throat contracts as if my body is trying to swallow the sentence before it can exist, and even though I know she is right I ask if she is sure, watching her keep her eyes on the image as she says she remembers the way she watched, like someone auditing a class rather than participating, assessing outcomes, and when I repeat the word outcomes she explains that it was which girls adapted, which girls fought, and which girls could be made to call it love, something cold moving through my ribcage that is not fear or rage but recognition, the sensation of a map being updated in real time, so I tell her to keep going.

She flips through the pages, mission statements, retreat descriptions, and testimonials that read like hostage letters rewritten in devotional language, pausing at the tagline to read it out loud, where obedience becomes freedom and being seen becomes healing, and she snorts softly as she says that is one way to describe making someone grateful for what is done to them, a line that makes something like nausea rise in me because gratitude in this context feels indistinguishable from weakness even though I am grateful she said it first. I tell her to look at the footer, and when she does her eyes widen at the word Meridian, so I tell her it is not just neurology grants but body and soul discounts and bulk rates on trauma, which makes her give a sound that could have been a laugh or a sob before she swallows it.

She tells me I worked with them, and I answer automatically that I thought I was above it before correcting myself to admit I worked with them because they spoke my native language, control dressed as cure. She flips to a page I marked, a section titled Raising Restored Daughters, and the phrasing lands like an old hymn buried in the spine as she reads lines about encouraging a daughter to delight in being noticed because attention is an invitation rather than a threat, about correcting modesty when it hides rather than when it honors, and about how a girl unwilling to be beheld is resisting her calling. She reads aloud that when she is chosen it should be celebrated as her first taste of holy power, and she looks up at me with eyes braided from fury and grief as she says this is what they told my mother, while I answer that it is what they told all of them, including the ones standing on the shore watching.

She traces one of the sentences with her finger and reads it under her breath, if a daughter is afraid stand firm and do not indulge cowardice or you will teach her to flee her own anointing, and something in my chest burns as I tell her I remember being afraid but I do not remember being allowed to stay that way, because fear was always something I was told to transform into obedience and performance. Clara says quietly that I was taught to turn it into those things, and when I add seduction she holds my gaze and tells me I did not invent that stance on the dock because it was coached into me, which should have felt like an indictment but instead lands like a diagnosis that finally gives the thing boundaries.

I tell her I need more than doctrine and that I need infrastructure, names, money trails, and ownership structures, and when she says it sounds like I am investigating I correct her by saying I am staging a pre-op consult, which makes her mouth twitch with something that is not quite affection but feels like permission all the same, as if she is saying fine, if I cannot feel it yet then we will map it.

At home that night I trade textbooks for public records, because there is something soothing about corporate registries that makes them feel almost honest, even though people think shell companies are sophisticated when they are really just lazy structures that leave repeating patterns behind. I make tea I do not drink and open so many tabs that the browser starts to look like a mind that cannot rest, and as I cross reference donation acknowledgments from the brochure with nonprofit databases and old articles about innovative partnership models between faith based wellness groups and private foundations I start to see the same names recur.

I find RV Foundation Trust and RV Shoreline Holdings, and sitting on the board of both are E Stone and M Niles, with Meridian Integrated Wellness Foundation listed as a strategic sponsor, which makes my jaw tighten because the shape of it is suddenly too familiar. When I click deeper I see that RV Shoreline Holdings is the majority owner of three properties, a lakeside campus, a retreat center in the hills, and a downtown entity categorized as hospitality and wellness, and the name of that last one makes the hair on my arms lift.

It is The Dockroom Collective, legally bland and commercially unremarkable but spiritually familiar, the same club with the encrypted archive and the wave logo that felt like home before I remembered why, and I stare at the screen long enough for time to become irrelevant. The girl who once stood barefoot on wet wood obeying on cue while her mother watched has grown into the woman who pays for the privilege of orchestrated reenactment in rooms designed by the same doctrine, which makes survival itself start to look like a business model.

I want to throw the laptop across the room but instead I do something more dangerous by continuing to read, copying a partnership agreement reference number into another search until a grainy scanned PDF marked confidential draft opens in front of me. It states that Meridian Integrated Wellness agrees to provide research funding, staff training, and clinical oversight to RV Shoreline's urban wellness initiative in exchange for anonymized behavioral data and co branded programming in somatic consent, embodied autonomy, and trauma informed power exchange, which are words designed to sound like ethics even as they disguise a doctrine.

They did not just groom us and let us go, they built a feedback loop where children were taught that being chosen was holy, where the ones who adapted too well were tracked into adult spaces marketed as liberation, and where data was collected on how we reenact what we learned before it was all called empowerment or science or anything but what it really is, which is weaponized autonomy. I press the heel of my hand into my sternum as if I can hold myself in place and then I pick up my phone.

Clara answers on the second ring, and the first thing she says is that I am awake, not as a question but as a fact, which makes me swallow before I ask if she has access to public corporate records. She snorts hello to you too and I say hello back out of habit before she admits that her brother is an accountant and that she once had a phase where forensic bookkeeping felt cool, so I tell her we are digging into RV Shoreline Holdings and anything linked to The Restored Vessel.

There is a stretch of silence long enough to feel like a held breath before she warns me that this is not a clinical trial but a legal minefield, and I answer that leaving a tumor in until it ruptures is not safer, telling her to check her email as I send the PDF and screenshots. A minute later I hear the muffled tapping of keys through the phone, like a second heartbeat, before she says she can see the trust and the retreat property and then stops with an oh that makes my skin tighten.

When I ask what she has found she murmurs that The Dockroom Collective is owned by RV Shoreline and that its primary lender is a shell company tracing back to Meridian's property arm, which makes my mouth go dry because I had believed Meridian only funded research. She laughs without humor and tells me they invest in holistic ecosystems, meaning clinics, retreats, and clubs, anywhere human vulnerability can be packaged and monetized, and when I ask about board overlaps she clicks again and says that E Stone is there along with two names she does not recognize and one more that makes my stomach drop.

Meridian's Trauma and Identity Research Lead is listed as a non voting advisor to the Dockroom board, which is Harrow, my colleague whose lab notes I once read as if they were neutral maps instead of roadways. I feel pressure build behind my eyes, not tears yet but something that wants to become shape, and I tell her that the lab note was never neutral, it was a roadmap, while she answers softly that this is not on me even though I insist that I gave them language, data, and clinical legitimacy by studying people like me and calling it research.

She counters that I studied survival and they weaponized it, which feels philosophical rather than practical but I let it sit because letting something sit without turning it into a performance is new, and when she asks what I want to do I pause longer than I ever would have before. I do not answer with what makes me sound powerful or what makes this hurt less, but with the next precise step, which is that I want to talk to her, not my mother but her teacher, Evelyn, and when Clara asks about Harrow I tell her he built the lab and she built the dock, so we start with the architect of the first incision.

She warns me that this is not safe and I reply that neither is letting them keep practicing, which leads to a long quiet before she says that if I am set on this we will do it like a procedure, with preparation, positioning, witnesses, and a plan for what happens if things go sideways. When I tell her she is offering to scrub in she answers that she was there for the first surgery and she is not leaving me alone for this one, and something in my chest tightens with the unfamiliar sensation of shared load and co authored survival.

The next day feels like pre op except that this time the patient is my history, and I wake before dawn with my heart hammering and my body remembering the sensation of being summoned to the dock, standing in front of my bathroom mirror with hair unstyled and eyes still ringed with the residue of sleep and adrenaline as I tell my reflection that control is choice and not performance. The woman staring back at me looks unconvinced, which feels honest enough to work with for now, so I pull on plain clothes, dark jeans, a black t shirt, and a jacket, nothing that shifts my posture into allure or invites being looked at as anything but present.

If I walk into that club in my usual armor, precision, aesthetic menace, and curated vulnerability, I will be halfway reenacting before the door closes, so I need to arrive as a surgeon and not a supplicant, which is why I keep my day at the hospital as ordinary as I can manage with rounds, charting, and one short consult but no cutting, even as my hands shake at unpredictable intervals like my nervous system is practicing rebellion in small doses. I do not tell anyone why my schedule is empty because hospitals are good at filling gaps, and if you leave a hole they will stuff it with support, protocol, or a committee with too many initials.

At lunch Clara sits opposite me with her tray like we are colleagues instead of co conspirators, telling me that I look like I am about to present at an M and M, which I answer by saying that in a way I am, except the mortality is twenty years old and the morbidity is my entire erotic template. She snorts into her coffee and says my ability to make that sentence sound like a discharge summary is terrifying, then asks if I slept, and when I say enough to show up she nods once and says that is all we need.

We go over the plan in low voices like we are discussing approach routes to a deep lesion where one wrong move could destroy something vital, reviewing when board meetings usually happen at The Dockroom based on corporate filings and staff gossip, noting the small administrative office behind the main floor where contracts are signed and NDAs are stored, and confirming that Evelyn still visits in person even though we do not know how she will react to seeing me or whether she will recognize me at all. Clara reminds me that I am not going there as a supplicant but as someone asking questions, and the word asking tastes wrong in my mouth because I prefer ordering and directing, anything where my voice is a scalpel instead of a plea, which is why her reminder about informed consent makes me twist my mouth as she points out that what we are doing is different because I get to leave at any time for any reason without being called a coward or a sinner. Leaving without having to transform it into moral failure feels so simple that it makes my throat sting, but I nod anyway and say okay, then tonight we go to church.

The hardest part is not deciding to confront but deciding how, because in surgery I always start by mapping vital structures, arteries, tracts, and functions I cannot afford to damage before I ever choose an approach, and here the vital structure is my own nervous system, which means every part of this plan has to pass a single test about whether it reclaims my agency or gives them another chance to choreograph me. We decide on constraints the way surgeons decide on margins, no alcohol, no private rooms, no contracts, and no scripts, with us walking in as civilians and staying where any member can stand while we ask to speak to management under the pretense of discussing Meridian ties, knowing that if that does not work I will use my name the way they have always wanted me to use my body, as leverage rather than invitation.

When Clara asks if I am okay weaponizing my credentials as we sit in my office after shift with the sun bleeding out behind the skyline, I tell her they are already using them, pulling up the Dockroom's anonymous testimonials on my phone and reading one aloud about how Dr. N saved a life in the OR and then showed someone how to surrender in here, which turns my stomach as I say I never wrote that, even as Clara answers that I created the conditions where they could believe it, calling it reenactment as liturgy. I mutter that I am going to burn that place down, and she says we are not starting with arson but with conversation, amending it to verbal arson because I can set things on fire with a sentence if I use that instead.

When I ask if she is afraid of them or of her, Clara admits she is terrified but already survived Evelyn once, which means the worst she can do now is lie, and when I tell her she should not have to do this she answers that neither should I, leaving us sitting in the office hum like two people who were once children on opposite sides of a dock about to walk together into the adult version of the same pattern, this time with witnesses because we are bringing our own.

At home an hour before we leave, I stand in front of my closet and realize I have no idea what to wear, because most of my clothes fall into two categories, surgical neutral or curated allure, and tonight needs a third option that feels like chosen presence rather than performance. I settle on black trousers, a charcoal shirt, and boots I can move in, with no heels and no jewelry that invites commentary, hair pulled back in a plain tie and my face bare, so that I look like someone heading to a difficult family meeting rather than a club, which feels fitting.

My phone buzzes with a message from Clara that reads, Downstairs. No turning back without telling me in person, and I almost smile as I pick up the folder with the printed photo of the lake, the dock, and the women on the shore, sliding it into my bag like an operative sliding a weapon into a holster. At the door I pause, because this is the moment I never had on the dock, the one my mother and Evelyn stole by calling obedience destiny, and I know that I can go or I can stay and either way the choice is mine as I open the door into a hallway that smells like detergent and someone else's dinner.

Clara waits by the curb when I step onto the street, hands in her pockets and posture neutral, and when she asks if I am ready I say no truthfully, which makes her reply that people who are ready walk in as offerings, while I ask what we are walking in as and she answers that we are the ones holding the scalpel.

The Dockroom looks different when you are sober, unarmoured, and not there to be touched, with the line outside shorter tonight and no themed event drawing a crowd, just the usual curated cluster of people who dress their damage in good fabric beneath the quiet stylised wave glowing above the door. Tonight I see it properly, not as ocean or freedom but as a shoreline, a boundary, a place where bodies are told where to stand.

The bouncer clocks us as we approach, thick forearms and a neutral gaze trained to be professionally un-intimidated, and when he greets us I tell him we are here to speak with management, which earns the standard reply about the app and the guest list until I ask him to tell them Dr. Jax Nile is here about Meridian. His eyes lift at my name and at the word Meridian, and after checking my ID and hospital badge he taps his earpiece with a jaw that tics once before he tells us to wait inside near the host stand until they clear it.

We step into the club where everything is dim and expensive, the music calibrated to be felt more than heard and the lighting designed for suggestion so that shadows can do the work of consent, and for the first time I recognize it as a lab built from my nervous system rather than a place that ever belonged to me. The hostess recognizes me immediately, surprise flickering into something like worship, but when she asks if I would like my usual I say no and tell her I want to speak with whoever handles their Meridian partnership, which makes her swallow and disappear through the side door.

Clara steps up beside me and murmurs that I am handling this like a complaint letter to Risk and Governance, and I tell her that is exactly what this is, except the risk is me, and we wait long enough for the choreography of the room to press against my skin without me slipping into it.

The hostess returns with a woman in her forties, sharp suit and sharper eyes, the kind of manager hired to ensure the police never have a reason to come inside, and when she introduces herself as Lisette and mentions strategic partnerships and compliance I tell her I would prefer to discuss my concerns somewhere quiet. Her gaze flicks to Clara until I say she is a witness, which earns a single nod before Lisette leads us down the admin corridor and into a small office with a desk, two chairs, a wall safe, and a framed black and white photograph of a lake at dawn with a dock extending into still water.

Lisette closes the door and gestures for us to sit, but I remain standing and tell her this will not take long if she is honest, which earns a comment about honesty being contextual here and people coming to explore versions of truth they cannot live anywhere else, a statement I flatten by telling her I helped design some of the language they use to justify it. When she blinks I mention Meridian's trauma and identity work and how they quote us in their training manuals, and when she tries to retreat behind proprietary materials I frame this as a privileged clinical conversation or else one that will involve counsel, which finally moves something beneath her composure.

I slide the Restored Vessel brochure across the desk and ask if she recognizes it, and when she confirms it as an early partner in Meridian's community engagement portfolio I name Evelyn Stone and ask if she is still on the board, which earns a careful explanation about layers and historic affiliations that I cut off by asking why the same woman who coached children on lakeside obedience is now architecting adult spaces that trade on trauma informed power exchange. Lisette exhales and insists they provide containers and safety until Clara says quietly that they provide alibis, and when Lisette asks who Clara is she answers that she is someone who stood on that dock, leaving the room very still.

Lisette's face tightens as if a muscle she forgot she had just engaged, and she says that if what we are implying is true then this is no longer an ethics issue but criminal exposure, which I agree with while telling her that is why I am allowing her to be careful with her next sentence. When she mutters that I sound like my mother rather than Evelyn I feel the words land like a delayed hemorrhage, and when I ask how she knows my mother Lisette explains that she was on the board and that Evelyn adored her, a word that tastes like bile in my mouth.

Clara asks whether Lisette ever went to the lake and Lisette admits to leadership intensives as an adult but resists the implication of childhood visits until Clara presses again, forcing a flicker of memory and anger across Lisette's face, and when she snaps back asking what we really want I tell her I want information. I step closer to the desk without looming and ask how they sell this place to Meridian and donors, which gets a rehearsed answer about embodied autonomy and adults reclaiming their narratives that I counter by asking whether their packets still quote a daughter unwilling to be beheld resisting her anointing, a silence that answers me well enough.

Lisette sags back and admits she was a teenager when they brought her in and that by the time she understood what they had done she was already one of them, which Clara reframes as survival built into a system designed to make leaving feel like self destruction, and when Lisette lashes out that I am their perfect product and that Evelyn never shuts up about me the room tilts because she confirms I was proof of concept. I state that I was a child, she agrees, and says that is why it sells so well.

I inhale and exhale instead of reacting, because the old pattern is to perform and call it control, and I refuse to give them that reflex any more. When I ask Lisette for Evelyn's current role she says Founding Director Emerita and Lead Advisor to RV Shoreline, adding that unofficially she is the one who shows up to remind everyone why they are here, which tells me exactly how much power she still holds.

I ask when Evelyn is next scheduled to be in the building and Lisette starts to deflect until I remind her I am not a member but a case study she built her theology on, and that Meridian's board will be very interested in what I have if she does not answer, while Clara quietly offers Lisette a way out by saying this is her chance to make it harder for them to keep doing this. Lisette looks between us and finally exhales before telling us about a Legacy Circle event in ten days, a private dinner with Meridian donors and old guard RV women, with doors at seven and a program from eight to eleven.

I tell her to add two names to the list and she warns that they will expect me to play the part and twist anything I say, which I counter by saying we will not give them improvisation because we will bring documentation, questions, and witnesses, while Clara states that if she is in that room it will be on her terms. Lisette looks exhausted and says we are going to blow this up, and I agree that eventually we will but that tonight we are only scheduling the surgery.

We leave through a side door into the alley like contraband being moved off site, and the night air hits my face clean and cold enough to feel real after the filtered atmosphere of the club. Clara walks beside me in silence until we are a block away and the wave logo has shrunk behind us, and when she says ten days I echo it back while she adds that we could still back out and tell ourselves we tried.

I tell her that I do not sleep and she replies fair, and under the harsh streetlight I admit that every cell in my body remembers what Evelyn turned me into and wants to run, even though I also do not want her telling my story for me or using my survival as marketing for other girls. Clara listens and asks so, and I answer that we go on purpose with a plan and not as offerings but as surgeons, which she reframes as wanting to open Evelyn up so that after decades of cutting into us she will finally have to hold still for a question she cannot rename.

She nods and tells me that the next ten days are prep, laying out rules that I do not see my mother, do not go to the club alone, and do not read Harrow's drafts at midnight, while she will worry about the paper trail, and I accept because what she is offering is shared load and distributed risk. We start walking again with the city humming around us and I think about ten days until Evelyn stands in a room she designed and I walk onto a different kind of dock, choosing where I stand this time and feeling what agency actually is, not power as performance but power as direction and a line I draw and refuse to let anyone else name.

Chapter Sixteen

———————— ∞ ————————

Refusal

W hen she says my name like a blessing, like ownership, like proof of her theology, I will look her in the eye and return it as something she has never expected from any of us, refusal, the word lands in my body before it lands in my mind. It isn't defiance, it isn't rebellion, it isn't even anger. When she says my name like a blessing, like ownership, like proof of her theology, I will look her in the eye and return it as something she has never expected from any of us, refusal, a word that lands in my body before it reaches my mind, not as defiance or rebellion or even anger, but as a shift in orientation that changes where I stand in relation to her.

Only weakness or mastery, collapse or control, this is neither, this is choosing to stop translating harm into meaning. As we walk, I feel my body searching for old cues, for the tightening in my shoulders that signals readiness, for the tilt of my chin that invites instruction, for the subtle rearrangement that tells the room I'm available to be shaped. I don't give it those cues, and that's the hardest part, not saying no out loud, but withholding the signals that made yes inevitable.

The city passes around us, indifferent and alive, windows lit with dinners, arguments, television glow, people making small choices that have nothing to do with power or proof, and I envy them in a way that surprises me. "Do you feel it?" Clara asks quietly, and I know what she means. "Yes," I say, "like my nervous system is waiting for permission to do something familiar," and when she says, "And?" I answer, "And it's not getting it." She nods and says, "That's refusal too."

I think about how often refusal has been aestheticized in the spaces Evelyn built, how saying no was allowed only if it was performed correctly, seductive, playful, temporary, a no that existed to make the eventual yes feel earned. This refusal isn't flirtation, it doesn't need witnesses, it doesn't ask to be understood, it doesn't improve anyone else's story. For the first time, my body doesn't feel like an argument, it feels like a boundary, and that frightens me more than obedience ever did.

Obedience gave me scripts, obedience gave me roles with applause built in, obedience meant I always knew what would happen next. Refusal is quiet, unscored, unrewarded, and refusal doesn't promise safety, only honesty. We stop at a crosswalk, the light is red, cars idle, engines humming, and a small, absurd thought crosses my mind, this is what consent actually looks like. Not desire surging forward, not endurance disguised as courage, just waiting until the signal changes.

I've spent years believing urgency was proof of authenticity, that if something pulled hard enough, fast enough, it must be true, but urgency was engineered. The dock trained it, the club monetized it, the lab intellectualized it, and refusal interrupts that circuit. When the light changes, I don't step forward immediately, neither does Clara, and we wait half a second longer than necessary, just long enough to feel the choice register in muscle. "This isn't bravery," I say, and she agrees, "No," then adds, "It's authorship."

That word settles differently. Authorship implies drafts, revisions, mistakes that don't invalidate the whole text, it implies identity isn't discovered intact, waiting to be unlocked, it's written, line by line, sometimes badly. Evelyn always spoke as if destiny was already complete, as if girls arrived as raw material and left as finished objects. Refusal dismantles that illusion, it says: I am not done.

My hands tremble again, softer this time, less like revolt, more like recalibration. I don't stop them, I don't interpret them, I let them be what they are. "You don't have to be steady," Clara says, as if reading the thought, and I answer, "I know," and for once, I actually do.

Refusal isn't the opposite of desire, it's the removal of coercion from the equation. What remains after that, wanting, not wanting, curiosity, fear, is allowed to be undefined. That may be the most radical thing of all.

I glance back once, at the street behind us, half-expecting to see the shoreline superimposed on asphalt, the dock ghosting out of concrete, but it isn't there. The past doesn't vanish, but it doesn't get to decide our direction anymore. We keep walking, not toward absolution, not toward justice, just forward, carrying refusal not as a weapon, but as a line we will not cross again. The confrontation isn't here yet, but for the first time, it's not chasing me out of the past, I'm walking toward it.

On the calendar, ten days is nothing, a bruise, a minor post-op recovery, a cluster of shifts you barely remember. In the body, ten days is a different unit, ten nights, ten mornings, ten times I wake up and decide whether I am a person making choices or a creature responding to cues. Agency is not a revelation, it's repetition.

Day One: I don't call my mother, that seems simple, it feels like amputation. My thumb hovers over her contact name more than once. Muscle memory: reach for the person who always explained reality for me, let her narrate, let her label, let her make me feel wrong in a way that feels familiar. Instead, I do what Clara said, I leave, not physically, not yet, I leave her voice where it belongs: outside my head.

It's strange, how the silence she leaves behind doesn't feel empty, it feels occupied. Like my own thoughts are finally allowed to take up space, and they don't know how. Day Two: I watch myself like a study, Patel's line returns from the emergency psych clinic: Study you like a scientist. I try, I keep a list in my notes app, not poetic, not dramatic, clinical.

Trigger: keys in hand at my apartment door, response: posture shift, chin lift, breath held, interpretation: preparing to be perceived. Trigger: male resident saying "Yes, Doctor," response: heat behind sternum, impulse to lean in, hand flex, interpretation: power cue; conditioning. Trigger: Clara's silence, response: panic; urge to perform to fill the space, interpretation: absence of script.

The list grows, so does my nausea, because the pattern is everywhere. Even in small things: the way I angle my body toward strangers in elevators, the way I adjust my tone on the phone with hospital admin, the way my eyes seek confirmation from faces I don't care about. Being watched is still my primary language, and the word refusal is not yet fluent, it is a stutter.

Day Three: I test my hands again in the simulation lab, but I do it differently. No audience, no stopwatch, no high stakes, just the instrument, the task, the breath. The tremor appears and disappears like a nervous animal deciding whether I'm safe, and when it comes, I don't punish it, I name it. You're not failure, I tell my fingers, you're information.

It doesn't stop, but it changes, less violent, more communicative. As if my body is trying to speak a truth it wasn't allowed to use language for. I practice a simple microvascular maneuver: clip placement on a synthetic vessel. The tremor flares at the moment of precision, not because the task is hard, because the task resembles obedience.

Hold still, be perfect, be praised for it. My jaw clenches, and then I do something I've never done with my own hands, I let them shake, not as surrender, as a controlled exposure. I let the tremor exist long enough that it stops being a catastrophe and becomes a sensation, a wave, a boundary, a line. The shaking eases a fraction, not because I forced it, because I stopped threatening it.

Day Four: Clara sends me a spreadsheet. Her brother has done what accountants do best: turned evil into columns, entities, directors, loan references, sponsorship agreements, event dates, board overlaps. Meridian isn't just funding research, Meridian is funding architecture. Spaces, staff training, co-branded "programming," a whole ecosystem designed to catch adult reenactment and call it healing.

I stare at the spreadsheet until my vision blurs. This is what I have been operating inside without seeing, an OR with velvet walls. I highlight lines with my cursor like I'm tracing tumor margins: RV Shoreline Holdings, Dockroom Collective, Meridian property arm. Harrow's title appears again like a stain that won't lift: Trauma & Identity Research Lead, non-voting advisor, a polite way of saying: architect with plausible deniability.

Day Five: I see Harrow in the hospital corridor, not planned, not staged, not courageous. He's leaving a meeting, smiling that crisp, controlled smile he uses when he wants people to feel grateful for his attention. "Jax," he says, and my spine tries to straighten like it's being tugged by a wire, "I heard you took some time off the schedule. I hope you're taking care of yourself."

There's the language, care, concern, the soft net of "support" that doubles as containment. "I'm fine," I start to say, because my mouth is a lying machine, then I stop, I look at him, I decide. "I'm not operating right now," I say, "and I'm not discussing my nervous system in a hallway."

Harrow's smile tightens. "Of course," he says smoothly, "whenever you're ready, my door is open. Meridian has resources," and I hear it like a trigger, not a sentence. Meridian, the ecosystem, the circulatory system. "No," I say.

His eyebrows rise. "No?" "No resources," I clarify, "no meetings. No drafts. No lab notes. Not from Meridian." He studies me, polite interest masking calculation. "Is there a reason?" he asks, and this is the moment where the old me would perform, offer a clever line, hint at vulnerability like a lure. Instead, I do something simpler. "I'm reviewing conflicts," I say, "that's all you need to know."

Harrow's smile doesn't move, but something behind it does, a slight cooling, a subtle retreat. Predators don't like prey that starts asking about doors. "Let me know how I can help," he says. "I will," I answer.

It's a lie, but it's a useful one. Agency, I'm learning, can be strategic without being manipulative. The difference is whose benefit it serves. Day Six: Clara and I rehearse, not seductively, not theatrically, procedurally. We sit in my living room with the folder spread out on the coffee table like imaging films before a case, and we map the dinner.

Who will be there, where Evelyn will stand, how the room will be staged: lighting, seating, the engineered moments for testimony and worship. The Dockroom isn't a club, it's a liturgy. "Do you think she'll recognize you?" Clara asks. "Yes," I say, and then, because honesty is now the only thing that makes my hands steady: "I think she's been recognizing me the whole time. I just didn't know what she was seeing."

Clara nods once. "Then we assume she's prepared," she says, "which means we prepare better." We develop rules: no improvisation with Evelyn, not yet, no private conversation, no physical contact, no accepting food or drink from her hand, no letting her frame the story first. And one more, the one that feels like swallowing glass: If I start to freeze, Clara speaks, not because I can't, because being seen while freezing is different than being frozen alone.

Day Seven: I almost break the rule. My mother calls. The phone lights up with her name, and my body does something humiliating: relief, as if the leash is being offered back, soft and familiar. I stare at it, ringing, ringing, and I think about the photo: her arms folded, chin lifted, not participating, assessing outcomes.

I let it go to voicemail. I don't listen, not yet, not because I'm brave, because I'm practicing something I was never taught: Not answering is a choice. Day Eight: I return to the observation booth above OR-2, not to punish myself, to remember what I actually love. Below the glass, a surgeon works, quiet, functional, unseductive.

The movement isn't worship, it isn't theatre, it's care in its purest form: attention applied to flesh, without the need to be adored for it. My hands tremble slightly on the railing, not because I want to cut, because I want to belong to myself while cutting. "I don't want to quit," I whisper, and Clara, beside me, doesn't say anything. She lets the sentence exist without being turned into performance.

Day Nine: I listen to my mother's voicemail. I do it at noon, in sunlight, sitting upright at my kitchen table with a glass of water beside me like I'm taking medication. Structure matters, if I'm going to hear her voice, I do it on purpose, not in the dark, not in my bed, not half-asleep, not as craving. The message is exactly what I expect.

Concern wrapped around control like a silk ribbon. "Jax, darling, I heard you had a... moment at work," she says, the pause between a and moment perfectly calibrated, "I'm worried about you. You've always carried too much. You don't have to be so... strong all the time. Call me. Let's talk. I love you." I sit very still. There it is again, love as leash, strength as accusation, and I don't call back.

Day Ten: We get confirmation. Lisette sends it from a burner address, three lines only: Added. Arrive 6:45 for pre-brief. Do not mention this email. Clara reads it over my shoulder. "She's choosing," Clara says quietly. "Or she's covering," I reply. "Both can be true," she says.

I look at my hands. They're steady, not because I'm calm, because the next step is precise. The night of the Legacy Circle arrives like weather, unavoidable, charged, full of pressure changes you can feel in your bones. I don't spend the day rehearsing, I don't feed the part of me that thinks performance will protect me, I do normal things: laundry, groceries, a walk outside, where nobody knows who I am and the sky doesn't care.

In the late afternoon, I sit in my car outside the hospital and watch staff stream in and out like ants, everyone with a role, everyone with a badge. For years, I used my badge like a shield. Tonight, I will use it like a scalpel, not to cut people, to cut through lies.

Clara meets me at my place at 6:10. She's dressed like she always is when she's serious: neutral, functional, ready to move. "You okay?" she asks. "No," I say. "Good," she replies, "then you're awake."

I pull the folder from my bag: the brochure, the corporate filings, the partnership draft, the wave logo comparisons, evidence. I also pull something else: a small index card, folded in half. Clara raises an eyebrow. "What's that?" she asks. "My script," I say.

She looks pleased and grim at the same time. "You wrote a script?" "Four sentences," I say, "anything beyond that becomes theatre." "Read them," she says. I unfold the card, my throat tightens, not from nerves, but from the unfamiliar intimacy of saying what I mean. "I will not be used as proof of your doctrine," I read. "I will not let you speak about my childhood as a success story." "I am not here to confess. I am here to ask questions." "And I will leave the moment this becomes a performance."

Clara exhales slowly. "That's consent," she says. We drive. The Dockroom's wave sign glows above the entrance like a halo drawn by someone who's never met a real god. This time, we don't wait in line.

Lisette has arranged a side entrance, a service door, the kind you use when you don't want to be seen arriving, because arrival is part of the performance. We're guided into a narrow corridor that smells like disinfectant and expensive perfume, two different ways of saying clean. Lisette meets us near the admin office. She looks paler than she did last time, more human.

"You're early," she says. "On purpose," Clara replies. Lisette nods. "Evelyn arrives at seven-thirty. Donors at seven. Program starts at eight. If you're going to do anything... do it before she takes the room." "She'll take it regardless," I say. Lisette's mouth tightens. "Yes. But there's a difference between her taking it and you giving it."

That surprises me. "Why are you doing this?" I ask. Lisette's eyes flick to the lake photograph on the wall and then away, as if she can't bear to look at the thing that taught her to call harm sacred. "Because you walked out of an OR to save a woman you could have killed," she says quietly, "and I've spent years walking people into rooms where they thought they were choosing, when really they were being steered."

She swallows. "I want one clean act," she finishes, "just one." "Clean acts are rare," Clara says. "Then let this be mine," Lisette replies. She opens the office door. "Pre-brief," she says.

Inside, the room is staged for intimacy that is not actually intimate: soft light, polished wood, water and neat little notebooks like this is a seminar, not a ritual. Lisette points to a door at the far end. "That leads to the private dining space. You'll be seated at the back."

"Back is fine," Clara says. "It won't feel fine when she's talking," Lisette warns. "I'm not here to feel fine," I say.

Lisette hands me a small card, a name badge, not Dr. Nile, just: Jax. My stomach turns. They're stripping the title, reducing the authority, returning me to the thing they prefer: a girl with a name, not a surgeon with a role. I look at Lisette. "Do I have to wear this?" I ask. Lisette hesitates. "Everyone does."

Agency isn't always grand. Sometimes it's adhesive paper. I tear the badge in half. Lisette's eyes widen. Clara's expression doesn't change, but something in her shoulders loosens, like she's just watched a chain snap. "I'm not participating in that," I say, and my voice is quiet enough that it's mine. Lisette nods once. "No badge," she says, "fine... be careful." "Careful is my profession," I reply.

We enter. The dining room is beautiful in the way predators love: warm lighting, velvet chairs, glassware catching light like jewellery, staff moving like shadows. The tables are arranged so the center is a stage, of course it is. We're seated at the back, as promised. Not hidden, observed.

I can feel the gaze in the room even before Evelyn arrives, the way people look when they think they're seeing something sacred. This is not a dinner, it's a sermon with table service. Clara sits beside me, not touching, close enough to be witness, far enough not to echo the dock. My hands tremble once under the table. Clara doesn't reach for them.

She shifts so her knee bumps mine, small contact that says: you are here. you are not alone. you are choosing. At 7:12 donors begin arriving in clusters, older couples, polished women, men with watches that announce their confidence. They greet one another with the easy warmth of people who have never had to worry that warmth might be transactional.

Lisette moves through the room like a competent ghost. Every time she passes our table, her eyes flick to mine, as if checking that I'm still solid. A waiter offers wine. "No," I say. He smiles, professional. "Sparkling water?" "No," I say again. He pauses, thrown for half a second by a woman who isn't selecting, isn't curating, isn't giving him a narrative he can serve. "Just water," Clara says gently, rescuing him from the discomfort.

The waiter nods and retreats. I watch the way my own body reacts to the simple act of refusing a drink. The old me would have accepted the wine for the ritual of it, held the glass properly, let it signal participation. Now I feel how hard my nervous system works to make refusal look normal. I don't have to make it look normal. That's the point.

At 7:28, the room quiets. Not because someone asks. Because the system expects the high priestess. At 7:31, she enters. Evelyn. Older than my body remembers, but not softer. Her hair is silver, but her posture is unchanged: serenity as dominance.

She smiles like she's blessing the air. Women turn toward her like flowers. Donors straighten. Staff become smaller. The room makes space without being told. That's what grooming does. It teaches bodies to anticipate.

My throat tightens. My vision narrows. For a fraction of a second, the dock overlays everything: wet wood, cold air, my mother's presence on the shore. I grip the edge of my chair until my fingers hurt. Clara's voice, low enough only I can hear: "Breathe. Not for her. For you."

Evelyn reaches the center and pauses, letting attention pool at her feet. Then she speaks. "Welcome, my darlings," she says. "Welcome to a night of legacy." Legacy. I taste blood.

She begins with the familiar arc: obedience disguised as freedom, being seen sold as healing, submission marketed as autonomy. She tells stories that are not stories so much as templates, each one designed to make the listener step into a pre-written role. Then she does what she always does. She looks around the room as if she's selecting people with her eyes, blessing them into significance.

"And we have among us tonight," Evelyn says warmly, "one of our most extraordinary restorations." Her gaze sweeps the room like a searchlight. It lands on me. Not confusion. Not surprise. Recognition. Ownership.

Her smile deepens. "Jax," she says, like she's tasting the word. "Our dock girl. Our miracle." The room turns to look at me. Attention floods my skin like acid. This is the moment the old me would stand, smile, perform humility, let them adore the narrative.

I don't move yet. I let the sensation happen without translating it into behaviour. Under the table my fingers curl around the index card like it's an instrument handle. Evelyn continues, voice honeyed. "She became a surgeon," she says, and the room murmurs appreciative awe, "a woman who saves lives with her hands, hands she once believed were only for trembling. Hands she learned to steady through faith and,"

I stand. The movement is simple. No drama. Just getting to my feet. The room freezes as if I've broken a spell. Evelyn's smile holds, but her eyes sharpen. I speak before she can. "I'm not here to be your miracle," I say.

My voice is steady. Not seductive. Not theatrical. Just true. A ripple of discomfort moves through the room. Some people glance away. Some lean in. Everyone is hungry for a scene.

Evelyn's mouth lifts slightly, indulgent. "Oh, sweetheart," she says softly, "you're nervous. That's all. This is a lot of love in one room." The word love lands like a hook. I feel the old reflex ignite: duel, perform, prove. Instead, I use the script.

"I will not be used as proof of your doctrine," I say, word for word. "I will not let you speak about my childhood as a success story." "I am not here to confess. I am here to ask questions." "And I will leave the moment this becomes a performance." Silence spreads, thick as surgical drape.

Evelyn's smile shifts. Not gone. Refined. "Questions are welcome," she says smoothly. "We are a community rooted in transparency and consent." Consent. I almost laugh. Clara stands up beside me.

Not in front. Not behind. With. Her presence changes the geometry of the room. It is no longer one woman speaking against a system. It is two people refusing the script together. "My question is simple," I say, and I pull the brochure from the folder. "Do you recognize this?"

I hold it up. Some donors frown, trying to place it. Evelyn's eyes flick to it, and something like caution flashes across her face. "That's an old document," she says. "A different era." "A different branding," Clara says, voice calm. "Same doctrine."

Evelyn's gaze slides to Clara. It sharpens with recognition, slower, like she's tasting a name she hasn't said in a while. "And who are you, dear?" Evelyn asks. Clara doesn't flinch. "A witness," she says. The word hits the room like a thrown object.

Evelyn's expression softens into practiced compassion. "Oh," she says, as if she's just remembered a sad story she can narrate. "Clara. You always were... sensitive." Clara's jaw tightens. I interrupt before Evelyn can turn Clara into an anecdote.

"Meridian," I say, and the word changes the air. Donors shift. Someone's face tightens. "Meridian funded The Restored Vessel. Meridian funds trauma research at my hospital. Meridian is tied to this club through RV Shoreline Holdings. I have the filings." A hiss of whispers. People don't like evidence. Evidence interrupts myth.

Evelyn's voice remains warm. "Jax," she says, "you're overwhelmed. You've been through stress at work. We've heard. And when women are under strain, they sometimes," Gaslighting with maternal frosting. Clara's voice cuts clean. "No," she says. "We're not doing that."

The room flinches. Evelyn looks at Clara with a smile that is almost affectionate. "Still so direct," she says. Clara doesn't move. "Still so practiced," she replies. My hands tremble at my sides, not from fear of Evelyn, but from the unfamiliar reality of standing up without performing it.

Evelyn returns her gaze to me, and the softness is gone now. The warmth remains, but it's weaponized. "This isn't the place for this," she says. "We can talk privately." No private rooms. No scripts. "No," I say.

One word. A cut. A boundary opened. Evelyn's mouth tightens almost imperceptibly. "You don't want to humiliate yourself," she says gently. There it is. Shame as leash. My body wants to respond the old way: prove I'm not humiliated by dazzling them.

Instead, I do the opposite. I let myself be plain. "I'm already humiliated," I say, "not by standing here. By realizing how long I let you tell my story as if it belonged to you." The room goes very still. Evelyn stares at me.

And in her eyes I see something worse than anger: satisfaction. As if my refusal is just another part in her drama. As if she can still use it. Clara's hand touches my elbow, brief, human, anchoring. "Do you want to leave?" she whispers.

The question is the purest agency I've ever been offered. Leaving is allowed. Leaving is not sin. Leaving is not cowardice. Leaving is choice. I look at Evelyn, at the donors, at the women watching like this is entertainment. I decide.

"Not yet," I whisper back. I lift the partnership draft, the grainy CONFIDENTIAL printout. "I have one more question," I say. Evelyn's eyes narrow. "This document," I continue, "describes 'anonymized behavioral data' collected through 'trauma-informed power exchange' programming. It reads like Harrow's language. Harrow is listed as a non-voting advisor to this board."

Now the donors truly shift. Meridian is money. Money is fear. "I want to know," I say, "how long Meridian has been collecting data on reenactment and calling it research." Evelyn's voice turns silky, dangerous. "Careful, darling," she says. "Accusations can ruin lives."

"I know," I reply. "Mine was ruined before I had a driver's licence." A gasp. Someone drops a fork. Clara's breath catches, not because she's surprised, but because she knows what I just did. I named it. Not poetically. Not obliquely. Plainly enough that the room can't pretend it's just story.

Evelyn's eyes harden. The warmth is gone now. Only control remains. And for the first time, I see her clearly: not mystic, not healer, not mentor. A system in a human shape. "You're tired," Evelyn says, voice cold under the sweetness. "You don't know what you're saying."

My hands tremble harder. Not because I'm losing control. Because I'm refusing to perform it. "I know exactly what I'm saying," I reply. And then, because agency is not endurance, and I don't need to prove I can stand on a dock forever: "I'm leaving."

The words land like a door shutting. Evelyn tilts her head, almost amused. "Jax," she says, and the way she says my name is a hook, "running away doesn't make you free." Clara's voice is a blade. "Leaving is not running," she says. "It's choosing."

I pick up my folder. I don't storm out. I don't perform exit. I walk. Clara walks beside me. Behind us, the room erupts, whispers, outrage, people trying to stitch the myth back together before it bleeds out.

At the threshold, I pause. Not for them. For me. I turn just enough to look at Evelyn one last time. She watches me with the same auditing gaze my mother wore in the photo: assessing outcomes. Measuring whether I will return. I don't give her a speech. I don't give her tears. I give her the simplest thing. Nothing.

I leave. Outside, night air hits me like oxygen after anesthesia. My hands shake violently now, full-bodied, honest. Clara doesn't touch them. She stands close, steady as a wall. "You did it," she says quietly. "I left," I correct, breath ragged. "Yes," she replies, "you left. On purpose."

The tremor continues. Not because I'm broken. Because something in me has finally stopped holding still on command. And that, terrifying as it is, feels like the beginning of agency, not the kind that dazzles, the kind that survives. We walk into the city. The wave sign glows behind us like a shoreline I'm no longer willing to stand on. For the first time, the past isn't dragging me, it's following, and I'm not turning around to let it catch me.

Chapter Seventeen

Legacy Circle

When she says my name like a blessing, like ownership, like proof of her theology, I will look her in the eye and return it as something she has never expected from any of us. Refusal. The word lands in my body before it lands in my mind. It isn't defiance. It isn't rebellion. It isn't even anger. When she says my name like a blessing, like ownership, like proof of her theology, I will look her in the eye and return it as something she has never expected from any of us, refusal, a word that lands in my body before it reaches my mind, not as defiance or rebellion or even anger, but as a shift in orientation that changes where I stand in relation to her.

Only weakness or mastery, collapse or control. This is neither. This is choosing to stop translating harm into meaning. As we walk, I feel my body searching for old cues, for the tightening in my shoulders that signals readiness, for the tilt of my chin that invites instruction, for the subtle rearrangement that tells the room I'm available to be shaped. I don't give it those cues.

That's the hardest part, not saying no out loud, but withholding the signals that made yes inevitable. The city passes around us, indifferent and alive, windows lit with dinners, arguments, television glow, people making small choices that have nothing to do with power or proof. I envy them in a way that surprises me. "Do you feel it?" Clara asks quietly. I know what she means. "Yes," I say.

"Like my nervous system is waiting for permission to do something familiar." "And?" "And it's not getting it." She nods. "That's refusal too." I think about how often refusal has been aestheticized in the spaces Evelyn built, how saying no was allowed only if it was performed correctly, seductive, playful, temporary, a no that existed to make the eventual yes feel earned.

This refusal isn't flirtation. It doesn't need witnesses. It doesn't ask to be understood. It doesn't improve anyone else's story. For the first time, my body doesn't feel like an argument. It feels like a boundary.

That frightens me more than obedience ever did. Obedience gave me scripts. Obedience gave me roles with applause built in. Obedience meant I always knew what would happen next. Refusal is quiet. Unscored.

Unrewarded. Refusal doesn't promise safety, only honesty. We stop at a crosswalk, the light is red, cars idle, engines humming, and a small, absurd thought crosses my mind, this is what consent actually looks like. Not desire surging forward, not endurance disguised as courage, just waiting until the signal changes. I've spent years believing urgency was proof of authenticity, that if something pulled hard enough, fast enough, it must be true.

But urgency was engineered. The dock trained it. The club monetized it. The lab intellectualized it. Refusal interrupts that circuit. When the light changes, I don't step forward immediately.

Neither does Clara. We wait half a second longer than necessary, just long enough to feel the choice register in muscle. "This isn't bravery," I say. "No," she agrees. "It's authorship." That word settles differently. Authorship implies drafts, revisions, mistakes that don't invalidate the whole text, it implies identity isn't discovered intact, waiting to be unlocked, it's written, line by line, sometimes badly.

Evelyn always spoke as if destiny was already complete, as if girls arrived as raw material and left as finished objects. Refusal dismantles that illusion. It says: I am not done. My hands tremble again, softer this time, less like revolt, more like recalibration. I don't stop them.

I don't interpret them. I let them be what they are. "You don't have to be steady," Clara says, as if reading the thought. "I know," I answer. And for once, I actually do.

Refusal isn't the opposite of desire. It's the removal of coercion from the equation. What remains after that, wanting, not wanting, curiosity, fear, is allowed to be undefined. That may be the most radical thing of all. I glance back once, at the street behind us, half-expecting to see the shoreline superimposed on asphalt, the dock ghosting out of concrete.

It isn't there. The past doesn't vanish. But it doesn't get to decide our direction anymore. We keep walking. Not toward absolution. Not toward justice. Just forward, carrying refusal not as a weapon, but as a line we will not cross again. The confrontation isn't here yet. But for the first time, it's not chasing me out of the past. I'm walking toward it.

On the calendar, ten days is nothing, a bruise, a minor post-op recovery, a cluster of shifts you barely remember. In the body, ten days is a different unit. Ten nights. Ten mornings. Ten times I wake up and decide whether I am a person making choices or a creature responding to cues. Agency is not a revelation. It's repetition. Day One: I don't call my mother.

That seems simple. It feels like amputation. My thumb hovers over her contact name more than once. Muscle memory: reach for the person who always explained reality for me, let her narrate, let her label, let her make me feel wrong in a way that feels familiar. Instead, I do what Clara said. I leave. Not physically. Not yet.

I leave her voice where it belongs: outside my head. It's strange, how the silence she leaves behind doesn't feel empty. It feels occupied. Like my own thoughts are finally allowed to take up space, and they don't know how. Day Two: I watch myself like a study. Patel's line returns from the emergency psych clinic: Study you like a scientist. I try.

I keep a list in my notes app. Not poetic. Not dramatic. Clinical. Trigger: keys in hand at my apartment door. Response: posture shift, chin lift, breath held. Interpretation: preparing to be perceived. Trigger: male resident saying "Yes, Doctor." Response: heat behind sternum, impulse to lean in, hand flex. Interpretation: power cue; conditioning.

Trigger: Clara's silence. Response: panic; urge to perform to fill the space. Interpretation: absence of script. The list grows. So does my nausea. Because the pattern is everywhere. Even in small things: the way I angle my body toward strangers in elevators, the way I adjust my tone on the phone with hospital admin, the way my eyes seek confirmation from faces I don't care about.

Being watched is still my primary language. And the word refusal is not yet fluent. It is a stutter. Day Three: I test my hands again in the simulation lab, but I do it differently. No audience. No stopwatch. No high stakes. Just the instrument. The task. The breath.

The tremor appears and disappears like a nervous animal deciding whether I'm safe. When it comes, I don't punish it. I name it. You're not failure, I tell my fingers. You're information. It doesn't stop. But it changes. Less violent. More communicative. As if my body is trying to speak a truth it wasn't allowed to use language for.

I practice a simple microvascular maneuver: clip placement on a synthetic vessel. The tremor flares at the moment of precision. Not because the task is hard. Because the task resembles obedience. Hold still. Be perfect. Be praised for it. My jaw clenches. And then I do something I've never done with my own hands. I let them shake. Not as surrender. As a controlled exposure.

I let the tremor exist long enough that it stops being a catastrophe and becomes a sensation. A wave. A boundary. A line. The shaking eases a fraction. Not because I forced it. Because I stopped threatening it. Day Four: Clara sends me a spreadsheet. Her brother has done what accountants do best: turned evil into columns. Entities. Directors. Loan references. Sponsorship agreements. Event dates. Board overlaps. Meridian isn't just funding research.

Meridian is funding architecture. Spaces. Staff training. Co-branded "programming." A whole ecosystem designed to catch adult reenactment and call it healing. I stare at the spreadsheet until my vision blurs. This is what I have been operating inside without seeing. An OR with velvet walls. I highlight lines with my cursor like I'm tracing tumor margins. RV Shoreline Holdings. Dockroom Collective. Meridian property arm. Harrow's title appears again like a stain that won't lift.

Trauma & Identity Research Lead. Non-voting advisor. A polite way of saying: architect with plausible deniability. Day Five: I see Harrow in the hospital corridor. Not planned. Not staged. Not courageous. He's leaving a meeting, smiling that crisp, controlled smile he uses when he wants people to feel grateful for his attention. "Jax," he says, and my spine tries to straighten like it's being tugged by a wire.

"I heard you took some time off the schedule. I hope you're taking care of yourself." There's the language. Care. Concern. The soft net of "support" that doubles as containment. "I'm fine," I start to say, because my mouth is a lying machine. Then I stop. I look at him. I decide.

"I'm not operating right now," I say. "And I'm not discussing my nervous system in a hallway." Harrow's smile tightens. "Of course," he says smoothly. "Whenever you're ready, my door is open. Meridian has resources, " I hear it like a trigger, not a sentence. Meridian. The ecosystem. The circulatory system. "No," I say. His eyebrows rise. "No?" "No resources," I clarify. "No meetings. No drafts. No lab notes. Not from Meridian."

He studies me, polite interest masking calculation. "Is there a reason?" he asks. This is the moment where the old me would perform, offer a clever line, hint at vulnerability like a lure. Instead, I do something simpler. "I'm reviewing conflicts," I say. "That's all you need to know." Harrow's smile doesn't move, but something behind it does. A slight cooling. A subtle retreat. Predators don't like prey that starts asking about doors.

"Let me know how I can help," he says. "I will," I answer. It's a lie. But it's a useful one. Agency, I'm learning, can be strategic without being manipulative. The difference is whose benefit it serves. Day Six: Clara and I rehearse. Not seductively. Not theatrically. Procedurally. We sit in my living room with the folder spread out on the coffee table like imaging films before a case.

We map the dinner. Who will be there. Where Evelyn will stand. How the room will be staged: lighting, seating, the engineered moments for testimony and worship. The Dockroom isn't a club. It's a liturgy. "Do you think she'll recognize you?" Clara asks. "Yes," I say. And then, because honesty is now the only thing that makes my hands steady: "I think she's been recognizing me the whole time. I just didn't know what she was seeing."

Clara nods once. "Then we assume she's prepared," she says. "Which means we prepare better." We develop rules. No improvisation with Evelyn. Not yet. No private conversation. No physical contact. No accepting food or drink from her hand. No letting her frame the story first. And one more, the one that feels like swallowing glass: If I start to freeze, Clara speaks. Not because I can't. Because being seen while freezing is different than being frozen alone.

Day Seven: I almost break the rule. My mother calls. The phone lights up with her name, and my body does something humiliating: relief, as if the leash is being offered back, soft and familiar. I stare at it. Ringing. Ringing. I think about the photo: her arms folded, chin lifted, not participating, assessing outcomes. I let it go to voicemail. I don't listen. Not yet. Not because I'm brave. Because I'm practicing something I was never taught: Not answering is a choice.

Day Eight: I return to the observation booth above OR-2. Not to punish myself. To remember what I actually love. Below the glass, a surgeon works. Quiet. Functional. Unseductive. The movement isn't worship. It isn't theatre. It's care in its purest form: attention applied to flesh, without the need to be adored for it.

My hands tremble slightly on the railing. Not because I want to cut. Because I want to belong to myself while cutting. "I don't want to quit," I whisper. Clara, beside me, doesn't say anything. She lets the sentence exist without being turned into performance. Day Nine: I listen to my mother's voicemail. I do it at noon, in sunlight, sitting upright at my kitchen table with a glass of water beside me like I'm taking medication.

Structure matters. If I'm going to hear her voice, I do it on purpose. Not in the dark. Not in my bed. Not half-asleep. Not as craving. The message is exactly what I expect. Concern wrapped around control like a silk ribbon. "Jax, darling, I heard you had a...

moment at work," she says, the pause between a and moment perfectly calibrated. "I'm worried about you. You've always carried too much. You don't have to be so... strong all the time. Call me. Let's talk. I love you."

I sit very still. There it is again. Love as leash. Strength as accusation. I don't call back. Day Ten: We get confirmation. Lisette sends it from a burner address, three lines only: Added. Arrive 6:45 for pre-brief. Do not mention this email. Clara reads it over my shoulder. "She's choosing," Clara says quietly. "Or she's covering," I reply. "Both can be true," she says.

I look at my hands. They're steady. Not because I'm calm. Because the next step is precise. The night of the Legacy Circle arrives like weather. Unavoidable. Charged. Full of pressure changes you can feel in your bones. I don't spend the day rehearsing. I don't feed the part of me that thinks performance will protect me.

I do normal things. Laundry. Groceries. A walk outside, where nobody knows who I am and the sky doesn't care. In the late afternoon, I sit in my car outside the hospital and watch staff stream in and out like ants. Everyone with a role. Everyone with a badge. For years, I used my badge like a shield. Tonight, I will use it like a scalpel. Not to cut people. To cut through lies.

Clara meets me at my place at 6:10. She's dressed like she always is when she's serious: neutral, functional, ready to move. "You okay?" she asks. "No," I say. "Good," she replies. "Then you're awake." I pull the folder from my bag. The brochure. The corporate filings. The partnership draft. The wave logo comparisons. Evidence.

I also pull something else: a small index card, folded in half. Clara raises an eyebrow. "What's that?" she asks. "My script," I say. She looks pleased and grim at the same time. "You wrote a script?" "Four sentences," I say. "Anything beyond that becomes theatre." "Read them," she says. I unfold the card. My throat tightens, not from nerves, but from the unfamiliar intimacy of saying what I mean.

"I will not be used as proof of your doctrine," I read. "I will not let you speak about my childhood as a success story." "I am not here to confess. I am here to ask questions." "And I will leave the moment this becomes a performance." Clara exhales slowly. "That's consent," she says. We drive. The Dockroom's wave sign glows above the entrance like a halo drawn by someone who's never met a real god. This time, we don't wait in line.

Lisette has arranged a side entrance. A service door. The kind you use when you don't want to be seen arriving, because arrival is part of the performance. We're guided into a narrow corridor that smells like disinfectant and expensive perfume, two different ways of saying clean. Lisette meets us near the admin office. She looks paler than she did last time. More human. "You're early," she says. "On purpose," Clara replies. Lisette nods. "Evelyn arrives at seven-thirty. Donors at seven. Program starts at eight. If you're going to do anything... do it before she takes the room."

"She'll take it regardless," I say. Lisette's mouth tightens. "Yes. But there's a difference between her taking it and you giving it." That surprises me. "Why are you doing this?" I ask. Lisette's eyes flick to the lake photograph on the wall and then away, as if she can't bear to look at the thing that taught her to call harm sacred. "Because you walked out of an OR to save a woman you could have killed," she says quietly. "And I've spent years walking people into rooms where they thought they were choosing, when really they were being steered."

She swallows. "I want one clean act," she finishes. "Just one." "Clean acts are rare," Clara says. "Then let this be mine," Lisette replies. She opens the office door. "Pre-brief," she says. Inside, the room is staged for intimacy that is not actually intimate: soft light, polished wood, water and neat little notebooks like this is a seminar, not a ritual. Lisette points to a door at the far end. "That leads to the private dining space. You'll be seated at the back." "Back is fine," Clara says. "It won't feel fine when she's talking," Lisette warns. "I'm not here to feel fine," I say.

Lisette hands me a small card. A name badge. Not Dr. Nile. Just: Jax. My stomach turns. They're stripping the title. Reducing the authority. Returning me to the thing they prefer: a girl with a name, not a surgeon with a role. I look at Lisette. "Do I have to wear this?" I ask. Lisette hesitates. "Everyone does." Agency isn't always grand. Sometimes it's adhesive paper.

I tear the badge in half. Lisette's eyes widen. Clara's expression doesn't change, but something in her shoulders loosens, like she's just watched a chain snap. "I'm not participating in that," I say, and my voice is quiet enough that it's mine. Lisette nods once. "No badge," she says. "Fine. Just... be careful." "Careful is my profession," I reply. We enter.

The dining room is beautiful in the way predators love: warm lighting, velvet chairs, glassware catching light like jewellery, staff moving like shadows. The tables are arranged so the center is a stage. Of course it is. We're seated at the back, as promised. Not hidden. Observed. I can feel the gaze in the room even before Evelyn arrives, the way people look when they think they're seeing something sacred.

This is not a dinner. It's a sermon with table service. Clara sits beside me, not touching, close enough to be witness, far enough not to echo the dock. My hands tremble once under the table. Clara doesn't reach for them. She shifts so her knee bumps mine, small contact that says: you are here. you are not alone. you are choosing. At 7:12 donors begin arriving in clusters, older couples, polished women, men with watches that announce their confidence.

They greet one another with the easy warmth of people who have never had to worry that warmth might be transactional. Lisette moves through the room like a competent ghost. Every time she passes our table, her eyes flick to mine, as if checking that I'm still solid. A waiter offers wine. "No," I say. He smiles, professional. "Sparkling water?" "No," I say again. He pauses, thrown for half a second by a woman who isn't selecting, isn't curating, isn't giving him a narrative he can serve.

"Just water," Clara says gently, rescuing him from the discomfort. The waiter nods and retreats. I watch the way my own body reacts to the simple act of refusing a drink. The old me would have accepted the wine for the ritual of it, held the glass properly, let it signal participation. Now I feel how hard my nervous system works to make refusal look normal. I don't have to make it look normal. That's the point.

At 7:28, the room quiets. Not because someone asks. Because the system expects the high priestess. At 7:31, she enters. Evelyn. Older than my body remembers, but not softer. Her hair is silver, but her posture is unchanged: serenity as dominance. She smiles like she's blessing the air. Women turn toward her like flowers. Donors straighten. Staff become smaller. The room makes space without being told.

That's what grooming does. It teaches bodies to anticipate. My throat tightens. My vision narrows. For a fraction of a second, the dock overlays everything: wet wood, cold air, my mother's presence on the shore. I grip the edge of my chair until my fingers hurt. Clara's voice, low enough only I can hear: "Breathe. Not for her. For you." Evelyn reaches the center and pauses, letting attention pool at her feet. Then she speaks. "Welcome, my darlings," she says. "Welcome to a night of legacy."

Legacy. I taste blood. She begins with the familiar arc: obedience disguised as freedom, being seen sold as healing, submission marketed as autonomy. She tells stories that are not stories so much as templates, each one designed to make the listener step into a pre-written role. Then she does what she always does. She looks around the room as if she's selecting people with her eyes, blessing them into significance. "And we have among us tonight," Evelyn says warmly, "one of our most extraordinary restorations."

Her gaze sweeps the room like a searchlight. It lands on me. Not confusion. Not surprise. Recognition. Ownership. Her smile deepens. "Jax," she says, like she's tasting the word. "Our dock girl. Our miracle." The room turns to look at me. Attention floods my skin like acid. This is the moment the old me would stand, smile, perform humility, let them adore the narrative.

I don't move yet. I let the sensation happen without translating it into behaviour. Under the table my fingers curl around the index card like it's an instrument handle. Evelyn continues, voice honeyed. "She became a surgeon," she says, and the room murmurs appreciative awe. "A woman who saves lives with her hands, hands she once believed were only for trembling. Hands she learned to steady through faith and, " I stand.

The movement is simple. No drama. Just getting to my feet. The room freezes as if I've broken a spell. Evelyn's smile holds, but her eyes sharpen. I speak before she can. "I'm not here to be your miracle," I say. My voice is steady. Not seductive. Not theatrical. Just true. A ripple of discomfort moves through the room. Some people glance away. Some lean in. Everyone is hungry for a scene.

Evelyn's mouth lifts slightly, indulgent. "Oh, sweetheart," she says softly, "you're nervous. That's all. This is a lot of love in one room." The word love lands like a hook. I feel the old reflex ignite: duel, perform, prove. Instead, I use the script. "I will not be used as proof of your doctrine," I say, word for word. "I will not let you speak about my childhood as a success story." "I am not here to confess. I am here to ask questions." "And I will leave the moment this becomes a performance."

Silence spreads, thick as surgical drape. Evelyn's smile shifts. Not gone. Refined. "Questions are welcome," she says smoothly. "We are a community rooted in transparency and consent." Consent. I almost laugh. Clara stands up beside me. Not in front. Not behind. With. Her presence changes the geometry of the room. It is no longer one woman speaking against a system. It is two people refusing the script together.

"My question is simple," I say, and I pull the brochure from the folder. "Do you recognize this?" I hold it up. Some donors frown, trying to place it. Evelyn's eyes flick to it, and something like caution flashes across her face. "That's an old document," she says. "A different era." "A different branding," Clara says, voice calm. "Same doctrine." Evelyn's gaze slides to Clara. It sharpens with recognition, slower, like she's tasting a name she hasn't said in a while.

"And who are you, dear?" Evelyn asks. Clara doesn't flinch. "A witness," she says. The word hits the room like a thrown object. Evelyn's expression softens into practiced compassion. "Oh," she says, as if she's just remembered a sad story she can narrate. "Clara. You always were... sensitive." Clara's jaw tightens. I interrupt before Evelyn can turn Clara into an anecdote.

"Meridian," I say, and the word changes the air. Donors shift. Someone's face tightens. "Meridian funded The Restored Vessel. Meridian funds trauma research at my hospital. Meridian is tied to this club through RV Shoreline Holdings. I have the filings." A hiss of whispers. People don't like evidence. Evidence interrupts myth. Evelyn's voice remains warm. "Jax," she says, "you're overwhelmed. You've been through stress at work. We've heard. And when women are under strain, they sometimes, " Gaslighting with maternal frosting. Clara's voice cuts clean. "No," she says. "We're not doing that."

The room flinches. Evelyn looks at Clara with a smile that is almost affectionate. "Still so direct," she says. Clara doesn't move. "Still so practiced," she replies. My hands tremble at my sides, not from fear of Evelyn, but from the unfamiliar reality of standing up without performing it. Evelyn returns her gaze to me, and the softness is gone now. The warmth remains, but it's weaponized. "This isn't the place for this," she says. "We can talk privately." No private rooms. No scripts. "No," I say.

One word. A cut. A boundary opened. Evelyn's mouth tightens almost imperceptibly. "You don't want to humiliate yourself," she says gently. There it is. Shame as leash. My body wants to respond the old way: prove I'm not humiliated by dazzling them. Instead, I do the opposite. I let myself be plain. "I'm already humiliated," I say. "Not by standing here. By realizing how long I let you tell my story as if it belonged to you." The room goes very still. Evelyn stares at me.

And in her eyes I see something worse than anger: satisfaction. As if my refusal is just another part in her drama. As if she can still use it. Clara's hand touches my elbow, brief, human, anchoring. "Do you want to leave?" she whispers. The question is the purest agency I've ever been offered. Leaving is allowed. Leaving is not sin. Leaving is not cowardice. Leaving is choice. I look at Evelyn, at the donors, at the women watching like this is entertainment. I decide.

"Not yet," I whisper back. I lift the partnership draft, the grainy CONFIDENTIAL printout. "I have one more question," I say. Evelyn's eyes narrow. "This document," I continue, "describes 'anonymized behavioral data' collected through 'trauma-informed power exchange' programming. It reads like Harrow's language. Harrow is listed as a non-voting advisor to this board." Now the donors truly shift. Meridian is money. Money is fear. "I want to know," I say, "how long Meridian has been collecting data on reenactment and calling it research."

Evelyn's voice turns silky, dangerous. "Careful, darling," she says. "Accusations can ruin lives." "I know," I reply. "Mine was ruined before I had a driver's licence." A gasp. Someone drops a fork. Clara's breath catches, not because she's surprised, but because she knows what I just did. I named it. Not poetically. Not obliquely. Plainly enough that the room can't pretend it's just story. Evelyn's eyes harden. The warmth is gone now. Only control remains. And for the first time, I see her clearly: not mystic, not healer, not mentor. A system in a human shape.

"You're tired," Evelyn says, voice cold under the sweetness. "You don't know what you're saying." My hands tremble harder. Not because I'm losing control. Because I'm refusing to perform it. "I know exactly what I'm saying," I reply. And then, because agency is not endurance, and I don't need to prove I can stand on a dock forever: "I'm leaving." The words land like a door shutting.

Evelyn tilts her head, almost amused. "Jax," she says, and the way she says my name is a hook. "Running away doesn't make you free." Clara's voice is a blade. "Leaving is not running," she says. "It's choosing." I pick up my folder. I don't storm out. I don't perform exit. I walk. Clara walks beside me. Behind us, the room erupts, whispers, outrage, people trying to stitch the myth back together before it bleeds out.

At the threshold, I pause. Not for them. For me. I turn just enough to look at Evelyn one last time. She watches me with the same auditing gaze my mother wore in the photo: assessing outcomes. Measuring whether I will return. I don't give her a speech. I don't give her tears. I give her the simplest thing. Nothing. I leave.

Outside, night air hits me like oxygen after anesthesia. My hands shake violently now. Full-bodied. Honest. Clara doesn't touch them. She stands close, steady as a wall. "You did it," she says quietly. "I left," I correct, breath ragged. "Yes," she replies. "You left on purpose." The tremor continues. Not because I'm broken. Because something in me has finally stopped holding still on command.

Chapter Eighteen

Repetition

When she says my name like a blessing, like ownership, like proof of her theology, I will look her in the eye and return it as something she has never expected from any of us. Refusal. The word lands in my body before it lands in my mind. It isn't defiance. It isn't rebellion. It isn't even anger. When she says my name like a blessing, like ownership, like proof of her theology, I will look her in the eye and return it as something she has never expected from any of us, refusal, a word that lands in my body before it reaches my mind, not as defiance or rebellion or even anger, but as a shift in orientation that changes where I stand in relation to her.

Only weakness or mastery, collapse or control. This is neither. This is choosing to stop translating harm into meaning. As we walk, I feel my body searching for old cues, for the tightening in my shoulders that signals readiness, for the tilt of my chin that invites instruction, for the subtle rearrangement that tells the room I'm available to be shaped. I don't give it those cues.

That's the hardest part, not saying no out loud, but withholding the signals that made yes inevitable. The city passes around us, indifferent and alive, windows lit with dinners, arguments, television glow, people making small choices that have nothing to do with power or proof. I envy them in a way that surprises me. "Do you feel it?" Clara asks quietly. I know what she means. "Yes," I say.

"Like my nervous system is waiting for permission to do something familiar." "And?" "And it's not getting it." She nods. "That's refusal too." I think about how often refusal has been aestheticized in the spaces Evelyn built, how saying no was allowed only if it was performed correctly, seductive, playful, temporary, a no that existed to make the eventual yes feel earned.

This refusal isn't flirtation. It doesn't need witnesses. It doesn't ask to be understood. It doesn't improve anyone else's story. For the first time, my body doesn't feel like an argument. It feels like a boundary.

That frightens me more than obedience ever did. Obedience gave me scripts. Obedience gave me roles with applause built in. Obedience meant I always knew what would happen next. Refusal is quiet. Unscored.

Unrewarded. Refusal doesn't promise safety, only honesty. We stop at a crosswalk, the light is red, cars idle, engines humming, and a small, absurd thought crosses my mind, this is what consent actually looks like. Not desire surging forward, not endurance disguised as courage, just waiting until the signal changes. I've spent years believing urgency was proof of authenticity, that if something pulled hard enough, fast enough, it must be true.

But urgency was engineered. The dock trained it. The club monetized it. The lab intellectualized it. Refusal interrupts that circuit. When the light changes, I don't step forward immediately.

Neither does Clara. We wait half a second longer than necessary, just long enough to feel the choice register in muscle. "This isn't bravery," I say. "No," she agrees. "It's authorship." That word settles differently. Authorship implies drafts, revisions, mistakes that don't invalidate the whole text, it implies identity isn't discovered intact, waiting to be unlocked, it's written, line by line, sometimes badly.

Evelyn always spoke as if destiny was already complete, as if girls arrived as raw material and left as finished objects. Refusal dismantles that illusion. It says: I am not done. My hands tremble again, softer this time, less like revolt, more like recalibration. I don't stop them.

I don't interpret them. I let them be what they are. "You don't have to be steady," Clara says, as if reading the thought. "I know," I answer. And for once, I actually do.

Refusal isn't the opposite of desire. It's the removal of coercion from the equation. What remains after that, wanting, not wanting, curiosity, fear, is allowed to be undefined. That may be the most radical thing of all. I glance back once, at the street behind us, half-expecting to see the shoreline superimposed on asphalt, the dock ghosting out of concrete.

It isn't there. The past doesn't vanish. But it doesn't get to decide our direction anymore. We keep walking. Not toward absolution. Not toward justice. Just forward, carrying refusal not as a weapon, but as a line we will not cross again. The confrontation isn't here yet. But for the first time, it's not chasing me out of the past. I'm walking toward it.

On the calendar, ten days is nothing, a bruise, a minor post-op recovery, a cluster of shifts you barely remember. In the body, ten days is a different unit. Ten nights. Ten mornings. Ten times I wake up and decide whether I am a person making choices or a creature responding to cues. Agency is not a revelation. It's repetition. Day One: I don't call my mother.

That seems simple. It feels like amputation. My thumb hovers over her contact name more than once. Muscle memory: reach for the person who always explained reality for me, let her narrate, let her label, let her make me feel wrong in a way that feels familiar. Instead, I do what Clara said. I leave. Not physically. Not yet.

I leave her voice where it belongs: outside my head. It's strange, how the silence she leaves behind doesn't feel empty. It feels occupied. Like my own thoughts are finally allowed to take up space, and they don't know how. Day Two: I watch myself like a study. Patel's line returns from the emergency psych clinic: Study you like a scientist. I try.

I keep a list in my notes app. Not poetic. Not dramatic. Clinical. Trigger: keys in hand at my apartment door. Response: posture shift, chin lift, breath held. Interpretation: preparing to be perceived. Trigger: male resident saying "Yes, Doctor." Response: heat behind sternum, impulse to lean in, hand flex. Interpretation: power cue; conditioning.

Trigger: Clara's silence. Response: panic; urge to perform to fill the space. Interpretation: absence of script. The list grows. So does my nausea. Because the pattern is everywhere. Even in small things: the way I angle my body toward strangers in elevators, the way I adjust my tone on the phone with hospital admin, the way my eyes seek confirmation from faces I don't care about.

Being watched is still my primary language. And the word refusal is not yet fluent. It is a stutter. Day Three: I test my hands again in the simulation lab, but I do it differently. No audience. No stopwatch. No high stakes. Just the instrument. The task. The breath.

The tremor appears and disappears like a nervous animal deciding whether I'm safe. When it comes, I don't punish it. I name it. You're not failure, I tell my fingers. You're information. It doesn't stop. But it changes. Less violent. More communicative. As if my body is trying to speak a truth it wasn't allowed to use language for.

I practice a simple microvascular maneuver: clip placement on a synthetic vessel. The tremor flares at the moment of precision. Not because the task is hard. Because the task resembles obedience. Hold still. Be perfect. Be praised for it. My jaw clenches. And then I do something I've never done with my own hands. I let them shake. Not as surrender. As a controlled exposure.

I let the tremor exist long enough that it stops being a catastrophe and becomes a sensation. A wave. A boundary. A line. The shaking eases a fraction. Not because I forced it. Because I stopped threatening it. Day Four: Clara sends me a spreadsheet. Her brother has done what accountants do best: turned evil into columns. Entities. Directors. Loan references. Sponsorship agreements. Event dates. Board overlaps. Meridian isn't just funding research.

Meridian is funding architecture. Spaces. Staff training. Co-branded "programming." A whole ecosystem designed to catch adult reenactment and call it healing. I stare at the spreadsheet until my vision blurs. This is what I have been operating inside without seeing. An OR with velvet walls. I highlight lines with my cursor like I'm tracing tumor margins. RV Shoreline Holdings. Dockroom Collective. Meridian property arm. Harrow's title appears again like a stain that won't lift.

Trauma & Identity Research Lead. Non-voting advisor. A polite way of saying: architect with plausible deniability. Day Five: I see Harrow in the hospital corridor. Not planned. Not staged. Not courageous. He's leaving a meeting, smiling that crisp, controlled smile he uses when he wants people to feel grateful for his attention. "Jax," he says, and my spine tries to straighten like it's being tugged by a wire.

"I heard you took some time off the schedule. I hope you're taking care of yourself." There's the language. Care. Concern. The soft net of "support" that doubles as containment. "I'm fine," I start to say, because my mouth is a lying machine. Then I stop. I look at him. I decide.

"I'm not operating right now," I say. "And I'm not discussing my nervous system in a hallway." Harrow's smile tightens. "Of course," he says smoothly. "Whenever you're ready, my door is open. Meridian has resources, " I hear it like a trigger, not a sentence. Meridian. The ecosystem. The circulatory system. "No," I say. His eyebrows rise. "No?" "No resources," I clarify. "No meetings. No drafts. No lab notes. Not from Meridian."

He studies me, polite interest masking calculation. "Is there a reason?" he asks. This is the moment where the old me would perform, offer a clever line, hint at vulnerability like a lure. Instead, I do something simpler. "I'm reviewing conflicts," I say. "That's all you need to know." Harrow's smile doesn't move, but something behind it does. A slight cooling. A subtle retreat. Predators don't like prey that starts asking about doors.

"Let me know how I can help," he says. "I will," I answer. It's a lie. But it's a useful one. Agency, I'm learning, can be strategic without being manipulative. The difference is whose benefit it serves. Day Six: Clara and I rehearse. Not seductively. Not theatrically. Procedurally. We sit in my living room with the folder spread out on the coffee table like imaging films before a case.

We map the dinner. Who will be there. Where Evelyn will stand. How the room will be staged: lighting, seating, the engineered moments for testimony and worship. The Dockroom isn't a club. It's a liturgy. "Do you think she'll recognize you?" Clara asks. "Yes," I say. And then, because honesty is now the only thing that makes my hands steady: "I think she's been recognizing me the whole time. I just didn't know what she was seeing."

Clara nods once. "Then we assume she's prepared," she says. "Which means we prepare better." We develop rules. No improvisation with Evelyn. Not yet. No private conversation. No physical contact. No accepting food or drink from her hand. No letting her frame the story first. And one more, the one that feels like swallowing glass: If I start to freeze, Clara speaks. Not because I can't. Because being seen while freezing is different than being frozen alone.

Day Seven: I almost break the rule. My mother calls. The phone lights up with her name, and my body does something humiliating: relief, as if the leash is being offered back, soft and familiar. I stare at it. Ringing. Ringing. I think about the photo: her arms folded, chin lifted, not participating, assessing outcomes. I let it go to voicemail. I don't listen. Not yet. Not because I'm brave. Because I'm practicing something I was never taught: Not answering is a choice.

Day Eight: I return to the observation booth above OR-2. Not to punish myself. To remember what I actually love. Below the glass, a surgeon works. Quiet. Functional. Unseductive. The movement isn't worship. It isn't theatre. It's care in its purest form: attention applied to flesh, without the need to be adored for it.

My hands tremble slightly on the railing. Not because I want to cut. Because I want to belong to myself while cutting. "I don't want to quit," I whisper. Clara, beside me, doesn't say anything. She lets the sentence exist without being turned into performance. Day Nine: I listen to my mother's voicemail. I do it at noon, in sunlight, sitting upright at my kitchen table with a glass of water beside me like I'm taking medication.

Structure matters. If I'm going to hear her voice, I do it on purpose. Not in the dark. Not in my bed. Not half-asleep. Not as craving. The message is exactly what I expect. Concern wrapped around control like a silk ribbon. "Jax, darling, I heard you had a...

moment at work," she says, the pause between a and moment perfectly calibrated. "I'm worried about you. You've always carried too much. You don't have to be so... strong all the time. Call me. Let's talk. I love you."

I sit very still. There it is again. Love as leash. Strength as accusation. I don't call back. Day Ten: We get confirmation. Lisette sends it from a burner address, three lines only: Added. Arrive 6:45 for pre-brief. Do not mention this email. Clara reads it over my shoulder. "She's choosing," Clara says quietly. "Or she's covering," I reply. "Both can be true," she says.

I look at my hands. They're steady. Not because I'm calm. Because the next step is precise. The night of the Legacy Circle arrives like weather. Unavoidable. Charged. Full of pressure changes you can feel in your bones. I don't spend the day rehearsing. I don't feed the part of me that thinks performance will protect me.

I do normal things. Laundry. Groceries. A walk outside, where nobody knows who I am and the sky doesn't care. In the late afternoon, I sit in my car outside the hospital and watch staff stream in and out like ants. Everyone with a role. Everyone with a badge. For years, I used my badge like a shield. Tonight, I will use it like a scalpel. Not to cut people. To cut through lies.

Clara meets me at my place at 6:10. She's dressed like she always is when she's serious: neutral, functional, ready to move. "You okay?" she asks. "No," I say. "Good," she replies. "Then you're awake." I pull the folder from my bag. The brochure. The corporate filings. The partnership draft. The wave logo comparisons. Evidence.

I also pull something else: a small index card, folded in half. Clara raises an eyebrow. "What's that?" she asks. "My script," I say. She looks pleased and grim at the same time. "You wrote a script?" "Four sentences," I say. "Anything beyond that becomes theatre." "Read them," she says. I unfold the card. My throat tightens, not from nerves, but from the unfamiliar intimacy of saying what I mean.

"I will not be used as proof of your doctrine," I read. "I will not let you speak about my childhood as a success story." "I am not here to confess. I am here to ask questions." "And I will leave the moment this becomes a performance." Clara exhales slowly. "That's consent," she says. We drive. The Dockroom's wave sign glows above the entrance like a halo drawn by someone who's never met a real god. This time, we don't wait in line.

Lisette has arranged a side entrance. A service door. The kind you use when you don't want to be seen arriving, because arrival is part of the performance. We're guided into a narrow corridor that smells like disinfectant and expensive perfume, two different ways of saying clean. Lisette meets us near the admin office. She looks paler than she did last time. More human. "You're early," she says. "On purpose," Clara replies. Lisette nods. "Evelyn arrives at seven-thirty. Donors at seven. Program starts at eight. If you're going to do anything... do it before she takes the room."

"She'll take it regardless," I say. Lisette's mouth tightens. "Yes. But there's a difference between her taking it and you giving it." That surprises me. "Why are you doing this?" I ask. Lisette's eyes flick to the lake photograph on the wall and then away, as if she can't bear to look at the thing that taught her to call harm sacred. "Because you walked out of an OR to save a woman you could have killed," she says quietly. "And I've spent years walking people into rooms where they thought they were choosing, when really they were being steered."

She swallows. "I want one clean act," she finishes. "Just one." "Clean acts are rare," Clara says. "Then let this be mine," Lisette replies. She opens the office door. "Pre-brief," she says. Inside, the room is staged for intimacy that is not actually intimate: soft light, polished wood, water and neat little notebooks like this is a seminar, not a ritual. Lisette points to a door at the far end. "That leads to the private dining space. You'll be seated at the back." "Back is fine," Clara says. "It won't feel fine when she's talking," Lisette warns. "I'm not here to feel fine," I say.

Lisette hands me a small card. A name badge. Not Dr. Nile. Just: Jax. My stomach turns. They're stripping the title. Reducing the authority. Returning me to the thing they prefer: a girl with a name, not a surgeon with a role. I look at Lisette. "Do I have to wear this?" I ask. Lisette hesitates. "Everyone does." Agency isn't always grand. Sometimes it's adhesive paper.

I tear the badge in half. Lisette's eyes widen. Clara's expression doesn't change, but something in her shoulders loosens, like she's just watched a chain snap. "I'm not participating in that," I say, and my voice is quiet enough that it's mine. Lisette nods once. "No badge," she says. "Fine. Just... be careful." "Careful is my profession," I reply. We enter.

The dining room is beautiful in the way predators love: warm lighting, velvet chairs, glassware catching light like jewellery, staff moving like shadows. The tables are arranged so the center is a stage. Of course it is. We're seated at the back, as promised. Not hidden. Observed. I can feel the gaze in the room even before Evelyn arrives, the way people look when they think they're seeing something sacred.

This is not a dinner. It's a sermon with table service. Clara sits beside me, not touching, close enough to be witness, far enough not to echo the dock. My hands tremble once under the table. Clara doesn't reach for them. She shifts so her knee bumps mine, small contact that says: you are here. you are not alone. you are choosing. At 7:12 donors begin arriving in clusters, older couples, polished women, men with watches that announce their confidence.

They greet one another with the easy warmth of people who have never had to worry that warmth might be transactional. Lisette moves through the room like a competent ghost. Every time she passes our table, her eyes flick to mine, as if checking that I'm still solid. A waiter offers wine. "No," I say. He smiles, professional. "Sparkling water?" "No," I say again. He pauses, thrown for half a second by a woman who isn't selecting, isn't curating, isn't giving him a narrative he can serve.

"Just water," Clara says gently, rescuing him from the discomfort. The waiter nods and retreats. I watch the way my own body reacts to the simple act of refusing a drink. The old me would have accepted the wine for the ritual of it, held the glass properly, let it signal participation. Now I feel how hard my nervous system works to make refusal look normal. I don't have to make it look normal. That's the point.

At 7:28, the room quiets. Not because someone asks. Because the system expects the high priestess. At 7:31, she enters. Evelyn. Older than my body remembers, but not softer. Her hair is silver, but her posture is unchanged: serenity as dominance. She smiles like she's blessing the air. Women turn toward her like flowers. Donors straighten. Staff become smaller. The room makes space without being told.

That's what grooming does. It teaches bodies to anticipate. My throat tightens. My vision narrows. For a fraction of a second, the dock overlays everything: wet wood, cold air, my mother's presence on the shore. I grip the edge of my chair until my fingers hurt. Clara's voice, low enough only I can hear: "Breathe. Not for her. For you." Evelyn reaches the center and pauses, letting attention pool at her feet. Then she speaks. "Welcome, my darlings," she says. "Welcome to a night of legacy."

Legacy. I taste blood. She begins with the familiar arc: obedience disguised as freedom, being seen sold as healing, submission marketed as autonomy. She tells stories that are not stories so much as templates, each one designed to make the listener step into a pre-written role. Then she does what she always does. She looks around the room as if she's selecting people with her eyes, blessing them into significance. "And we have among us tonight," Evelyn says warmly, "one of our most extraordinary restorations."

Her gaze sweeps the room like a searchlight. It lands on me. Not confusion. Not surprise. Recognition. Ownership. Her smile deepens. "Jax," she says, like she's tasting the word. "Our dock girl. Our miracle." The room turns to look at me. Attention floods my skin like acid. This is the moment the old me would stand, smile, perform humility, let them adore the narrative.

I don't move yet. I let the sensation happen without translating it into behaviour. Under the table my fingers curl around the index card like it's an instrument handle. Evelyn continues, voice honeyed. "She became a surgeon," she says, and the room murmurs appreciative awe. "A woman who saves lives with her hands, hands she once believed were only for trembling. Hands she learned to steady through faith and, " I stand.

The movement is simple. No drama. Just getting to my feet. The room freezes as if I've broken a spell. Evelyn's smile holds, but her eyes sharpen. I speak before she can. "I'm not here to be your miracle," I say. My voice is steady. Not seductive. Not theatrical. Just true. A ripple of discomfort moves through the room. Some people glance away. Some lean in. Everyone is hungry for a scene.

Evelyn's mouth lifts slightly, indulgent. "Oh, sweetheart," she says softly, "you're nervous. That's all. This is a lot of love in one room." The word love lands like a hook. I feel the old reflex ignite: duel, perform, prove. Instead, I use the script. "I will not be used as proof of your doctrine," I say, word for word. "I will not let you speak about my childhood as a success story." "I am not here to confess. I am here to ask questions." "And I will leave the moment this becomes a performance."

Silence spreads, thick as surgical drape. Evelyn's smile shifts. Not gone. Refined. "Questions are welcome," she says smoothly. "We are a community rooted in transparency and consent." Consent. I almost laugh. Clara stands up beside me. Not in front. Not behind. With. Her presence changes the geometry of the room. It is no longer one woman speaking against a system. It is two people refusing the script together.

"My question is simple," I say, and I pull the brochure from the folder. "Do you recognize this?" I hold it up. Some donors frown, trying to place it. Evelyn's eyes flick to it, and something like caution flashes across her face. "That's an old document," she says. "A different era." "A different branding," Clara says, voice calm. "Same doctrine." Evelyn's gaze slides to Clara. It sharpens with recognition, slower, like she's tasting a name she hasn't said in a while.

"And who are you, dear?" Evelyn asks. Clara doesn't flinch. "A witness," she says. The word hits the room like a thrown object. Evelyn's expression softens into practiced compassion. "Oh," she says, as if she's just remembered a sad story she can narrate. "Clara. You always were... sensitive." Clara's jaw tightens. I interrupt before Evelyn can turn Clara into an anecdote.

"Meridian," I say, and the word changes the air. Donors shift. Someone's face tightens. "Meridian funded The Restored Vessel. Meridian funds trauma research at my hospital. Meridian is tied to this club through RV Shoreline Holdings. I have the filings." A hiss of whispers. People don't like evidence. Evidence interrupts myth. Evelyn's voice remains warm. "Jax," she says, "you're overwhelmed. You've been through stress at work. We've heard. And when women are under strain, they sometimes, " Gaslighting with maternal frosting. Clara's voice cuts clean. "No," she says. "We're not doing that."

The room flinches. Evelyn looks at Clara with a smile that is almost affectionate. "Still so direct," she says. Clara doesn't move. "Still so practiced," she replies. My hands tremble at my sides, not from fear of Evelyn, but from the unfamiliar reality of standing up without performing it. Evelyn returns her gaze to me, and the softness is gone now. The warmth remains, but it's weaponized. "This isn't the place for this," she says. "We can talk privately." No private rooms. No scripts. "No," I say.

One word. A cut. A boundary opened. Evelyn's mouth tightens almost imperceptibly. "You don't want to humiliate yourself," she says gently. There it is. Shame as leash. My body wants to respond the old way: prove I'm not humiliated by dazzling them. Instead, I do the opposite. I let myself be plain. "I'm already humiliated," I say. "Not by standing here. By realizing how long I let you tell my story as if it belonged to you." The room goes very still. Evelyn stares at me.

And in her eyes I see something worse than anger: satisfaction. As if my refusal is just another part in her drama. As if she can still use it. Clara's hand touches my elbow, brief, human, anchoring. "Do you want to leave?" she whispers. The question is the purest agency I've ever been offered. Leaving is allowed. Leaving is not sin. Leaving is not cowardice. Leaving is choice. I look at Evelyn, at the donors, at the women watching like this is entertainment. I decide.

"Not yet," I whisper back. I lift the partnership draft, the grainy CONFIDENTIAL printout. "I have one more question," I say. Evelyn's eyes narrow. "This document," I continue, "describes 'anonymized behavioral data' collected through 'trauma-informed power exchange' programming. It reads like Harrow's language. Harrow is listed as a non-voting advisor to this board." Now the donors truly shift. Meridian is money. Money is fear. "I want to know," I say, "how long Meridian has been collecting data on reenactment and calling it research."

Evelyn's voice turns silky, dangerous. "Careful, darling," she says. "Accusations can ruin lives." "I know," I reply. "Mine was ruined before I had a driver's licence." A gasp. Someone drops a fork. Clara's breath catches, not because she's surprised, but because she knows what I just did. I named it. Not poetically. Not obliquely. Plainly enough that the room can't pretend it's just story. Evelyn's eyes harden. The warmth is gone now. Only control remains. And for the first time, I see her clearly: not mystic, not healer, not mentor. A system in a human shape.

"You're tired," Evelyn says, voice cold under the sweetness. "You don't know what you're saying." My hands tremble harder. Not because I'm losing control. Because I'm refusing to perform it. "I know exactly what I'm saying," I reply. And then, because agency is not endurance, and I don't need to prove I can stand on a dock forever: "I'm leaving." The words land like a door shutting.

Evelyn tilts her head, almost amused. "Jax," she says, and the way she says my name is a hook. "Running away doesn't make you free." Clara's voice is a blade. "Leaving is not running," she says. "It's choosing." I pick up my folder. I don't storm out. I don't perform exit. I walk. Clara walks beside me. Behind us, the room erupts, whispers, outrage, people trying to stitch the myth back together before it bleeds out.

At the threshold I pause, not for them but for myself, and turn just enough to look at Evelyn one last time. She is watching me with the same auditing gaze my mother wore in the photograph, measuring outcomes, calculating whether I will return, already placing me back into her ledger. I do not give her a speech or a final declaration, and I do not offer her tears or defiance that she could turn into meaning. Instead I give her the only thing she cannot metabolise, which is nothing at all, and then I leave.

Outside, the night air hits me like oxygen after anesthesia, sharp and bracing and suddenly real, and my hands begin to shake in a way that is full-bodied and honest. Clara does not touch them, but she stands close enough to steady the space around me, solid as a wall without becoming another surface I have to lean on. When she says quietly, "You did it," I correct her through a ragged breath and tell her, "I left," and when she answers, "Yes, you left on purpose," the words settle in me with a weight that is both frightening and relieving. The tremor continues, not because I am broken, but because something in me has finally stopped holding still on command.

Outside, the night air hits me like oxygen after anesthesia, and my hands shake violently now, full-bodied and honest in a way that no performance ever was. Clara does not touch them, but she stands close, steady as a wall, and when she says quietly, "You did it," I correct her through a ragged breath, "I left," and she answers, "Yes. You left on purpose." The tremor continues, not because I'm broken but because something in me has finally stopped holding still on command.

We walk several blocks without speaking while the city remains loud in the ordinary way, traffic and people laughing and a siren far away, the world continuing its indifference as my nervous system keeps waiting for a consequence. I expect a hand on my shoulder, a voice calling my name like a hook, some form of punishment, but nothing happens, and when Clara stops under a streetlight and looks at me she asks, not suggestive or leading but real, "Tell me what you need," and I blink because my throat hurts and all I can say is, "I don't know."

"That's fine," she says. "Then we choose something small. Drink water. Go home. Sleep if you can. No autopsy tonight," and when I echo, "No autopsy," it sounds almost funny, and she adds, "Tomorrow we document," and I nod as she tells me to text when I'm inside. We part ways like colleagues after a hard case, no ritual, no comfort performance, just shared reality.

I get home, lock the door, and stand in the entryway with my folder still in my hands, evidence, and I set it on the table like it might bite before doing something I haven't done in years, which is sitting on the floor, not collapsing, just lowering myself to a position that doesn't require me to look competent. The tremor slows, my breathing drops, and for a few minutes I simply exist without being watched.

I sleep in pieces. The dreams are less cinematic than I expected, no screaming, no dock, no Evelyn with her hand on my neck, just paperwork, seating charts, a name badge torn in half, and my mother's hands folded in her lap. When I wake, my phone is lit with messages, three missed calls from an unfamiliar number, two emails from Meridian addresses I recognise but have never been contacted by directly, and one text from Lisette saying, Are you okay. And also... thank you. We will need to talk.

I stare at the screen until my eyes sting, a part of me wanting to answer immediately to manage and control outcomes, while another part, the newer part, remembers that urgency is engineered, so I do not respond yet. I shower, eat something small, dress in scrubs, and at the hospital the day proceeds with its usual indifference to personal rupture, trauma not pausing because you confronted it publicly and schedules not flexing around narrative arcs. In the locker room I catch my reflection in a metal door and realise I look the same, no visible transformation, no signifier that something foundational has shifted, which I understand now is the point.

The first case is routine and the second is not, a cavernous malformation near the insula with tight corridors and elevated risk of language deficit, exactly the kind of surgery that used to calm me, high stakes, narrow margins, total immersion. As I scrub, the old creed hums in my muscles, ritual equals safety, precision equals control, control equals worth, and my hands tremor once as I turn off the tap, not enough to stop me but enough to register. I breathe through it slowly and deliberately, not suppressing or indulging, and when the tremor passes what remains is not confidence exactly but permission.

In OR-2, Rivera looks at me a half-second longer than usual and asks, "You good?" and when I say, "Yes," for the first time I do not mentally qualify the answer. The surgery unfolds with its usual intimacy, the narrowing of the world to field and fibre, the careful navigation of vessels that do not forgive arrogance, and my hands are steady without being rigid or performative, just responsive. At one point I feel the familiar surge of satisfaction when a difficult plane opens cleanly, the old pleasure flickering as competence becomes relief and mastery becomes safety, but then something else overlays it, not pride or triumph, just usefulness, because the patient will wake up able to speak and that is all, and that is enough.

Afterward, Rivera says, "You felt... different today," and when I ask how, she shrugs and says, "Less tense. Like you weren't trying to prove anything," and I nod as I dry my hands and tell her, "I wasn't." In my office, between charts, I open the Meridian email, the subject line soft enough to be plausible and sharp enough to be a warning, Request for Clarification re: Public Remarks, and I recognise the cadence immediately, concern dressed as policy, empathy framed as liability, requests for meetings, reminders of partnership values, mentions of wellness resources and cohesive messaging.

My jaw tightens as I feel the familiar pressure to respond beautifully, articulate and devastating and composed, but I remember what happened in that room, the way I refused to be reframed, and how this is the same room, just fluorescent. I type one sentence, No, and I do not explain or justify or give them my nervous system in a memo before I hit send, and my hands shake afterward not because I'm afraid of them but because I did something my body was trained to believe was unsurvivable, I said no to an institution without offering myself as compromise.

I sit very still and then do something else, opening a blank document as the cursor blinks accusatory and expectant in the place where I usually translate experience into something legible and impressive, a framework or paper or narrative arc with a clean thesis. I do not do that. I type a title and stop, My Dock Story, not a subtitle or a claim, just possession, and the cursor blinks beneath it like a heartbeat as I write one line, I was twelve when they taught me that being watched could feel like safety, and I stop, letting the sentence exist without turning it into performance.

Chapter Nineteen

---∞---

A Cut That Heals Wrong

S ome wounds don't break you. They just heal wrong. Bone sets off-angle. Skin pulls tight. Nerves find a new route and call it "fine," and the body keeps going, even as you pay in reach, feeling, or ease. Brains do it too, and we call it plasticity, like it's a gift, although often it is and sometimes it's just a fast way to cope that leaves you bent.

Mine healed like that. Fear built a crooked bridge, and want grew over it like ivy. It worked. It even looked like strength from far away. Up close, it was still a break, and you can't erase the damage or get that kind of clean, you only get to see the scar's shape and then decide what you do with it.

That's what I'm telling myself when the consult request lands in my inbox and the subject line reads: Complex Case Review, Limbic Resection Candidate / Meridian Referral. Of course it's Meridian. They've been hovering since Harrow's paper started making the rounds, and "Trauma-Induced Memory Excision" makes grant panels hungry while it also makes lawyers sweat, which is why every email now carries the same line: The intention of this surgery is seizure control and quality-of-life improvement, not targeted memory erasure.

Intent matters to boards, to donors, to risk teams. To patients, intent is noise. They care what happens, and when I open the file I see Female. Thirty-two. Lila Kerr. Childhood trauma. Refractory temporal lobe epilepsy. Flashbacks that track with seizure clusters. Meds failed. One aborted ablation three years ago, too close to key tracts.

MRI, PET, EEG. The hot spot sits in the right mesial temporal lobe, brushing the hippocampus and leaning on the amygdala, the exact ground people want and fear. Under "Referring body" there are two names: Meridian Institute and The Restored Vessel Trust. Of course. The same doctrine that broke me, now helping pay to cut near other people's stories.

I scroll to the clinical note. Patient states: "If you could take the memories and leave everything else, I would sign anything." Below that, a line from Harrow: Recommend Nile for surgical opinion. She understands the narrative load of these regions. Narrative load, like memory is freight and I'm back on a dock.

I tap the intercom. "Teasdale." He's in my doorway in half a minute, tablet in hand and tie already loosened. "Case from Meridian," I say. "Kerr. I want raw scans. I want all psych notes, printed and digital, and I want the consent talks recorded, audio and transcript."

His eyebrows lift. "You expecting trouble?" "I'm expecting layers," I say. "I don't want any 'misreads' later." He nods, understanding the part I didn't say, that I don't trust Restored Vessel money near this line of work, not without witnesses.

"Book an in-person pre-op consult," I add. "Forty-five minutes. Not twenty." "With you?" "Yes." He hesitates. "And... Clara?" I don't ask how he guessed. Word travels when a surgeon steps away from a meningioma mid-case and still keeps their job. "Offer," I say. "If she can." He gives a small smile. "She'll make it work."

Some wounds don't break you. They just heal wrong. Bone sets off-angle. Skin pulls tight. Nerves find a new route and call it "fine," and the body keeps going, even as you pay in reach, feeling, or ease. Brains do it too, and we call it plasticity, like it's a gift, although often it is and sometimes it's just a fast way to cope that leaves you bent.

Mine healed like that. Fear built a crooked bridge, and want grew over it like ivy. It worked. It even looked like strength from far away. Up close, it was still a break, and you can't erase the damage or get that kind of clean, you only get to see the scar's shape and then decide what you do with it.

That's what I'm telling myself when the consult request lands in my inbox and the subject line reads: Complex Case Review, Limbic Resection Candidate / Meridian Referral. Of course it's Meridian. They've been hovering since Harrow's paper started making the rounds, and "Trauma-Induced Memory Excision" makes grant panels hungry while it also makes lawyers sweat, which is why every email now carries the same line: The intention of this surgery is seizure control and quality-of-life improvement, not targeted memory erasure.

Intent matters to boards, to donors, to risk teams. To patients, intent is noise. They care what happens, and when I open the file I see Female. Thirty-two. Lila Kerr. Childhood trauma. Refractory temporal lobe epilepsy. Flashbacks that track with seizure clusters. Meds failed. One aborted ablation three years ago, too close to key tracts.

MRI, PET, EEG. The hot spot sits in the right mesial temporal lobe, brushing the hippocampus and leaning on the amygdala, the exact ground people want and fear. Under "Referring body" there are two names: Meridian Institute and The Restored Vessel Trust. Of course. The same doctrine that broke me, now helping pay to cut near other people's stories.

I scroll to the clinical note. Patient states: "If you could take the memories and leave everything else, I would sign anything." Below that, a line from Harrow: Recommend Nile for surgical opinion. She understands the narrative load of these regions. Narrative load, like memory is freight and I'm back on a dock.

I tap the intercom. "Teasdale." He's in my doorway in half a minute, tablet in hand and tie already loosened. "Case from Meridian," I say. "Kerr. I want raw scans. I want all psych notes, printed and digital, and I want the consent talks recorded, audio and transcript."

His eyebrows lift. "You expecting trouble?" "I'm expecting layers," I say. "I don't want any 'misreads' later." He nods, understanding the part I didn't say, that I don't trust Restored Vessel money near this line of work, not without witnesses.

"Book an in-person pre-op consult," I add. "Forty-five minutes. Not twenty." "With you?" "Yes." He hesitates. "And... Clara?" I don't ask how he guessed. Word travels when a surgeon steps away from a meningioma mid-case and still keeps their job. "Offer," I say. "If she can." He gives a small smile. "She'll make it work."

The morning of surgery, the hospital feels calm. Maybe it's the place, maybe it's me, maybe I've stopped running on anxiety like it's fuel. Pre-op bay, Lila in a gown, lines taped, hair braided back, her partner sitting close with his thumb moving in slow circles on her wrist, steady, not possessive.

"Last chance to run," I say, light on purpose. She snorts. "I fainted once during a blood draw. If I was going to run, it would've been then." "Fainting is honest," I say. "You don't owe anyone brave." "Too late," she says. "I signed forms. That's legal brave." I let the corner of my mouth lift.

Anesthesia does final checks. Clara stands near the curtain, not assigned, she swapped shifts to be here. "Any questions?" I ask. "One,"

Lila says. "When I go under... what do you want me to think about?" Old reflex rises in my mouth. Look at me. Don't move. Good girl. Instruction as trance. Obedience as comfort. The dock in scrubs. I swallow it.

"Nothing," I say. "You don't owe this a performance. Think about anything you want. Or nothing." She nods, and I see two feelings at once, relief and a strange disappointment. "That feels wrong," she admits. "Like I should do something." "You already did," I say. "You showed up." They wheel her away.

In the scrub room, I stand at the sink and don't pray. I narrate, fingers, palms, wrists, forearms. I'm not asking a force outside me to steady my hands, I'm telling my nervous system this is water, this is soap, this is not the lake. Clara steps in, tying up her hair. "Hands?" she asks. I flex my fingers in the air between us, no tremor, just a low hum.

"They're listening," I say. "Good," she replies. "I'd like them to stick around." We gown, we glove, we step into theatre. The OR air sits at the exact cold some policy group calls sterile, machines hum, navigation shows Lila's brain in clean 3D, tracts glowing like threads laid under skin.

"Morning," I tell the room. "Right mesial temporal malformation with seizure focus. Priority is seizure control with maximal preservation of memory structures." Fernandez stands opposite me, eyes sharp above her mask. She remembers my old line, protect the fornix at all costs, she wrote it down like law. "Approach?" I ask her.

She straightens. "Trans-sylvian corridor. Minimal retraction. Map the hippocampal tail. Spare as much anterior tissue as possible. Stay superficial to the fimbria when we can." "Good," I say. "And if we can't clear the focus without taking more hippocampus than planned?" She hesitates, then answers. "We stop and reassess. We follow consent and best interest. Not ego."

Good. "We'll monitor language and memory in case," I add. "If she starts losing herself, we adjust." We position. We drape. Anesthesia nods. Knife in hand, I draw the incision. Muscle. Bone. Dura. Each layer gives the same way it always does. I could do this part half asleep. I don't. I track it.

"Craniotomy," I say. "Bring the window to us." The bone flap lifts. Under the scope, the brain pulses with each heartbeat, pink-grey, alive. We split the Sylvian fissure, veins, arachnoid, slow tese I'm soft, because retraction can turn into s, t gle with exact pressure, enough to make a corridor, not enough to bruise.

We reach the the screen like a warning. "There," I say. The malformation presses against the hippocampue removed without cost.

A cut that heals wrong. "We go slow," I say, mostly to myself. Microdissector. Suction. Coag. My hands move in small arcs, not chasing perfect, chasing clear. Inside my chest, an old script stirs, hold still, look at me, good girl, and I let it rise, I name it, I let it go.

No. Look at her. Keep her intact. Good enough. "Stay lateral," I tell Fernandez. "Don't cling to the hippocampus because it makes you feel safe. Respect the line." She nods and follows the plane. A small venous branch oozes. Years ago I would have snapped out an order with a blade in my voice, not anger, a performance of command. Today I just say, "Irrigation. Suction," and wait for a clean field before I move.

The malformation comes away in fragments, each piece one less storm waiting to happen. We map as we go, stimulate, watch for slur, confusion, the blank look that means you took too much. Lila's answers come through the speaker in a thin, sedated voice. "Name this," the neuropsych tech says, holding up a card. "Apple." "I, apple," Lila murmurs.

"Where do you live?" She answers, slow but oriented. "Tell me something that makes you feel safe." A pause. Then: "My dog. The sound he makes when he... sighs in his sleep." Good. We work around that answer like it's part of the anatomy. At the deepest point, my instrument sits a millimetre from the fimbria. Navigation crosshairs hover over territory that could steal years, or soften their edges in ways you don't see until months later.

My hand is steady, not because I've killed fear, because I've stopped treating fear as weakness. "We can stop here," I say. "This is enough."

Levin, observing from the back for once, clears his throat. "Seizure margins, " he starts. "Are reachable without turning her into a different person," I cut in. "We're not chasing purity." He huffs behind his mask. He doesn't push. We cauterise lightly, no scorched-earth "just in case," we irrigate, blood runs clear, and the malformation sits in the basin, small and ugly. I don't feel victory. I feel right. We close.

Lila wakes in recovery three hours later. Clara and I stand at the foot of the bed as she surfaces, eyes fluttering, hand twitching toward the bandage. "Hey," I say. "You're post-op. It's done. Hands down." She lowers her hand, not like a trained girl, like someone bargaining with pain. "How..." Her voice cracks. "Did it... work?"

"Too early," I say. "You came through well. No clear deficits. We watch for seizures. The rest takes time." She closes her eyes for a beat. When she opens them, her eyes are wet. "Do I..." She swallows. "Do I still remember?" I don't ask what. We all know. "Do you?" I ask.

She stares at the ceiling, like she's testing doors in her mind. "Yes," she whispers. "But it's... quieter." "How?" Clara asks, gentle. "It's like someone turned the volume down," Lila says. "Like it happened in another room. I can see it. My body still knows it. But it's not drowning everything." She looks at me. "Is that real? Or am I making it up because I want it?"

"It can be real," I say. "We didn't cut your story out. We may have interrupted the replay." "Will it come back?" she asks. "Maybe," I say. "Brains like old paths. But now you can build new ones without getting jumped every time." Tears slide into her hair. "I thought I'd wake up empty," she says. "Or... not me."

"You didn't," I say. "You woke up you. With a scar." "Is that good?" she asks. "It's honest," I say. "Good is yours to decide." Clara steps closer and rests a hand on the bedrail, not skin, metal, presence without claim. "You don't have to decide today," she says. "Rest. Let your brain knit around what happened."

Lila gives a small, tired laugh. "Feels like you moved furniture in the dark." "We tried to leave the important pieces," I say. She studies me. "Do you have scars like this?" she asks. "Not the skin kind. The wrong-healed kind." "Yes," I say. "I'm just now seeing where they pulled me out of shape." "And you can still do this?" she asks, nodding weakly toward the OR doors. "I can," I say. "I just don't do it for the wrong god anymore."

Her eyelids sink. As sleep pulls her under again, she whispers, "If it heals wrong... can we fix it?" "No," I say. "But you can choose what you do with it." She nods, already gone.

In the corridor outside recovery, Levin catches my arm. "You left tissue," he says. "I did." "Recurrence risk goes up." "Yes." He watches me like he expects me to flinch. "If she seizes again," he says, "they'll say you were too cautious." "They might," I say. "You okay with that?" "No," I say. "I'm more okay with that than turning her into a case study Meridian drags through conferences."

His jaw tightens. "This will shape your name," he says. "You stepped away from one meningioma. Now you spare tissue in a high-profile limbic case. People will say you've gone... soft." There it is. The old charge, wearing a suit. I think of the dock. Evelyn. My mother on the shore, arms folded, calling hardness holy. "Good," I say. "Let them call it soft. Scar tissue is soft. It's still stronger than what tore."

He snorts, half annoyed, half impressed, and walks off. Clara appears a moment later. "He'll complain over drinks," she says. "I know." "And the board will call," she adds. "Because Meridian will call them." "Probably." "And?" she asks. "And I'll tell them what I did and why," I say. "Then I go back to work."

She nods. "How did it feel?" "The cut?" I ask. She shakes her head. "Doing it this way. Without using the room." I look through the recovery window at Lila, asleep. "Like setting a bone that already started healing wrong," I say. "It hurts. It's needed. It's quiet." "Any tremor?" Clara asks. "A little," I admit. "Before we started. Right when I thought about being perfect." I flex my fingers. "It stopped when I decided I didn't have to be."

Clara's mouth tilts. "That'll ruin your brand." "Good," I say again. We stand there for a few breaths, sharing the same over-filtered air. When Clara leaves for rounds, I go back into recovery. I take the empty chair by Lila's bed and sit.

I don't watch her like data. I watch her like a person who trusted me to make new scar tissue inside who she thinks she is. Her monitor beeps steady. The incision line along her scalp is neat, almost delicate. In months it will fade into her hairline. The deeper scar won't. None of mine did.

I think of what Evelyn said we were doing on that dock. Purifying. Initiating. Refining. What we were doing was making scars without consent. What I'm doing now isn't the opposite. It's just honest about the price.

Lila shifts. Her lashes flutter. She doesn't wake, but some part of her hears sound. An old line rises in me, fast as a reflex: Look at me.

Don't move. Good girl. I break it apart. I keep the shape. I change the meaning.

"Don't look at me," I whisper. "You don't have to move. You don't have to be good. You're already here." Her breathing deepens. Then evens. For the first time in a long time, the words I speak over a vulnerable body don't belong to the woman on the shore. They belong to me.

In the corridor outside recovery, Levin catches my arm. "You left tissue," he says. "I did." "Recurrence risk goes up." "Yes." He watches me like he expects me to flinch. "If she seizes again," he says, "they'll say you were too cautious." "They might," I say. "You okay with that?" "No," I say. "I'm more okay with that than turning her into a case study Meridian drags through conferences."

His jaw tightens. "This will shape your name," he says. "You stepped away from one meningioma. Now you spare tissue in a high-profile limbic case. People will say you've gone... soft." There it is. The old charge, wearing a suit. I think of the dock. Evelyn. My mother on the shore, arms folded, calling hardness holy.

"Good," I say. "Let them call it soft. Scar tissue is soft. It's still stronger than what tore." He snorts, half annoyed, half impressed, and walks off. Clara appears a moment later. "He'll complain over drinks," she says. "I know."

"And the board will call," she adds. "Because Meridian will call them." "Probably." "And?" she asks. "And I'll tell them what I did and why," I say. "Then I go back to work." She nods. "How did it feel?" "The cut?" I ask. She shakes her head. "Doing it this way. Without using the room."

I look through the recovery window at Lila, asleep. "Like setting a bone that already started healing wrong," I say. "It hurts. It's needed. It's quiet." "Any tremor?" Clara asks. "A little," I admit. "Before we started. Right when I thought about being perfect." I flex my fingers. "It stopped when I decided I didn't have to be."

Clara's mouth tilts. "That'll ruin your brand." "Good," I say again. We stand there for a few breaths, sharing the same over-filtered air. When Clara leaves for rounds, I go back into recovery. I take the empty chair by Lila's bed and sit.

I don't watch her like data. I watch her like a person who trusted me to make new scar tissue inside who she thinks she is. Her monitor beeps steady. The incision line along her scalp is neat, almost delicate. In months it will fade into her hairline. The deeper scar won't. None of mine did.

I think of what Evelyn said we were doing on that dock. Purifying. Initiating. Refining. What we were doing was making scars without consent. What I'm doing now isn't the opposite. It's just honest about the price.

Lila shifts. Her lashes flutter. She doesn't wake, but some part of her hears sound. An old line rises in me, fast as a reflex: Look at me. Don't move. Good girl. I break it apart. I keep the shape. I change the meaning.

"Don't look at me," I whisper. "You don't have to move. You don't have to be good. You're already here." Her breathing deepens. Then evens. For the first time in a long time, the words I speak over a vulnerable body don't belong to the woman on the shore. They belong to me.

The resident today is Patel. Third year. Smart hands. Late timing. She knows the steps. She hasn't learned why yet. I remember being that surgeon, mistaking precision for purpose, thinking the body was there to prove I could handle it.

Patel stands across from me, gloved, waiting. Her eyes flick between my hands and the tract maps on the screen. The patient's name, Vera Marin, sits printed on the wristband above the drape. Forty-eight. Bilingual teacher. Early-stage lesion in the dominant temporal lobe. Small mass. Big risk.

I speak low, mostly to Patel, not fully to her. "In places like this, you don't carve," I say. "You negotiate." She starts to nod, then stops, remembering the eye shield will fog. Good. She's learning.

I place my hands over the field. The brain pulses in time with the heart, mine and hers, slow, steady, not braced. The tremor I expect doesn't come. The stillness feels strange, not because it's new, but because it isn't forced.

Patel whispers, "Should I retract more medially?" "Not yet," I say. "Watch the vessels. They're telling you how much space you get." She hesitates. "The fissure's tight." "Then don't pry it," I say. "Follow what opens on its own."

That would have sounded like dock talk to me once, like a line, like faith. It isn't. Tissue has limits. It shows you where harm starts. I advance the microdissector along the sulcus as Patel watches my wrist, not my tool, waiting for a show, for strength to look like force.

I soften pressure instead. Her eyes widen. "Watch the fibers," I say. "Not me." She shifts her gaze, then steadies. We isolate the lesion, its borders uneven, like something trying to pass as normal tissue, almost shy, a mistake, not a monster.

A lot of things that hurt us start that way. Patel holds suction a touch off target, nervous. "Trust yourself," I tell her. "I don't want to damage function," she whispers. "You won't," I say. "You're listening. That's harder than cutting."

She steadies. We work. The OR is quiet in a new way, not silent, machines still hum, nurses still talk, quiet because I'm not using the room to prove anything. I'm here. I'm useful.

When the final piece comes loose, pale, wet, plain, it slips into suction almost too easily. I feel a small satisfaction, not triumph, correction. No one claps. No one praises. We irrigate. We check bleeding. We close.

As I place the last suture, Patel breathes out like she's been holding it for months. "That was..." she starts. "Routine," I finish. Her eyes shine with something mixed, relief, pride, a new idea forming.

"You're different now," she says. "When you operate." Am I. I could deny it, pretend I don't hear her, keep the mask on. That would be another act.

"I stopped confusing control with who I am," I say. She studies my face like she wants a key. I don't give her one. Some lessons need time.

We strip gloves. We peel masks. We wash until the iodine smell lifts from our wrists. In the scrub room, Patel waits, unsure if she's allowed to speak again.

Then she asks, "How do you stay steady when it matters this much?" A year ago I would've given her the old lines, stillness as power, precision as proof, control as worth. Those words don't fit my mouth anymore.

I dry my hands. I let my weight settle in my feet, not posed, not staged, just standing. Then I look at her as a surgeon, not a performer. "You don't hold still for the room," I tell her. "You hold still for you."

Patel's breath catches. She nods, not because I ordered it, but because she hears it. She repeats it under her breath, not like prayer, like a tool. "For me."

No big moment. No spark. Just a small shift that will matter later. We leave the scrub room. No applause. No doctrine. No shore. Just the work of keeping someone alive. And that is enough.

Chapter Twenty

---◆◇◆---

Who Remembers Whom

There is a kind of silence that does not remove sound. It rearranges it. Hospitals have that silence. Monitors still murmur. Ventilators still exhale. Fluorescents still buzz. But something underneath shifts, and noise turns into meaning.

After Evelyn. After the lake drained. After the dock collapsed in memory instead of myth, the hospital feels like it is allowed to be what it is, a hospital, not an altar, not a stage, not a place where desire gets dressed up as ritual.

I walk these halls differently now, not with dominance, not with that polished certainty I used as armor, but with something quieter. Choice. No one notices, why would they. The outside version of me still looks the same, my scrubs still sit crisp, my badge still taps my pocket, my pace still reads as sure.

To them, the surgeon stays the surgeon. Staff nod as I pass. Residents keep a careful distance. They respect competence more than charm. What they cannot see is this, I do not walk like I am being watched anymore, I walk like I am here.

We start early. My team crowds the whiteboard, notes stacking across it like layers of bone. Fernandez runs through overnight neuro consults. Teasdale cuts in twice. Julie mutters corrections at the pace of caffeine. Levin tries to take the room with a technique question he has not used in ten years.

Before, I would have ended it fast, sharp, smooth, efficient. People would have called it leadership. It was choreography. I was performing knowledge the way I used to perform consent, let me show you how cleanly I can do this.

Today, I let them work, not to punish them, to respect them.

"Fernandez," I say. "Walk us through your plan again." She does, not perfect, not a mess. Julie adds, "Try posterior first. Not lateral." Fernandez pauses, thinks, then says, "Yeah. That makes sense."

Before, I would have grabbed the reins. Now I just say, "Good." A small word, no hook, no sting. Levin frowns like he cannot find his role. Teasdale loosens. Fernandez brightens.

Power can be shared without thinning out. Control is only worth anything when it is optional. We move on, a subdural, a consult for a brainstem glioma. The board fills with writing that is not mine, the day taking shape in loops of marker I did not draw.

For the first time in years, I notice it. I am not the center of that board. I am part of it.

I step into the break room to refill my tea. Levin follows. "You are... different lately," he says, not hostile, curious, a little threatened. "People change," I say. "That is not what I mean." He rubs the back of his neck. "You are less..." He gestures. "Less Nile." I smile without turning it into a weapon. "You mean I am less theatrical." He blinks. "I did not say that." "You did not have to."

He watches me like he cannot decide if we are sparring or talking. "Just do not lose your edge," he mutters. "I am not losing it," I say, pouring hot water. "I am choosing where to use it." He has no reply, not because he disagrees, but because the idea lands in a place he has not mapped. He only knows control as display, control as proof.

Choice does not fit his system. Maybe it will someday. Maybe he will resent me forever. Either way, it is not my stage anymore.

I leave him by the fridge, staring at the magnet schedule as if it is written in a language he cannot read. I do not hide in my office. I do not retreat to the surgeons' lounge where hierarchy tastes like burnt coffee. I take my sandwich, plain, edible, forgettable, to a bench near the courtyard. There are trees here, real ones, their leaves moving without witnesses, no ritual, no script.

Clara finds me there. She does not announce herself. She sits, not beside me, not across from me, diagonal, close without claiming. She bites into a granola bar and studies the courtyard like it is a scan. "How did the tumor case go?" she asks. "Clean," I say. "Margins held. No speech hit expected." She nods, not impressed, not performing anything, just present.

"And your hands?" she asks. "Steady," I say. "Not because I forced them. Because I did not." A small smile. "The body tells the truth," she says. "We are the ones who lie." "I am trying not to," I say. She looks at me then, really looks, not like a clinician checking a symptom, not like a witness waiting for confession, not like someone holding my name hostage, just here.

"Do you want help finding what honesty looks like?" she asks. I do not rush it. I breathe. "I would like company while I figure it out," I say. "Company," she repeats. "That I can do." She does not reach for my hand. I do not act interested. We just eat, slowly, quietly. It feels more intimate than anything that ever happened on the dock.

Later that afternoon, a resident, Collins, stands too close behind me while I review scans. Young, bright, earnest, he leans in, breath near my shoulder, eager to be seen. Before, I would have used it, shifted the room, turned attention into currency. Now my body responds with clarity, not compulsion.

"Step back," I say, not sharp, not cruel, clear. He flushes. "Sorry, just wanted to point at." "You can point from a professional distance," I say. He nods, steps back, learns. Nothing charged, nothing covert, no reenactment, just a boundary. It feels like washing my hands in real water, not ritual.

He points from where he should. "Do you think tractography underestimates spread here?" "Probably," I say. "The brain rarely lies. It just tells the truth slowly." He pauses, unsure if that is metaphor. Good. Let him think. Let him understand instead of obey.

He tries again. "If you do not mind me asking, when you step back from a case now, is that about your hands?" I keep my eyes on the images. "It is about knowing when I am operating," I say, "and when I am reenacting." He frowns. "Reenacting what?" "It does not matter," I say. "If I cannot tell the difference, I do not cut." He sits with that longer than most would. Maybe he will carry it. Maybe it will save someone. Maybe it will save him.

That night, I call my mother, not to confront, not to confess, to calibrate. She answers on the third ring, her voice bright the way fear can be bright. "Jax, how is my brilliant girl?" For a beat, my body reaches for the old part, the part that makes her feel safe, the part that turns my life into her trophy. I do not give it.

"Fine," I say. "Busy. I want to say something clearly." On her end, silence snaps into place. She braces for blame. "I know you thought you were helping," I say. "I also know you did not protect me." Her breath catches, not tears, shock. "I... Jax, I kept you close." "You handed me over to someone you trusted more than yourself," I say. "That is the truth. I am not asking you to fix it. I am not asking you to punish yourself. I am not pretending anymore."

She swallows. "I did not know what else to do," she whispers. "I know," I say. "And I am choosing to do better." No forgiveness. No punishment. A boundary between two adults. We hang up and something settles in me.

For years I wanted an apology she cannot give. I wanted her to remember what I remember. She will not. She remembers a dock where her daughter was brave. I remember a dock where I learned how to disappear. Both memories exist. Only one gets to shape me.

Two days later, Psych consults me. A woman with chronic facial pain insists it defines her. She fears surgery will steal her identity. "I do not know who I am without it," she says. "The pain proves I survived." It hits like a mirror. "It does not prove survival," I tell her. "What you built around it does."

She trembles, not from fear but from the idea of being something else. "If we reduce the pain," I say, "you will have space to choose who you are next." "Choice scares me," she whispers. "Good," I say. "That means it is yours." She agrees to treatment, not because she trusts me but because she believes she will not be emptied out. We schedule surgery. I do not walk out feeling like a savior. I walk out feeling human.

Later, in pre-op, she looks at me through wet eyes. "If I wake up and it is gone," she says, "will you stay until I know what is left?" Once, I would have answered with a line built to be remembered. "Yes," I say. "I will stay until you know it is you." When she goes under, neither of us performs.

The surgery is careful and unshowy, no conference talk, no glossy case report, we interrupt the circuit without cutting everything nearby. In recovery, she winces, blinks, and whispers, "It is quieter." "Good," I say. "Quiet does not mean you are gone. It means there is space." "For what?" she asks. "For whatever you choose," I say.

Her eyes close, not from sleep but from relief edged with terror. I know that look, not destiny, transition.

On Friday, I run a skills lab. Microsutures on simulated tissue. Residents bent over their stations, too focused to pose. Before, I hovered, I intimidated, I made mastery into spectacle. Today, I speak the way I operate now. "Precision does not come from force," I say. "It comes from alignment. You do not dominate tissue. You listen to it."

Collins raises a hand. "But is not control the point?" "Control is a tool," I say. "Not a personality. Not a signature. Not bait." Julie smirks. She knows who the last word is for. "Authority should make people safer," I add. "If it makes them perform, you are not teaching. You are reenacting." A few heads lift. The room shifts. Fernandez murmurs, "Surgery without choreography." "Yes," I say. "This is not theatre. If you need applause, find another room." They laugh, not at me but with me, and something rises in my chest that is not hunger or the old pull, just the want to be understood.

Park asks, "How do you know when you are reenacting instead of just being good?" The room stills. That is the question. "In my case," I say, "reenactment feels urgent, like if I do not prove something I will vanish. Doing my job feels different. It is tight and focused, but it is not about me, it is about the person on the table." "So if you are thinking about yourself..." Park says, slow. "Sometimes," I say. "Brains are not clean rooms. You will always be in there. But if what you are doing serves your need to feel powerful more than their need to be safe, stop." Julie whistles. "Put that on a poster." "I would rather you put it in your hands," I say, and they go back to suturing with less show and more care, because teaching does not feel like building an audience, it feels like building a future.

Clara and I eat together again, not a date, not a dodge, dinner. Soup for her, noodles for me, no wine, no poses, no ritual, we talk about small things, a new study, resident gossip, a terrible haircut in Radiology. Then she asks, "Are you scared of wanting things now?"

"Yes," I say. "Good," she answers. "Wanting without fear would not be honest yet." "What do you want?" I ask. She thinks. "I want to want things without needing them to define me." We sit with that, the most intimate exchange of my life because it is not trying to be.

"And us?" I ask. She takes a sip of tea and sets the cup down like a normal person, no slow choreography. "Let us not reenact anything," she says. "If we want something, it should be new, not a sequel." New, not a sequel, and my chest aches cleanly. "Then we go slow," I say. "Slow," she agrees. "And honest." No vows, no claims, no hooks, just direction.

Outside, the air is cold and blunt. At the crosswalk the signal changes and people surge forward, but we do not move yet. Clara asks, "If there were no lake, no dock, no Evelyn, who do you think you would want?" The question cuts clean. "I do not know," I say. "That is the point." She nods. "I would rather walk next to the person who does not know than the one who is certain because someone else wrote the script." The light turns red again before we cross, and we laugh for no reason, which feels like the smallest kind of freedom.

Later she comes to my apartment, not late, not secret, eight p.m. on a Tuesday, journals under one arm and cheap takeout under the other. "I brought three papers that will annoy you," she says, "and one that might help." We sit at my kitchen table in socks under overhead fluorescent light that makes us both look tired, no candles, no wine, no mood. She slides over an article on Somatic Empowerment in Ritual Contexts, which reads like marketing for the lake, and we mark it up like a tumor board, circling the phrases that soften harm and underlining the places it almost gets it right and then flinches.

"This part," Clara says, tapping a line, "where they say participants reported agency despite discomfort." "That is reenactment," I say, and we move to Harrow's revised draft, where he has added a section on integration instead of excision, on choosing how to narrate what will not undo. "Do you feel seen by it?" Clara asks. "No," I say. "But I feel understood." "Is that enough?" "For a paper, yes," I say. "For a life, no." She grins. "Good. Papers should not be enough."

We argue about method until midnight. At one point she tells me, flat and calm, "You are wrong," and I laugh. "You want memory to behave like a clean margin," she says. "It does not. It bleeds." "Of course it bleeds," I say. "I just want to know where to suture." When she leaves, the table is a mess of journals, notes, and takeout boxes, less like a set and more like a life, and I go to bed alone, not as punishment but as practice.

That night I dream of the lake one last time, not as a nightmare and not as a ritual, just as an image. I stand on the dock with water in front of me and no one behind me, no voice correcting posture, no hand on my neck, no mother on the shore, no woman waiting to call me strong. There is only wood and water and cold. My feet shiver and no one tells me to hold still, so I sit at the edge and let my legs drop into the water, the cold biting without caring who I am or what I deserve.

"I am not your good girl," I whisper, not to Evelyn, not to my mother, not even to the memory, but to myself. The dock does not respond. There is no magic, no lesson, no transformation, only creaking wood and temperature, only memory with nothing added. I wake up not shaking, not acting, not gone, just awake, which feels like a small and durable victory.

The next week Meridian emails with praise and polite language and a review of historical partnerships that reads like the corporate version of we looked away and now we might glance. I skim it and reply with three sentences and one attachment. "I expect my name, story, and surgical career removed from any Restored Vessel or legacy materials, effective immediately. I do not consent to being referenced as a beneficiary of that community. Attached is a formal statement." Then one more line, "You may want to review more than wording," and when I hit send I do not imagine their faces or picture spin or panic because their reaction is not part of my body anymore.

The email leaves like shrapnel finally worked out of tissue, and it will scar, but the wound can close. In my office I meet Harrow, not as a subject but as someone who knows where the body is, and he sits across from me with his notebook open and his face careful. "You read the paper," he says. "I did," I say. "You wrote about narrative substitution like you observed it from a distance." "It needs distance," he replies, "clinically," and I hold his gaze. "You know it closer than that." He does not deny it.

We talk about children who learn to call coercion choice and adults who polish harm until it reflects light. "And now?" he asks. "What do you do with what you remember?" "Operate," I say, "but not on myself, not anymore." He nods and tells me once a memory is integrated you cannot go back, and I tell him I spent decades not knowing and it almost killed people, so I will take knowing. He closes his notebook and says he will update the next paper because they are obsessed with excision and forget the other path. "What path?" I ask. "Teaching people to live with what they know," he says with a faint smile. "It is hard to sell." "Good," I say. "We have had enough selling."

After he leaves I finish the document I have been writing, my Dock Story, and I read it once without polishing or prettifying, letting it be accurate. Three versions sit side by side, the girl's version in fragments and sensation without language, the cult's version scripted and sanctified and used as myth, and mine integrated and ugly where it needs to be and mine where it matters. I do not submit it or send it to Meridian or hand it to Clara. I save it with one note, for reference, not worship, and then I write one last line beneath it, drafting and rewriting not as surrender but as authorship.

Memory is not what happened to me, it is what I carry forward. I close the file, the story is mine, and this time I am the one who remembers, because it is what I refuse to hand back.

www.ingramcontent.com/pod-product-compliance
Lightning Source LLC
Chambersburg PA
CBHW070858180626
46817CB00003B/820